KT-144-613

DARK QUEEN WATCHING

DARK QUEEN
WATCHING

Paul Doherty

SEVERN
HOUSE

First world edition published in Great Britain and the USA in 2021
by Severn House, an imprint of Canongate Books Ltd,
14 High Street, Edinburgh EH1 1TE.

Trade paperback edition first published in Great Britain and the USA in 2022
by Severn House, an imprint of Canongate Books Ltd.

severnhouse.com

British Library Cataloguing-in-Publication Data
A CIP catalogue record for this title is available from the British Library.

ISBN-13: 978-1-78029-138-3 (cased)
ISBN-13: 978-1-4483-0586-5 (trade paper)
ISBN-13: 978-1-4483-0585-8 (e-book)

All Severn House titles are printed on acid-free paper.

MIX
Paper from
responsible sources
FSC
www.fsc.org   FSC® C013056

Typeset by Palimpsest Book Production Ltd.,
Falkirk, Stirlingshire, Scotland.
Printed and bound in Great Britain by
TJ Books, Padstow, Cornwall.

To my good friend Lady Grace for all her
support and encouragement.

HISTORICAL NOTE

I n two brilliant victories at Barnet and Tewkesbury in the early summer of 1471, Edward of York (soon to be proclaimed Edward IV) totally annihilated the power of Lancaster. Edward became 'Master of his House', ably supported by his wife, Elizabeth Woodville, as well as his two brothers, Richard and George, and a host of veteran war captains, such as Hastings and Norfolk. Edward's rule at home went virtually unchallenged. However, Edward's victories also chilled the other great powers of Europe. France in particular was deeply worried. Once again, a powerful England might unleash invasion and war in Normandy as it had earlier in the century, before the English, under the inept Henry VI, were driven from France by Joan of Arc, the 'Maid of Orleans'. Other powers like Burgundy and Brittany were also watchful and wary. Would Edward resurrect English dreams of pillaging France and occupying its major cities? The drama was about to unfold. Edward, however, was slightly distracted by one remaining shadow of the House of Lancaster. Margaret Beaufort, Countess of Richmond, was a living reminder of Lancaster's claims, which had now fallen to her own son Henry Tudor. This young prince had fled to hide in Brittany in the hope of better days to come. Margaret, Tudor's mother, was ruthlessly determined that, however long it took, that day would dawn!

www.paulcdoherty.com

HISTORICAL CHARACTERS

House of York
Richard Duke of York and his wife Cecily, Duchess of York, 'The Rose of Raby'.
Parents of:
Edward (later King Edward IV),
George of Clarence,
Richard Duke of Gloucester (later King Richard III).

House of Lancaster
John of Gaunt: son of Edward III, founder of the Lancastrian dynasty.
John Duke of Bedford: Gaunt's grandson, regent of the kingdom during the early minority of his infant nephew, Henry VI.
Henry VI, Henry's wife Margaret of Anjou and their son Prince Edward.

House of Valois
Louis XI, King of France.
Others:
Duke Francis of Brittany.
Duke Charles of Burgundy.
Joan of Arc, 'La Pucelle', 'The Maid', Saint and heroine, who played a most significant role in driving the English out of France.
Pedro the Cruel: King of Castile.
John May: Abbot of Chertsey.
Sir Thomas Urswicke: Recorder of London.

House of Tudor
Edmund Tudor, first husband of Margaret Beaufort, Countess of Richmond, and half-brother to Henry VI of England.
Edmund's father Owain had married Katherine of Valois, French princess and widow of King Henry V, father of Henry VI.

Jasper Tudor, Edmund's brother, kinsman to Henry Tudor (later Henry VII).

House of Beaufort

Margaret Beaufort, Countess of Richmond, married first to Edmund Tudor, then Sir Henry Stafford and finally Lord Thomas Stanley.

John Beaufort, first Duke of Somerset and Margaret's father.

Christopher Urswicke, Margaret Beaufort's personal clerk and leading henchman.

Reginald Bray, Margaret's principal steward and controller of her household.

The comments before each part attest to the power and utter ruthlessness of the Garduna.

PROLOGUE

'The Garduna were a secret army licensed by God'

Lucien Barras, a high-ranking clerk in the King's Secret Chamber, the Cabinet Noir deep in the Palace of the Louvre, did not realise that he would die so swiftly and so barbarously that day. The words of scripture, so far as Monsieur Barras was concerned, were certainly fulfilled! 'I shall come like a thief in the night and you do not know the day nor the hour.'

Lucien rode towards his death, spurring his horse along the winding highway between Paris and the embattled town of Provins. Lucien had a meeting at The Salamander, a lonely auberge deep in the woods which fringed the highway on either side. At the crossroads Lucien immediately turned his horse off the main thoroughfare, guiding it along a coffin path which snaked between the ancient oaks. Lucien sighed in relief when the oppressive green darkness gave way to the auberge's high curtain wall, its iron-studded gates pulled back in welcome. Lucien dismounted, led his horse into the stable yard and handed the reins to a cheery-faced ostler. The royal clerk then stood for a while staring around. Nothing was amiss. Nothing out of place. No hint of danger. Lucien stared up at the light blue sky. Despite the freezing winter cold, the day was a good one for travelling. No rain, no blustering breeze, only meagre wisps of crawling mist whilst the air was clear and bracing, the ground underfoot ideal for riding.

Lucien realised he was early but he still had to break his fast. The clerk walked through the main door and along a stone-paved passageway. He entered the taproom, which smelled deliciously of cooked salted ham, ripening onions, fresh vegetables, the fragrance mingling with those from the great bowl of potage suspended neatly over the flames in the taproom's massive hearth. Other customers were there. Four gamblers arguing over the hazard cup and a group of ferreters with their cages, traps and sacks. These sat cheek by jowl with labourers from the fields and cottages which ringed the tavern. The floor was clean and clear, the tables well-scrubbed.

Lucien took one of these in the far corner beneath a shuttered window. A scullion hurried across. Lucien ordered some wine, a platter of hot spiced meats and a bowl of potage from the great cauldron. He glanced around. No one seemed interested in him. Good! He glanced at the tall tallow candle; its flame had not yet reached the agreed hour ring. He still had time to relax. Lucien sipped the wine and pulled his warbelt closer. He was a member of the Luciferi. François, his captain, always insisted on constant vigilance, especially now. The Luciferi, busy in the Cabinet Noir, had received good intelligence that a battle group of the Garduna, that legion of professional killers, had left Toledo, hired by Heaven knew who, to carry out some malevolent mischief across the Narrow Seas. Edward of England might well be no friend of France, but the Garduna were deeply hostile to the French Crown and the House of Valois. The Garduna were a cancer in the body politic. A coven which constantly conspired against France, be it within or without. Had not the Garduna been instrumental in the assassination so many years ago of the Duke of Orleans on the streets of Paris? A murder which divided France, leaving it vulnerable and exposed to the Goddams and all the power of England. Rumour had it that the Garduna were also responsible for the capture of the saintly Joan of Arc at Patay, which had led to La Pucelle being publicly burned in Rouen. The Garduna had meddled in all of this; hired by the Duke of Burgundy and, at his insistence, the Holy Maid had been handed over to the English, who were determined on her death.

François had no real information about the battle group except that they were moving to England where they would set up camp. Little more than that, François could not say, except to add that someone very powerful and very rich must have hired them. The Garduna were not cheap. They fielded a highly organised battle group, organised in different ranks and divided by specific functions. The Luciferi had been ordered to seek out any information they could. Lucien had cast his net far and wide, desperate to discover any scrap of information from his many informants, men and women across Paris and beyond. One of these, Etienne, a merchant who plied his wine trade between the city and Provins, had written to him urgently about a conversation he'd overheard in this very tavern. How the person he'd been watching had spoken fluently in Spanish in the rash belief that no eavesdropper would understand what he was saying. He was wrong. Etienne's mother hailed from Castile and Etienne could speak and understand the Spanish tongue easily enough. He had eavesdropped on the conversation of the two travellers, apparently journeying to meet comrades. Apparently they were all involved in some bold enterprise which would inflict great hurt to France, England, and above all the House of Lancaster.

'Monsieur?'

Lucien broke from his reverie and stared at the taverner, garbed in a thick leather, blood-stained apron.

'Are you Monsieur Lucien?'

'Perhaps, why?'

'My apologies, Monsieur Lucien, but I did not want to make a mistake. You are expecting to meet someone called Etienne?'

'Certainly.'

The taverner pointed to the ceiling.

'Your friend arrived an hour ago. He said he was early. He hired a small chamber where he could rest until he met with you. I am sorry, monsieur; I should have spoken earlier.'

'Never mind, never mind.'

Lucien rose and picked up his cloak and warbelt. The taverner gestured across to the stairs on the far side of the taproom.

'Go up there and look for the chamber with the letter "A" painted on its door.'

Lucien thanked him and climbed up onto the dusty, dimly lit gallery. He found the chamber easily enough and knocked. No answer, so he pressed on the latch and quietly opened the door. In the murky light, Lucien glimpsed Etienne sprawled face down on the bed.

'Etienne, Etienne?'

Lucien went and leaned across the bed. He gripped his informant's shoulder, his fingers brushed Etienne's face. Lucien felt the wet sticky blood and abruptly turned to confront the two cowled figures who slipped out of the shadows. Lucien fumbled with his warbelt but it was futile. One of the hooded shapes lunged with his own dagger; a killing blow to Lucien's throat, slashing it open in a few heartbeats. Lucien crumpled to the floor, jerking and shivering as he choked on his own blood. His two attackers watched him die. Once he had, they crouched down, emptying Lucien's pockets and purses before taking the dead man's cloak and warbelt. They did the same to Etienne and, using the light from the small table lantern, carefully searched the chamber for anything else of value.

'So, Manelato, everything comes in full circle.' The speaker, a tall, thick-set man with long black hair, his heavy, swarthy face almost concealed by a thick moustache and beard.

'Yes, Master.'

'Sit down,' the other declared, pointing to a stool. Manelato did so. The Master, as he called himself, picked up another stool and squatted close. He leaned forward, staring into Manelato's eyes. 'As I said,' he declared, 'everything comes full circle and here we are back at this tavern. They are the Luciferi,' he pointed at the two corpses, 'but we are the Garduna, sacred to ourselves, devoted to our cause. Now, my friend, we shall wait.'

'For whom?'

'For Juan, yes? The comrade you were talking to when this one,' he pointed to the corpse Lucien had found, 'when this one overheard you. Yes?'

'Yes.'

'Good. I have summoned him here along with you. There was no one else, was there?'

'No, Master.'

'You are certain, you are sure?' The Garduna leader grasped Manelato's hand and squeezed hard. 'You are certain about that?'

'Master, I am. So why are we here?'

The Garduna leader withdrew his hand to comb his moustache and beard with his fingers, time and again as he held Manelato's gaze. 'Manelato, we have business here, and then we are done.'

'And we leave for the coast?'

'We certainly do, followed by swift passage to England. Exciting days, Manelato!'

'Why are we going?' Manelato fought to keep the tremor out of his voice. Yet, try as he must, he could not hide the secret dread sweeping over him as he sat in this dark, dank chamber with those two corpses, cold and stiffening, and this enigmatic leader, the

Master of his battle group, sitting so calmly yet so menacingly. A man of hot temper, ruthless and ferocious. Yet that was true of all of the Garduna, especially its leaders.

'To England, Master?'

'We are going there because we are needed. Our services have been purchased.'

'For what?'

'Manelato, have you ever heard of the topsy-turvy world?'

'Where dogs fly and birds chase cats?'

'Precisely, Manelato, well said, for that is the world of the Garduna. We turn everything like a wheel. We have no allegiance to prince, prelate or people. We have our own laws and customs and we tolerate no other. You must know this? You are a recent recruit?'

'Only last Michaelmas . . .'

The Master lunged forward to press a finger against Manelato's lips.

'Michaelmas, All Saints,' he snarled, 'All Souls, Corpus Christi, and all the other nonsense of the Catholic Church does not concern us. We do not measure our time as they do because we are Garduna. Am I not right?' The Master turned slightly, watching Manelato out of the corner of his eye. He then gently rubbed the furrowed scar – long-since healed – behind his right ear. 'A slash,' he explained in answer to his comrade's stare. 'The thrust of a dagger from an assassin despatched by the so-called Holy Inquisition. Holy indeed!' He grinned. 'The Catholic Church is our enemy, as are all the princes of this world. We are the Garduna and we answer to no one. So my friend,' he leaned over and patted Manelato on the shoulder, 'make no reference to Catholic feasts and practices.'

'Very good, Master, I agree, but forgive my ignorance, I have only been a member of our order since September last.'

'I know that.' The Master continued. 'You are in the lowest rank, a chivatos, a goat. We always hoped you'd be a nimble one. As for what we intend? Yes, our battle group is bound for England and the power of Edward of York. We have been hired to provoke the very terrors into an ageing countess, and so we shall. However, we Garduna are hired for our cunning as well as our ferocity so, as always with us, there is a plot within a plot.'

'Master?'

'Oh, let me put it this way. You unlock one casket and there's another one sealed inside. And so it is with this business. We have our plans. We will adhere to the two compacts we reached in Arras.'

'Two, Master?'

'Oh yes I can tell you that,' the Master smacked his lips, 'because you can tell no others. Yes, we reached two compacts, one with Edward of York's emissary and the second with Duke Charles of Burgundy.'

'And we have friends, allies in England? A grim place, a freezing cold island. They say its citizens cannot be trusted.'

'Like us,' the Master joked.

Manelato forced a smile. He felt relaxed, comforted by the Master's confidence in him, chatting as if Manelato was his equal.

'Oh yes, we have friends and allies awaiting us.'

'And where shall we stay?'

'The place already chosen is most suitable.'

'And then what, Master?'

'We shall inflict terror upon terror on those chosen for us, then we hunt for the remains of a dead King.'

'Why is that, Master?'

'The dead are also powerful, Manelato, or so it would appear. We shall be busy . . .' He paused at a noise outside. 'Our visitor,' he declared, 'has arrived.'

Both men rose at a sharp knock at the door. The Master nodded at Manelato, who carefully opened it and allowed his friend and comrade Juan into the chamber. The newcomer bowed to the Master and gaped at the two corpses laid out on the bed, the blood of one soaking them both in a sticky, glistening mess.

'Strange,' the Master muttered, clasping Juan by the hand. 'I was just talking about the dead. Some are important; most, like these two, are not. Now, Juan, you and Manelato visited this tavern just a few days ago during your toing and froing as we prepared to move to the coast, yes?'

'Yes, we did.'

'And you discussed our secret enterprise, which would do great damage not only to the House of Lancaster but to the power of both England and France.' ·

'Yes, Master, we have heard rumours amongst our brethren and we have listened attentively to your speeches.'

'Aye, as others have listened to you.' The Master turned and pointed to the corpses. 'One of these is Etienne Langlois, a hired informer in the pay of our enemies, the Luciferi, who spin their tangled web from the Cabinet Noir in Paris. The Luciferi are the servants – no, I should really say slaves – of our deadliest foe, Louis of France. The other corpse is Lucien Barras, a high-ranking clerk in the Luciferi, despatched here to discover exactly what Etienne overheard.'

'Master, how did you find out about this?'

'Oh, quite simple, Juan. Etienne stayed here until after you both left. Once you had, Etienne informed Minehost downstairs that he wished to buy a parchment sheet, a quill pen, ink and some sealing wax. Minehost of course, as is customary, happily obliged. Etienne wrote his message describing what he'd heard, as well as fixing a time and date for Lucien and him to meet here in The Salamander. Once he had finished his message, Etienne sealed it and hired an ostler from this tavern to take the letter to the chancery at the Louvre Palace. Now, unbeknown to Etienne, Minehost of The Salamander, like so many taverners on the approaches to Paris, are in the pay of the Garduna, as they probably are,' he added wearily, 'deep in the pockets of the Luciferi.'

'We were careful,' Manelato declared.

'Most prudent,' Juan answered. He sat down on the chamber chest and glanced quickly at Manelato, who crouched, wetting his lips nervously.

'Ah well, on with my story. Minehost downstairs, as is quite common, intercepted this letter, unsealed it and read the contents. Once satisfied, he resealed the letter and let the ostler go, probably telling him that if he valued his job he would keep his mouth shut about what had happened. The ostler left on his errand and Minehost, who realised the importance of Etienne's message, hastened along the road to the Prospect of Jerusalem, a splendid hostelry near the gate of Saint Denis, where one of our company constantly lodges. He heard Minehost out and then brought the message to me. Etienne's message gave the day, the hour and the place where Lucien should meet him. I and my company journeyed here,' he drew a deep breath, 'and so we are ready to take care of business. I thought it was appropriate that only Manelato should join me here.'

'And me?'

'Of course. You and Manelato will take care of Minehost; you will remove that problem for good. Pass me the sack.'

Manelato, now agitated, rose and went into a darkened recess, and brought out the sack his leader had carried into the chamber. The Master grabbed it, undid the cords and shook out two hand-held arbalests and a squat quiver of bolts. He primed both crossbows, winching back the cords and sliding the barbs into the grooves. He placed one weapon on the floor beside him whilst cradling the other in his lap.

'Master?'

'Manelato, Minehost deserves to be punished. He is supposed to be in my pay. True he sent me that message, but he also let it reach the Luciferi.' The Master wagged a warning finger. 'That treacherous turd expects to be rewarded by them as he does by me. Moreover, this sly mouldering maggot has seen all our faces. Wouldn't you agree?'

Both of his companions nodded.

'Good, but first, you must be punished.' The Master abruptly lifted the crossbow he was cradling and aimed it at Juan. He released the catch and, before either startled Garduna could react, loosed the bolt, which smashed into Juan's face, crumpling skin and bone, turning the flesh into a blood-spurting mess. Manelato tried to rise but the Master was already lifting the second crossbow.

'You are Garduna,' he hissed. 'Not old washer-women gossiping around the tub. In the name of all we hold sacred, what were you doing? You broke the omertà, the law of silence. You dare to sit in a tavern proclaiming what we plot.'

'No, mercy.'

'Judgement made, judgement passed. Farewell.'

The Master pulled the catch, releasing the cruel-edged barb into Manelato's forehead, shattering skin, bone and flesh. The Master watched the blood spurt out then rose as Manelato's corpse lurched to the floor. The Master went through the dead men's possessions, quickly pocketing anything of value. He placed the arbalest back in the sack, gazed around that room of slaughter and quietly left.

Minehost, his fat face and bald head all glistening with sweat, was waiting for him in the taproom. The Master stared around at the few customers before turning back to the taverner. He slipped a silver piece into Minehost's greasy hand, watching the man pocket it in a purse hanging on a cord around his fat neck.

'Good business,' the Master murmured. 'My friends will soon join you.' He then nodded and walked out of the taproom to collect his horse from the stables. He checked its harness, mounted his powerful destrier and left the tavern yard. He did not follow the trackway but crossed into the fringe of trees. He urged his mount forward until he reached a glade where others, about twenty in number, were waiting for him, sitting like cowled and hooded statues on their horses. The Master called across his henchman.

'Alphonso, take our beloveds into The Salamander. Close the gates then take care of everyone. Kill them all and burn that place to the ground. They'll think it's the work of outlaws; others will suspect different, however, so lessons will be learnt.'

'No prisoners, Master?'

'As always no prisoners. Go now. Oh,' the Master exclaimed in a jingle of harness, 'you will meet Minehost. He has a purse hanging around his neck, make sure you take it, it holds my silver piece. Seize it,' he repeated, 'make sure you do.'

'And anything else of value?'

'Of course, as always.'

Alphonso raised a hand and led the horsemen out of the glade, filing through the trees like shadows. The Master sat, eyes half shut, listening to the birdsong fade as the clamour and noise of the tavern carried through the trees: screams, yells and pleas for pity. The Master ignored them. He stared up, half smiling, as he glimpsed the dark plumes of smoke rise to blot the sky and tinge the breezes with the acrid smell of burning.

'We are the Garduna,' he whispered. 'And we answer to no one.'

Margaret, Countess of Richmond knelt on her prie-dieu before the triptych in the recess of her private chamber. This place was her Holy of Holies and the triptych, depicting St George of England wearing the Beaufort colours, was the reason for this. Margaret gazed at the painting. She could even swear that the saint looked like her father, John Beaufort, first Duke of Somerset. Margaret

crossed herself. She recalled that day, what she called 'the beginning of the haunting', Margaret's gnawing sense of unease that
the Beauforts were cursed. The fate of her father seemed to prove
that. Recalled from France where he had suffered one military
disaster after another, John Beaufort had been found dead in his
chamber. Some said he had been poisoned. Others claimed that
he had suffered a stroke of the heart. A few whispered that John
Beaufort, unable to accept his recall from France, had committed
suicide. Margaret had never really discovered the truth of the
matter. Nevertheless, her father's death seemed to herald others,
culminating in the devastating bloody defeat at Tewkesbury
where the Beaufort dream had been consigned to the dark.
She was the last true descendant of the Beauforts. She would prove
the curse wrong! She would restore her family honour and the
glory of her house.

'So powerful,' Margaret murmured, threading the ave beads
through her slender fingers. 'We were so powerful, yet so swiftly
annihilated.' Margaret closed her eyes as she recalled the ferocious,
bloody battle-storms which had dominated her life: Townton,
Wakefield, Tewkesbury and Barnet. 'So sudden, so swift,' she
breathed. 'So violent a change.'

The last great bloodletting had occurred six months ago in the
West Country, where York had culled the opposition. Margaret's
son, the only true Lancastrian claimant, had no choice but to flee
with Uncle Jasper and the latter's half-sister, the Lady Katarina.
They had been successful; Lady Katarina, in particular, was
cunning and shrewd. Henry was now safe in Brittany, but Margaret
realised that York would do anything to seize or kill him, whilst
the young prince himself was constantly being urged by others to
go here or shelter there. 'As I am,' she murmured, staring at the
triptych. 'And I am tempted to do so.'

She was not welcome in England. York despised her. Edward
and his brothers regarded her as a malignant but, at this moment
in time, they dared not move against her. 'And there's the rub,'
she declared to herself. Margaret drew a deep breath. She had just
buried her second husband, Sir Henry Stafford, a sickly man who
had sustained grievous wounds in the recent murderous clashes
between York and Lancaster. While Sir Henry lived, Margaret had
enjoyed the support and protection of the powerful Stafford family

under their leader, the ever-mighty Duke of Buckingham. Now Sir Henry was gone, what protection could be offered? Margaret paused in her reflections as she heard voices and the laughter of her brother-in-law in the gallery beyond. Sir John Stafford, together with two others, had journeyed from Burgundy to attend Sir Henry's funeral. 'That was good of him,' Margaret murmured. She and Sir John had never really enjoyed the best of relationships. He had not been too happy with his brother's marriage to Margaret, or any alliance with the hated Beauforts.

Margaret realised the power the Staffords offered her was now limited. She was vulnerable, exposed. She had her henchmen and her retainers, but she could not field troops as swiftly and easily as the great lords could. 'Ah well, all things drain away.' She prayed to the triptych. 'Nothing lasts, everything changes.' She closed her eyes and pleaded for what she considered one of the greater virtues; to be cunning and resolute in dealing with her enemies.

Margaret got to her feet. She opened her psalter and picked out the letter. Margaret held this up as reverently, as a priest would a pyx. Margaret truly believed this letter was her best protection. A shrewd move across the chessboard of court intrigue, least expected by either friend or foe. Only she, and the person she was writing to, knew about the great surprise she was preparing. Not even – at least not yet – her two stalwart henchmen, Christopher Urswicke and Reginald Bray, knew of her plans. She would inform them but not now, as they were busy in other parts of this deadly dance. The murderous masque would only end when Margaret's son Henry received the Crown of the Confessor at Westminster Abbey. In the meantime, Margaret was determined to continue to act the role of the rather bewildered, lonely, widowed countess, secretly cherishing a hope shared by few others. Margaret would creep, not advance. She would wait and watch. One of her favourite phrases was 'never to hang an enemy, for they did such a good job in hanging themselves'. So it was here. The Brothers York enjoyed supreme power but, at the same time, they were sowing the seeds of their own destruction. One day those seeds would truly sprout. In the meantime, Margaret and her household had to survive until harvest time.

Margaret knelt back on the prie-dieu, threading her rosary beads through her fingers, each bead being a problem or a challenge. First she needed to see her beloved son Henry: that was now in hand. The Lady Katarina, that redoubtable woman, along with Henry's trusted uncle, Jasper Tudor, would bring the young prince safely to her. Secondly, there was the pressure from Sir John Stafford, her good brother-in-law. He had arrived in London seeking shelter, along with his body servant, Squire Lambert, and close friend, Guido the physician. They loudly maintained she should flee the kingdom. In truth, as Margaret often confessed to herself, she'd never really liked Sir John, and she was not too keen on his companions either but – Margaret let the beads fall through her fingers – such problems paled against the newly emerging danger confronting her.

Margaret drew a deep breath. She was concerned, deeply so, by those hideous broadsheets posted on St Paul's Cross and at the Standard in Cheapside. The broadsheets were nothing more than a foul litany of filthy allegations against the countess. The publication of such anonymous broadsheets was becoming increasingly common throughout the city. Only recently her personal clerk, Christopher Urswicke, had attended the execution of Simon Chilen, an ardent Lancastrian, a former clerk in the chancery of Lord Faucomburg. Chilen had posted the most heinous remarks about King Edward's wife, Elizabeth Woodville. He had depicted her as a common whore, 'a palfrey' ridden by many. Chilen had eventually been caught and paid the supreme penalty. He was dragged on a sledge from Newgate to the gallows above Tyburn stream: half hanged, his body was cut open, his entrails plucked out and burned before him.

Margaret whispered a prayer. Who would pursue or hunt down the author of the broadsheets maligning her? Ostensibly they were published in the name of Merlin the Magician, but the true author remained hidden, the litany of heinous accusations against her being repeated time and again. She had appealed to the authorities, but the Brothers York and their coven couldn't give a fig. Indeed, they'd been only too delighted at her discomfiture. They would cry false tears then giggle behind their fingers. Margaret had no faith in the court, or indeed York's creature, Christopher Urswicke's own father, Sir Thomas Urswicke, the devious Recorder of London. Despite her worries, Countess Margaret half smiled. The wheel of fortune would surely turn and she would use one Urswicke to confront and resolve the chilling challenges posed by another. Margaret abruptly recalled her visitor waiting in the chamber downstairs. She really must go down to speak to him whilst it was nearly time to meet with her henchmen. 'First things first,' Margaret whispered to herself.

The countess crossed herself and left her chamber, pattering swiftly down the staircase into the hallway where Hardyng, her steward, was waiting. He bowed, whispered a salutation, and opened the door to the visitors' chamber. Margaret swept in. The Benedictine monk, crouched on the chair like a black moving shadow, made to rise.

'No no, Father Abbot, please.' Countess Margaret waved the monk back to his chair and sat down on another. She leaned against the table and smiled at her visitor. The thin, bony-faced, austere-looking John May, abbot of Chertsey Abbey, was one of her most treasured confidants. 'My friend, you look tired. This is a great honour; I mean, to visit me. You would like some refreshment?'

'No no.' The abbot's ascetic face creased into a smile; an old man deep in the autumn of his life, his still, clear eyes twinkling with amusement. 'I'm getting fat, Margaret, even though we no longer feast as we used to in your family home.'

'You're not fat,' she repeated. 'You must be hungry.'

'Lady Margaret, rest assured I've eaten and drunk to my fill. Let us move to the business in hand.'

'Abbot John, I do appreciate you coming so silently, so unobtrusively. Nobody saw you?'

'None except Hardyng, yet all he saw was a Benedictine monk with his cowl pulled up.' Abbot John tapped the muffler now pushed down beneath his chin. 'And this.'

Lady Margaret stretched out both hands. The abbot clasped these, then administered a blessing. Margaret crossed herself and moved her chair closer.

'I did not come down immediately, Abbot John, just in case my eagerness to meet you was glimpsed by those who should not glimpse such things.'

'Yorkist spies here?' the abbot exclaimed. 'Surely not?'

'Surely so, Father Abbot. They are everywhere. I am certain

York has paid good coin to servants greedy enough to rise to the
bait. Father Abbot, I have known you for years, decades even; my
manor of Woking lies close to your abbey. You know the ways of
York. They will keep a sharp eye on someone like you.'

'True, true,' the abbot agreed. 'Even on my journey from
Chertsey I had to be careful. People would wonder why I would
journey midwinter. I made it clear that I had to speak to my good
brothers the abbot and prior of Westminster.' He shrugged. 'That
was easy enough; we Blackrobes love to talk. I am summoned
here and summoned there and, in truth, I am very grateful for it.
I used that as an excuse to come to London and visit you.' He
paused. 'My Lady what do you want me to do?'

'My beloved son Henry, together with his protectors, Jasper
Tudor and the Lady Katarina Fitzherbert, are already on their way
to England aboard a Hainault cog. They will land,' Lady Margaret
raised a hand to still the abbot's startled gasps, 'they will disembark
and make their way as pilgrims to Chertsey Abbey, where I and
my trusted henchmen will meet them.'

'In God's name, my Lady, why?' The abbot lifted up his hands
as if in prayer. 'Journeying through both the city and the forest
could be most dangerous. I cannot, for the life of me, say which
is the more perilous.' He lowered his hands. 'And my abbey too.
If York has spies here in your household, and I now believe they
do, York certainly has informants at Chertsey Abbey. It's logical.
Listen.' The abbot used his fingers to emphasise his points. 'First,
you and I are old friends, good comrades. York knows this, as he
does that I am a fervent supporter of you, your father and the
House of Lancaster. Secondly, Chertsey Abbey houses – allegedly,
I do concede – the mortal remains of the last Lancastrian king,
the saintly Henry. Over the years, his tomb could emerge as a
shrine, a rallying point for Lancastrians, as well as a constant
reminder of how poor Henry was murdered, or martyred, by Yorkist
henchmen, a deep eternal stain on all their immortal souls.'

The abbot joined his hands in prayer. 'They know you visit me.
They know you honour the shrine and, above all, they know you
take secret counsel with me. They would pay good silver and shed
even more blood to discover what passes between us.'

'Great danger I admit, Father Abbot.' Margaret leaned over and
clasped the Benedictine's right hand. 'All you say is true, but I

need to see Henry urgently. He will come to Chertsey. You will receive him? You will protect him?'

'As I would my own but, my Lady, his arrival will be fraught with peril.'

'I have lived with such dangers since my birth,' Lady Margaret retorted. 'I was only twelve years old when my beloved Edmund took me as his wife, and I became pregnant with Henry, our future king. There's danger all around me, Lord Abbot. Peril in all guises, be it scurrilous stories about me, the assassin with his sharpened dagger lurking behind a silken arras or in the mouth of some murky alleyway. Rest assured, I know I walk a perilous path. All kinds of monsters lurk in the darkness either side of it. They glare at me and I certainly glare back.'

PART ONE

'The Garduna were free to plot killings and perpetrate any kind of secret treachery'

The Chasuble – or so the woodsmen claimed – truly was an ancient tavern, standing close to the forest crossroads. The woodsmen believed it was once a royal hunting lodge, used by successive kings in their furious forays against stag, boar and, in years long gone, even the wolf. Here, so locals declared, the royal princes would let loose falcon and hawk to bring down birds on the wing or some fat coney caught out of the dark shadows. Afterwards the royal party would not travel on to Woking or back to London but adjourn to The Chasuble to feast on their prey, washed down with goblets of the best Bordeaux or blackjacks brimming with a strong frothy ale, brewed by some local vintner before being barrelled and casked for the great majestic lodge. Times, however, had changed. The magnificent three-storey manor had been neglected. The hunting parties never returned. The Chasuble had slowly decayed, being sold from hand to hand by a litany of would-be taverners who had hoped in vain to resurrect the former glories of the place.

Master Henry Islip was the last of these. A former alehouse owner, Islip had plied his trade along the Mile End road leading into London. Islip had decided he could do better. He had bought The Chasuble and moved into the tavern with his large family and household. Matters had not gone well. Islip had to concede that local lore spoke the truth. The former hunting lodge seemed to be under some form of malignant spell. However, on 2 November, the Feast of All Souls, the year of our Lord 1471, Islip could hardly believe his eyes when he opened the tavern door and stepped out into the cobbled, wall-enclosed stable yard. A large company had arrived. Men and women on horse or in great covered carts. Master Islip spread his hands in welcome, not realising – at least not yet – that Murder had arrived to set up house in that ancient tavern. Islip, totally unaware of who the Garduna really were, warmly welcomed his guests. He clapped his hands, gesturing at the leader of these new arrivals, standing hooded and visored before him, to accompany the taverner back into the cavernous taproom.

The stranger followed him in and stood staring up at the hams, onions and other vegetables clasped in sacks which were nailed to the blackened rafter beams. Islip's guest pulled back his hood and lowered the visor that had been hiding the bottom half of his face to reveal a swarthy man, his hair and beard black and silvered. His skin was tawny, a scar marking the neck behind his right ear. The stranger's eyes were dark and hooded, constantly flickering, as if wary of some hidden enemy. He pulled his cloak further back, and Islip glimpsed the broad leather warbelt, sword- and knife-sheath either side. The stranger's hand fell to the ornate pommel of his dagger, tapping his fingers as if wondering whether he should draw it or not. A spasm of cold fear clenched the taverner's belly. He stared around. Others of the company had now crowded in, cloaks and hoods pulled back, all armed to the teeth. For a while there was silence, an uneasy silence. Then the leader of the arrivals abruptly turned back to Islip, his face transformed by a smile which softened his harsh features.

'My friend, I am the Master, the leader of the Garduna.' The man's English was slightly tinged by a harsh accent. He then turned away and spoke swiftly in a guttural voice to one of his companions, who hurried out on some errand.

'My tongue.' The Master glanced back at Islip. 'My tongue is Castilian; we are a travelling troupe from Spain. We seek comfortable lodgings for a long time, or at least for some time. Rest assured we pay good coin. See.'

The Master beckoned Islip over to a table and, in one deft movement, plucked a coin purse from the folds of his cloak. He shook out the silver pieces to glint in the light. Islip caught his breath, licking his lips in anticipation, wiping sweaty hands on his blood-spattered apron.

'Let me.' The Master leaned over and clasped Islip on the shoulder. 'Let me first meet all your family, your entire household so we know with whom we lodge. Summon everyone. Would you do that, Master Islip?' The stranger rubbed his hands together then gestured at the silver coins, winking so enticingly in the light of torch and lanternhorn. 'This will soon be yours,' he added. He spoke something in Spanish and glanced over his shoulder at the three Floreadores, the foragers who had slipped into England two months earlier to prepare the ground and search out all the possibilities.

'You did very well,' he called out in Spanish. 'Very well indeed.'

The three Floreadores had been most successful organising the horses, carts and supplies, all ready when Hermano and his entourage had landed on a stretch of deserted Essex coastline. A peaceful disembarkation from the pirate cog, *The Hidalgo*, which had taken them from Corunna. They had travelled swiftly and silently into the English countryside to lodge in this dilapidated though still majestic tavern deep in the forest. An ideal lair, within striking distance of Woking as well as the roads and waterways into London.

'You did well,' Hermano repeated.

The three, dark-faced Floreadores bowed in thanks at such praise.

'Well, Master Taverner.' Again the pat on the shoulder. 'My friend, let us meet your kith and kin.' He smilingly held up a warning finger. 'All of them now. Quickly, quickly!'

Islip hastened to obey. Hermano scooped the silver back into his purse and went out into the courtyard where the rest of his retinue patiently waited.

'Now!' he called out in Spanish. 'Now my beloveds, let the Ponteadores and Floreadores,' he pointed back at the tavern, 'go in and join your brothers and sisters.' Men and women, cowled and visored, dismounted from horses and carts. They left the reins to others as, cloaks thrust back, they entered the taproom of The Chasuble.

The Master went and stood in the open gateway of the tavern. He shivered at the freezing cold breeze which swept out from the nearby forest to send the black branches rustling, whipping up the piles of dead leaves and frozen gorse. He glanced up at the sky, iron-grey and lowering.

'It might snow,' he murmured to himself. 'All to the good, but I do miss the orange groves of Seville. Ah well.'

He turned back, tugging his cloak closer against the freezing chill. He caught the smell of cooking wafting from the tavern kitchen and smacked his lips. He and all his household would certainly feast like kings, but first there was business to do. He went back into the now crowded taproom. Islip had gathered wife, sons and daughters and all the tavern servants. The Master, smiling and courteous, introduced himself then turned to Islip.

'Is this all?' he demanded. 'Everyone?'

'Yes sir.'

'Good, good.' The Master walked to the door then paused, hand on the latch.

'Alphonso,' he called out to his henchman.

'Yes, Master?'

'Kill them all.'

The Master went out into the stable yard, the door slammed shut behind him. Locks were turned. Bolts pulled across. The slaughter began. The noise and clamour were heart-rending; screams and shrieks, yells and shouts. A woman pleaded for mercy, her voice brutally cut off. A window shutter flew open; a young man struggled to get out, only to be dragged back. Those waiting in the stable yard remained impassively silent, despite the freezing cold and the hideous killings taking place only a few yards away. The massacre continued then abruptly ended. The Master stared at the door and glimpsed the blood seeping out from underneath to drench the cobbles and so create more rivulets to twist and snake, the still hot blood cooling in the icy air. The Master stood, head slightly cocked, listening intently. No sound, not a whimper or a groan. He banged on the taproom door. It swung open. Alphonso stood there, his sword bloodied from tip to hilt.

'It is done,' the henchman murmured. 'It is over.'

The Master brushed by him, walking deep into the darkness. The taproom lay eerily still. The corpses of the slain had been pulled to lie next to each other, a gruesome, gore-stained sight. All the dead bore death wounds to the throat, chest and stomach. The air was no longer bitter-sweet but reeking of the flesher's yard, some filthy Newgate slaughterhouse.

'Good, good,' the Master breathed. 'My children.' He extended his arms as he turned to take in all the company ranged around the taproom. 'My beloveds, well done. However, your companions are in the cold outside. Collect the corpses and strip them. You know where there is a deep forest marsh?' The Master pointed at the Floreadores who had chosen this place.

'Deep and broad,' one of them murmured.

'Take the corpses there. Hide them well. We will then take lodgings here. We have become taverners, ale masters.' He laughed and his entourage chuckled in agreement. 'If anyone asks, we will declare how Master Islip,' he went over and kicked the taverner's corpse, 'sold The Chasuble to me and my extended family, then they left for pastures new.' The Master laughed. 'They certainly did. So let us send them on their way. Let us feast and rejoice. Afterwards, we shall present our compliments to the Lady Margaret both at her manor of Woking, as well as her fine townhouse in the city. Indeed, we must send reinforcements and supplies to our comrades who are already there.' The Master's smile faded as he held up a warning hand. 'Remember, my beloveds, how easy it is for the hunters to become the hunted. True we are well protected here, but the Luciferi are also busy, ready to interfere in our affairs.' He paused at the murmured curses. 'Our enemies,' the Master continued, 'to the very death. We must be vigilant and prudent. Do not forget the danger which lurks at noon-time, and the horrors that can crawl by night. In the meantime, my beloveds, let us feast. Let us rejoice at our success but let us not forget the darkness all around us.' He beckoned over his henchman. For a while they just stood, watching the corpses being removed, the splashes of blood cleared away along with the pathetic possessions of those they'd massacred. They then took one of the tables in a window embrasure, far enough away from those now cleaning and setting the taproom right. Wine was served. The Master and Alphonso toasted each other then sat for a while in silence.

'Alphonso,' the Master declared. 'A cohort of our battle group has already swiftly advanced before us and now hide in London.'

'Where?'

'We are the Garduna, my friend, we make do with what we can. There are certainly enough derelict houses in the city. Rafael will find a suitable place, as we have here. He will turn it into his nest. He and his companions are well armed, with plenty of coin to buy food, drink and other necessities. Rafael's mother was English; he is skilled in the tongue. Rafael has some knowledge of the city; he has also been furnished with charts depicting the main routes and principal wards. We shall communicate with him and, as I said, ensure he remains well supplied.'

'And here?'

'Ah yes, here my good friend. Tonight, between the sixth and seventh hour, loose three fire arrows up over the trees. Our comrades expect us. They did so last night as they would tomorrow. I gave them clear notice that we would reach The Chasuble on one of these three days. We have. You should be answered by three fire arrows; if so, let me know immediately.'

'And then?'

'And then tomorrow, Alphonso, a journeyman, a traveller, a tinker, hooded and visored, will enter our tavern and ask for the sweet wines of Spain. If he does, he is to be ushered to this table and I am to be immediately informed. No one else but myself will deal with him. Understand?'

'Yes, Master.'

'I want scouts despatched into the forest, but for the moment keep well away from Chertsey Abbey – we have learnt enough about that place for the moment. We will only move against it when we have to, when we are ready to take what has been asked of us. Understood?' He clinked his goblet against Alphonso's. 'Do not fear the English, they will not pose any danger; but, for all our sakes', Alphonso, keep the sharpest eye out for the Luciferi. They hunt us, as we do them.'

Margaret, Countess of Richmond, sat in the high-back chair in her bedchamber, which stood off the first gallery of her elegant river-side mansion. The chamber, like everything else in that opulent house, was exquisitely refined, be it the blue and gold arras hanging against the sheened, pink-washed walls, or the thick scarlet turkey rugs which adorned the finely polished elm-wood floor. The gold-edged four-poster bed, tables, aumbries, cabinets and caskets were a dark oaken brown.

This finely carved furniture gleamed in the fluttering light of a host of beeswax candles on silver-chased spigots, placed judiciously around the room. The sweet fragrance of the pure melting candles mingled with the perfumed smoke curling from the small herb pots. Further fragrance was provided by the braziers, their fiery charcoal laced with a dust of crushed flowers, plucked and prepared the previous summer.

Countess Margaret, dressed in a sky blue veil and gown, her lean, expressive face framed by a starched, snow-white wimple, sat as composed and collected as any nun at her prayers. Indeed, the countess threaded a set of pearl ave beads through her long thin fingers. She looked as if she was at prayer, but in truth her mind was spinning like a wheel. Margaret stared intently at the two men seated before her. These were her council; the only men she could really trust. Now was the time for such loyalty. Margaret had received fragmented reports about this and that. She had not shared all her fears with these two henchmen, or informed them about exactly what was planned – that would have to wait. Margaret played with the ave beads. She'd had fresh reports out of Brittany. Her beloved son Henry, fiercely protected by her brother-in-law Jasper, former Lord of Pembroke, and his cunning and capable half-sister Katarina, was on his travels. Margaret had yet to decide what to do when Henry came to England. She drew comfort from her recent meeting with Abbot John. Henry would be safe in Chertsey, but more than that she couldn't say. Margaret had not revealed all her fears to the Benedictine, nor would she now to these two confidants.

Lady Margaret trusted both her henchmen, though she wondered what would happen if they were put to the torture. Sometimes the bravest men, the most loyal and devoted, would simply yield to the pain. Margaret knew that she was also being shadowed but she would not react. She would sit, she would wait, and she would watch. Margaret blinked, shaking her head slightly and went back to her reflections.

A log broke noisily in the fire, cascading out of the grate in a shower of sparks. Bray went to deal with it. Margaret shifted her gaze to Christopher Urswicke; her chancery clerk looked every inch the professional scrivener, his shirt pulled high under his clean-shaven chin. A good-looking, almost beautiful young man, Urswicke had a smooth, shaven boyish face, blue-eyed and full lipped. Indeed, he looked much younger than his twenty-six years, an impression heightened by his tousled auburn hair. Urswicke sat languidly, his cloak and warbelt laid over a coffer, his spurred riding boots placed in a tiled windowed embrasure next to those of his companion Reginald Bray. The latter was close-faced with deep, hooded eyes. Bray was swarthy, even sallow, his moustache and beard were closely trimmed, his hair, black as a raven's wing, tied neatly in a queue behind him.

Margaret continued to sit and stare as her sharp mind turned over the business in hand. Despite the danger, she was confident that this chamber was sealed. No eavesdropper could lurk, no Judas man desperate for reward could slink close, hungry for any juicy titbit to pass on to his masters. God knows there was enough for them to feast upon. As Margaret had once conceded to these two confidants, she was steeped in treason and the danger of discovery; arrest and punishment hung over her like the executioner's axe. Margaret, however, would not be deterred, her hour would come. For the time being she recognised what the times and the place really were. This was not the occasion for sharp sword-play and blood-soaked conflict. The kingdom was tired of war, of invasion, of disruption. No, this was the time for intrigue, plot and counter-plot, deceit and deception. She must wear masks to face others who wore masks. She must move cautiously as she threaded her way through a truly murderous maze to celebrate her vision, her dream of a Tudor, her beloved son Henry, enthroned at Westminster wearing the Confessor's Crown as his right.

'Mistress,' Urswicke cleared his throat. 'Mistress, we are waiting.'

'Yes, yes we are. We all wait and watch, Christopher.'

She drew a deep breath.

'My friends, what we say here might be deemed high treason, which could provoke all the dire, dreadful penalties of the law. Of course,' Margaret's voice turned sarcastic, 'if what we plot is successful then it will not be treason. Remember that, my friends. If we fail, men will condemn us. If we succeed, those same men will applaud. So let us begin. Let us review what we face. Today is the fourth of November, the year of our Lord 1471, the feast of some saint or other – but to be quite honest, I have forgotten. Autumn has come and gone and the horrors of last summer with it. Here in this kingdom, the Brothers York reign supreme. Edward, our noble warrior King, is supported by his Woodville wife and a host of henchmen, be it his wife's wolf pack or the likes of Hastings, Howard of Norfolk and the rest. So far Edward has kept the support of the city, the kingdom and, above all, Holy Mother Church, who views Edward as sitting on the right hand of the power, God's anointed, vindicated by battle. In the meantime,' Margaret tried to keep the bitterness out of her voice, her raging anger against what was, when it should be so different, 'We of the House of Lancaster, now eat the hard bread of disgrace. We sip the bitter wine of defeat. Lancaster has been devastated. My kinsman, Beaufort of Somerset and the rest are no more. The bloody defeat at Tewkesbury saw to that. The same is true of possible allies such as Neville, Earl of Warwick, the self-styled kingmaker, killed outright at Barnet. The legitimate King, my son Henry, now shelters in Brittany, the guest of Duke Francis who, I pray, will keep him safe. Yet dangers threaten him constantly.' She sighed. 'But what I say is true, yes?'

'Undoubtedly, mistress,' Bray replied. 'Our enemies wax powerful.'

'But York is not so strong,' Urswicke retorted. 'True, Edward is supported by his henchmen, in particular Richard of Gloucester, but the other brother,' Urswicke smiled bleakly, 'George of Clarence, is as treacherous as they come.'

'True, true. We must watch him as we do the rest.'

'You have news of your son, mistress?'

'Yes, Brittany still protects him, but kinsman Jasper and the latter's half-sister fear for him. They do wonder how long Brittany will support them.'

Margaret rubbed the side of her head.

'I need,' she whispered, 'to see my beloved son. I feel new dangers are emerging. Fresh challenges and threats. I have lost my husband, so my ties to the Duke of Buckingham and the whole Stafford brood have been sorely weakened. Now I face attacks on my manor in Woking whilst filthy proclamations about me are posted throughout the city. Sir John Stafford, my brother-in-law, who lodges here with me, is also deeply worried. He has heard about these broadsheets,' she paused at a knock on the door, 'and this must be them.'

The door opened. The countess's house guests, followed by Squire Lambert, swaggered into the chamber and took the proffered seats. Margaret shifted her gaze to the three guests now sitting expectantly at the far end of the table. Sir John Stafford, her brother-in-law, had a plump, rubicund, jolly face, framed by neatly clipped white hair, moustache and beard. A bon viveur who had supped deeply from the cup of life, Sir John now looked decidedly uneasy and anxious. Next to him, Sir John's squire and body servant, the blond-haired, smooth faced Squire Lambert, was turned out so elegantly in his blue and gold jerkin with its high, silver-encrusted collar and puffed sleeves. Margaret noticed the rings and bracelets, which adorned his fingers and wrists to create a brilliant sheen around the squire whenever he moved his hands, as he did quite often. A young man, Margaret reflected, who found it difficult to keep still. Studying Squire Lambert's slender, smooth face, Margaret wondered for the umpteenth time about the true relationship of Sir John with this very handsome young man. The third guest, sitting on Sir John's right, was his personal physician, a graduate of the great medical faculty of Montpellier, Guido Verres. The physician was a close personal friend of Sir John's, an old comrade who had stood next to him in the shield wall on a host of battlefields both here and abroad. Guido was clean-shaven; even his head was closely shorn, as the physician fervently believed that hair caught and carried a myriad of infections. A pleasant-looking, soft-eyed man, Guido, as customary, was garbed in black from neck to toe like some professional mourner at a funeral. He laughingly called these 'the garb of Castile' where he had been born.

Margaret glanced up at the ceiling. She had now finished the burial rites for her late husband, Sir Henry Stafford. Sir John and his friends had been her principal guests, enjoying their stay, until recently, in her luxurious manor of Woking. A self-proclaimed chronicler, Sir John had been keen to continue what he called his 'magnum opus', his great work on the history of the Stafford family. He was using his stay in England to study whatever records he could find. Perfect guests, until matters had taken a truly sinister turn.

'Mistress,' Urswicke whispered hoarsely, breaking into her reverie. 'Shall I read the proclamation again?'

'No!' Margaret forced a smile to counter the sharpness of her voice. 'I shall read it once again for all of you to hear.'

'Mistress,' Bray intervened. 'It is . . .'

'Hurtful? Very much so. But let's read the atrocious lies again.' She picked up the parchment before her, closed her eyes and drew a deep breath. She crossed herself, opened her eyes, staring at the manuscript. 'Know ye,' she began, 'know ye citizens of London that the widow Margaret Beaufort, who styles herself Countess of Richmond, the mother of the traitorous rebel Henry Tudor, now skulking and afeared, as he should be, at Rennes in Brittany. Yes, she with all her titles and pretensions is no more than a murderous whore. She is directly responsible for the untimely death of her husband, that paladin knight Sir Henry Stafford. The Beaufort bitch kept this man of honour a virtual prisoner at her opulent but desolate manor of Woking in Surrey, while she lasciviously cavorted in London with her two catamites whom she retains for her own illicit pleasure, namely Reginald Bray and Christopher Urswicke. Know ye also,' Margaret kept her voice firm, 'know ye also,' she repeated, 'that this Beaufort bitch has murderous designs on her late husband's brother, Sir John, or so it is bruited throughout the city. A traitor, the wife of a dead traitor Edmund Tudor, the mother of a traitor Henry Tudor, and the daughter of the traitorous Beaufort who took the coward's way out. This perfidious whore nurses horrid designs against our present glorious King, his family and his court. Know ye well, good citizens, the true nature of the woman you harbour so close to your loyal hearts. Remember, be on your guard. I shall return to you on this matter. However, for the moment, *pax et bonum* to you all. Given and sealed in the House of Truth, Merlin the Prophet, the Ancient of Days.'

Margaret let the proclamation slip from her hands. She simply sat staring down at the table.

Urswicke, clerk of her chancery, leaned over and picked up the parchment. He realised every word of these disgusting allegations was a lie, a poisoned arrow to his mistress's heart. According to this perjured proclamation, all the men the countess had ever loved were damned and despised while she, who had lived a life above reproach, was depicted as a killer, an assassin, a cheap city whore. Even its signature at the end of the proclamation was a heinous insult, a nasty jibe at the way the Tudors proclaimed themselves to be the direct descendants of King Arthur, at whose court the magician Merlin had flourished.

'Where were these proclamations posted?' Bray asked.

'At the Cross in St Paul's Churchyard and the Standard along Cheapside,' Urswicke replied. 'I took both down but,' he tapped the document, 'copies have been made and distributed the length

and breadth of the city. I am sure,' he added bitterly, 'that the
King and his . . .' Urswicke paused at a sharp kick under the table.
He glanced quickly at his mistress. Margaret was warning him
with her pale grey eyes. Urswicke nodded in agreement. He must
not be rash; he must not say anything which could be used against
them. He could only truly trust two people in this chamber. His
mistress and his good friend and ally, Reginald Bray.

'You were saying,' Sir John barked. 'Come on, Urswicke, who
else knows about this? Indeed,' he breathed out noisily, 'I am sure
everyone does – the King, his council. I also understand copies
have been posted in Lambeth on the archbishop's door, as well as
outside St Stephen's Chapel in Westminster. Who could do this?'

'Easy enough to arrange,' Urswicke retorted. 'The perpetrator
has probably hired some scrivener to provide good parchment and
night-black ink. The letters are well formed, round and eye-
catching. In truth, the malicious Merlin has prepared a poisonous
brew for others to stir.'

'Who?' Margaret snapped.

'Mistress, their name is legion for they are many. Clarence, or
any of those at court who hate you.'

'Why did they do this?'

'Mistress, to besmirch your name, to drive a wedge between
you and the powerful Stafford family. Sir Henry has died. Your
relationship with Buckingham and others of the Stafford family
has weakened. True, Sir John?'

'True, true,' the knight replied. 'But it will not work. The head
of our house, the Duke of Buckingham, knows the real value and
worth of the Lady Margaret. He will view these for what they are:
malicious, scurrilous lies.'

'But why now?'

'You are exposed,' Urswicke replied. 'You are a woman alone,
a widow. You may wish to marry again so they malign your every
marriage as well as yourself. You are depicted as some spider
lurking in the dark. They hint that you are an assassin, a lecher.
Oh, for the love of God,' Urswicke faltered, 'it's obvious what
they are implying and they heap hurt upon hurt.'

'Lady Margaret.' Sir John leaned against the table as he spread
his hands towards the countess. 'Squire Lambert, Guido and myself
would go on solemn oath before any prince or prelate to defend

your innocence in all these matters. Your husband, my late brother Sir Henry, was a truly sick man even before he was sorely wounded at the Barnet fight. After that battle, you took Henry to your exquisitely beautiful and most comfortable manor house of Woking. You provided every comfort and the best physicians possible.' He turned to his companion. 'Yes, Sir Guido?' The physician nodded vigorously.

'In the end, despite all this,' Sir John continued, 'my good brother died of his sickness, fortified by all the rites of Holy Mother Church. If you can use such a phrase, Sir Henry died a good Christian death. We are witnesses to this, as are the priests who came to shrive and anoint him.'

Lady Margaret tapped the table and smiled. 'Sir John, I thank you for that but these present troubles . . .?'

'They may well all be connected, my lady, to what happened at Woking.'

'You had trouble at the manor house?' Urswicke demanded. 'After the funeral, we left all three of you at Woking, and then what?'

Sir John shook his head. 'As I said earlier to Lady Margaret on our arrival here, at first nothing. When you visit Woking, ask your own retainers, who cared for us so well. For a while, all was calm, then the malevolent mysteries descended. Fire arrows loosed during the dead of night above the manor. A stag's head impaled on the pillar of the main gate; that's supposed to symbolise death and destruction, the emergence of dark forces, the presence of the demon lords of the air. The warning proved to be accurate. The rain of fire arrows continued. The corpses of dead animals were left around the manor, all discovered by servants. Ghastly gruesome sights: a dog with its head severed; a deer, its swollen belly ripped open. Matters turned from bad to worse. On one occasion we left the manor to hunt in the nearby woodlands. We were escorted by two of Lady Margaret's verderers as well as your principal huntsman. We entered the trees, making our way to Elfin glade.'

'Yes, yes, I know it well,' Margaret murmured. 'Most hunts gather there.'

'Well, we'd scarcely entered the glade when we were attacked. A flight of arrows hissing through the trees. Fortunately, wounds were slight.'

'Outlaws?' Bray demanded.

'We don't know because nothing happened.'

'What?'

'As I said, a flight of arrows then silence. Of course, by then we'd all dismounted, using our horses as shields. We waited for a fresh assault but then nothing. The huntsmen, who had been slightly wounded, agreed with the verderers that the danger had passed. Birdsong returned, the usual forest noises. We were alone so we went back to the manor.'

'And there was more?' Bray demanded.

'Four days after this, we left for Woking. The weather was freezing though the ground underfoot was hard and good for riding. We left the manor, taking the Woking road, when two of our horses were brought down by caltrops.'

'Caltrops?'

'Yes, Master Christopher. Someone had strewn barbed horse traps across our path. Two of our mounts stumbled and fell. I was thrown, so was Squire Lambert. Doctor Guido, riding behind us, managed to avoid the ambuscade. We were not injured, but two of our horses had to be given the mercy cut. My Lady, I am sorry for your loss. Two fine mounts from your stables.'

'Never mind, never mind.' Margaret shook her head. 'How did your assailants know on two occasions when you would leave the manor and what direction you would take?'

'Lady Margaret, we asked ourselves the same question. Perhaps our assailants had an informant in your household, someone they had suborned. Or they might have set up watches at the manor gates and acted accordingly. My Lady, in truth I cannot answer that.'

'And yet,' Urswicke cleared his throat, 'despite all those preparations, the arrow attacks, the caltrops, the strange sights and sounds in the dead of night, no real harm was done.'

'None, Master Christopher.' Sir John scratched his head. 'And that truly puzzles me. Strange sounds and shapes but nothing really substantial.'

'I agree,' Urswicke retorted. 'As if someone was trying to frighten you, nothing more, nothing less. But what is truly dangerous are these anonymous proclamations, the rantings of this malevolent Merlin. He,' Urswicke paused, 'is trying to fashion a link between Henry's death and you, Sir John. Because there is an implicit allegation that you are under threat and the attacks at Woking prove this.'

'True, true,' Sir John agreed. 'Yet my health, like that of my two comrades here, is hale enough.'

'And you intend to stay here.'

'Yes, Master Bray, we do – at least for a while. As you know, I now live in Burgundy. In my younger days I campaigned in France, where I met Guido, who hails from Castile.' Sir John's smile widened whilst the physician beamed expansively. 'We travelled to London to attend my good brother's funeral, but we also hoped – and we were not disappointed – to be invited by my Lady to reside here in this splendid townhouse, and in her richly endowed manor at Woking. What wonderful places to celebrate Advent, Yuletide, Christmas and Twelfth Night.'

'We have,' the countess replied, 'including your good selves, Sir John, been invited to court. His Grace the King, not to mention Queen Elizabeth and all the Yorkist princes, have insisted on that.'

'Good, good.' Sir John rubbed the side of his face.

'But there's something else, isn't there?' The countess's voice took on a lighter tone. 'We've referred to it already.'

'You know, good sister, there is.'

'Which is what?' Urswicke asked.

'Master Christopher, Master Bray.' Sir John took a deep breath. 'I am a scion of the red and gold retinue of Stafford. I am a member of a very powerful family. In my golden days, a knight banneret who has stood in the battle line of the royal array and,' Sir John became more expansive, 'as my good sister has said, and we have touched on this a little earlier, I style myself a chronicler. I have read, nay devoured, the great chronicles, copied carefully time and again for those who want to understand the past. You know the manuscripts – *Lanercost*, *Scalacronica*, Froissart, *The Great Chronicle of London*,' he waved a hand, 'and so on and so on.'

'For what purpose?' Urswicke, now intrigued, asked.

'Why, Master Christopher, I want to draw up my own chronicle, a detailed history of the Staffords, with all our glories and,' he shrugged, 'all our family failures. London,' he continued excitedly, 'is a veritable treasure house of history. I have applied for licence to study the records and archives of the great offices of state, the chancery, the Exchequer and King's Bench.' Sir John bowed towards Lady Margaret. 'And thanks to you sweet sister, I have also obtained licence to wander Westminster. Squire Lambert and Physician Guido will assist me. I do think—' He broke off as loud banging, shouts and cries echoed through the chamber.

Urswicke and Bray sprang to their feet, snatching up warbelts and fastening them on. There was a pounding of feet along the gallery outside, a swift knock on the door, which was then flung open as Lady Margaret's messenger Fleetfoot, accompanied by her new steward Hardyng, burst into the chamber.

'My Lady,' the steward gasped, 'you'd best come. The Frenchman, the stranger who came to the door—'

'Calm yourself, man.' Urswicke resheathed his sword.

'Hardyng,' Urswicke patted the steward's round, sweaty face, usually so cheerful, now twisted in concern. 'Slowly now,' Urswicke urged, gesturing both men to chairs around the table. 'Sit and tell us what happened.'

'Yes, yes,' the steward gasped, mopping his face with a kerchief he plucked from under the cuff of his jerkin. 'Fleetfoot and I were having morning ales in the buttery about an hour after your meeting began. A servant told me that a stranger – French, by the sound of him – was at the main door. Fleetfoot and myself went out. We brought the stranger into the house. He looked of sober appearance, fluent in the English tongue, though now and again he lapsed into French. I asked him his business; he replied that he needed to speak with you, my Lady, that it was urgent. I asked for his name, he said Bernard, then I asked him his business. He replied it was for the countess only. My Lady, I know from what you told me that you already had important affairs to deal with, so I asked him to wait. He said he would, so I put him in one of the waiting chambers. As a courtesy I brought him a goblet of wine and left him be. He seemed most respectable, orderly and law-abiding, he posed no danger. Now my Lady, as you know, our waiting chambers can be locked and bolted both within and without. I informed Bernard of that, adding for safety's sake, I would lock and bolt the door from the outside and that he should do the same on the inner. He listened to me carefully, nodded and replied that, in the circumstances, that would be most prudent. I left him for a while. Indeed, I almost forgot him, then I remembered and decided to ensure all was well. I knocked on the door, there was no answer. I undid the clasps, turned the lock, but Bernard had bolted it from within, I called Fleetfoot for help.' Hardyng gestured at the lanky, pale-faced courier. 'We knocked and we knocked,' Fleetfoot declared. 'We shouted and yelled – you must have heard the commotion. The door remained sealed and locked with no sound from within. My Lady, there is something very wrong. We need your permission to break that door down.'

'Do it.' Urswicke rose. 'My Lady, it is best . . .'

'No, I will come.' The countess pushed back her chair. 'All of you may come. Christopher, hurry ahead. You and Reginald do what you have to.'

A short while later, Bray and Urswicke had organised two burly scullions armed with hammers to break down the door. Swinging their heavy mallets, the scullions smashed the hinges and forced the door back, until the inside bolt snapped and the door crashed down like a drawbridge. Urswicke and Bray, both carrying lanterns, stepped across the threshold. Bernard lay sprawled in a chair, a wine goblet on the table beside him. Urswicke and Bray edged closer, their lanterns casting bobbing circles of light; these caught Bernard's face and both men groaned. A youngish man, Urswicke thought, certainly not yet past his thirtieth summer, Bernard must have died most cruelly and swiftly. He had not even tried to rise but died in the chair. The Frenchman's face was truly gruesome. The skin had a yellowish hue, eyes popping, his half-opened mouth filled with a dirty-white, frothy foam. Guido the physician stepped tentatively into the room.

'I'll state the obvious,' he murmured. 'The poor man is dead.'

'He certainly is,' Urswicke replied over his shoulder. 'A most horrid death.'

'Let me see.' Guido came between them. He crouched before the stricken man and felt for the blood beat in wrist and neck. 'Long gone,' he muttered. 'Whoever Andre Bernard was, he has gone to God. He is now before Heaven's judgement seat.' The physician rose and picked up the goblet from the table. He carefully dipped his finger in, swilling the dregs around. 'In my humble view,' he murmured, 'having witnessed the shock of death on the man's face and other symptoms, such as his ice-cold skin, Bernard was poisoned. I believe he was fed a most noxious potion.'

'Such as?' The countess stood framed in the doorway, Urswicke and Bray now standing either side of her.

'Such as, my Lady? Oh, simple enough. I would wager something very common, cultivated in many a herb garden.'

'Such as?' Urswicke snapped.

'My friend, this is only a guess, but I would suggest belladonna, juice of the lily, or an arsenic.'

'But how was it administered?' Bray came back into the chamber.

'The logical answer to that is this goblet,' Guido retorted.

'My Lady,' Hardyng's voice was almost a screech, 'the wine I brought was from a cask of the best Bordeaux. I tasted it myself, a generous sip. It warmed my belly and gladdened my heart. I suffered no ill-effects.'

'So,' Urswicke gestured at the door for Guido – clutching the goblet – to leave, 'it's best if this chamber was guarded.'

'I will arrange that,' Bray declared. 'As well as make a thorough search.'

Urswicke murmured his thanks and joined the rest outside on the gallery. Sir John looked agitated, Squire Lambert frightened. Guido the physician just stood sniffing at the goblet and shaking his head. Hardyng, still shocked, kept moaning about the wine until the countess dismissed both him and Fleetfoot.

'Christopher and Reginald,' she declared, 'search that room from floor to ceiling, then join me in my chamber.'

'And I will take this,' Guido held up the goblet, 'down to the cellars. I'll mix in a little *doucette* and see how the rats fare, yes?'

Urswicke absentmindedly agreed as he wondered who Bernard really was and why and how he had been so mysteriously murdered?

The countess posed the same question when Urswicke and Bray met in her privy chamber. Margaret sat in a high-cushioned chair before a roaring fire, Bray and Urswicke either side. The light outside had faded early as an icy rainstorm swept in from the river. The hailstones hammered the mullioned painted glass, as if desperate to break in.

'A true mystery,' Margaret declared. 'So what do we have here? Christopher, you have been sifting what we all saw and heard.'

'I have, mistress. But first, an obvious question. Are all your servants trustworthy?'

'No,' Margaret half laughed, 'of course not.'

'I would agree,' Reginald murmured. 'I am sure some of them are in the pay of the Brothers York. You know how it is, Christopher. One of our spit-boys visits a brothel, an alehouse or a tavern, where someone offers good silver for any gossip about the countess. Some might refuse but a few could be bribed. Oh yes, souls can be purchased for a pittance.'

'True, true,' Urswicke murmured, staring into the leaping flames. 'But first, let's deal with the mysterious Bernard. We searched his corpse. The man's clothing was fustian, his shirt and linen-shift underclothes of good quality. His boots were sturdy and the same could be said of his warbelt, on which both sword and dagger were sheathed. He had a woollen cloak with a hood and mittened gloves. Most of these items were found hanging on pegs in the waiting chamber. Bernard carried good pounds sterling but also French coins – *livres-tournois*. Now,' Urswicke leaned down and fished in his chancery satchel, 'we found nothing else on him. No rings, no bracelets, no neck chains. Nothing except these two items.'

Urswicke opened his hands and he held up a small medallion shaped like a pilgrim's badge. One side displayed the severed head of Saint Denis, the patron saint of Paris. On the other side were etched the three lilies of the French Crown. 'Then there's this.' Urswicke undid the small slender leather pouch and shook out what looked like a candle with a wick on one end, but the stem was painted blue and gold.

'I have seen and heard of similar,' Bray muttered. 'But for the life of me I cannot recall. Anyway, we have now established that Bernard is a skilled, experienced courier.'

'Reginald, how do you know that?'

'Mistress, he carries very little to betray him or his masters to anyone else. Oh yes, he has the insignia and the French pounds, but no documents, nothing that could be seized and examined. No memorandum in a secret cipher. No warrant, no licence, nothing! Now we know this man definitely came here to speak to you, but what about? A danger? Some issue connected with the troubles we now face? I suspect he meant well. He was polite, patient, self-effacing and prepared to wait.'

'Nor must we forget his words to Hardyng,' Urswicke declared.

'That in the circumstances it would be prudent to lock and bolt the door to the waiting chamber both within and without.'

The countess and Bray murmured their agreement.

'So,' Urswicke continued, 'Bernard.' He then paused.

'Christopher?'

'Nothing, mistress. Something amiss but it eludes me. Well, never mind. Let us concentrate on what we know or at least what is reasonable. I suggest Bernard came here to deliver a warning message. He would do it through a personal meeting with you, my Lady. We have no knowledge of the message he carried. He was placed in that chamber. Hardyng locked and bolted the door from the outside, a common enough practice so a stranger cannot go wandering the place. Bernard, however, also secured the door from within, which means he was being very cautious, most prudent, possibly aware of danger close by.'

'And there was,' the countess murmured. 'Bernard was correct. Murder sniffed at his heels but how was it done?'

'Three possibilities,' Urswicke replied. 'And all three are dictated by logic but with little or no evidence. First, the possibility that Bernard could have been poisoned before he entered this house. However, I doubt this. If the poison was as noxious as Guido maintained, it would have manifested itself immediately. Oh, by the way,' Urswicke added, 'our beloved physician did as he proposed and mixed the wine dregs with crushed sweetmeat. He went back a short while later to discover the rats had feasted without any harm.'

'And the second possibility?'

'My lady, that someone crept into this house, persuaded Bernard to open the door and somehow poisoned our mysterious visitor.' Urswicke shook his head. 'Highly unlikely, as is the third possibility that someone in this household gained access to that chamber. But why?' Urswicke sighed. 'How did the assassin murder a vigorous young man?'

'A true mystery,' Bray murmured. 'And there's the other tangle. The filthy proclamations posted at Cheapside and St Paul's. Vicious rumours which will snake through the city, repeated and embellished by the heralds of the alleyways and their flocks of street swallows. Who's responsible for that?' Bray pulled a face. 'I have looked again. The parchment and ink are of a high quality, the words well-formed and clear.'

'London houses a host of scriveners and clerks,' Urswicke declared. 'If the perpetrator hired such a scrivener, he would leave himself very vulnerable. I suspect the author of these libels wrote those proclamations himself.'

'Again,' Margaret murmured, 'the who, the why and the how are shrouded in mystery. As are those attacks on my good brother Sir John. In the meantime . . .' Margaret fell silent as the tocsin bell, close to the water-gate, began to toll. Shouts and exclamations echoed through the house. Urswicke and Bray hastily pulled on boots, warbelts and cloaks and hurried out to meet a fearful Hardyng standing at the top of the stairs.

'It's the water-gate,' the steward gasped. 'Sirs, we are under attack.'

'What?'

'Master Urswicke.' Fleetfoot now joined Hardyng. 'I could not believe it myself, but fire arrows are being loosed at the jetty and our water-gate.'

Urswicke and Bray brushed by the two retainers, hastening down the stairs, Urswicke shouting back at Fleetfoot to guard their mistress. The household was now alarmed, servants, scullions and others fleeing from the back of the house. Urswicke and Bray, followed by a reluctant Hardyng, reached the water-gate. Urswicke cautiously drew back the bolts. He opened the gate but slammed it shut as more fire arrows smacked into the wooden jetty, the flames sizzling as the water swirled around them.

'Notice,' Bray hissed, 'how the shafts are loosed up at the sky. In truth they pose no real harm.'

'Except to the jetty,' Urswicke snapped. 'Why all this nonsense?'

They stayed shivering in their cloaks until the arrow storm ceased. Urswicke sent Hardyng to their small armoury to bring back two long kite shields. Once he had, Urswicke and Bray strapped these on, opened the water-gate and, shields locked, edged onto the jetty. Here and there a fire arrow still flickered, small dancing pools of light in the encroaching dark. They reached the end of the jetty, bracing themselves against the bitterly cold breeze, whilst the fast-flowing river surging beneath them cast up a freezing spray.

'Nothing.' Urswicke stared across the turbulent waters. He could see nothing amiss, only the glow from lanterns fixed to the stern and prow of different river craft. The sound of horns and bells, warning other boats approaching, carried across the water.

'You are correct,' Bray agreed. 'There's nothing but the darkness.'

'And that's what I fear,' Urswicke retorted. 'Let us return to the countess.'

Lady Margaret was waiting for them in her chamber, now guarded by armed servitors. Hardyng assured them that the house had been thoroughly searched. All doors, gates and shutters were firmly locked and bolted. The countess, sitting on her chair before the fire, exuded that same formidable icy composure she had shown during the ferocious battle and its bloody aftermath at Tewkesbury. A most dangerous time, when she had been forced to witness the wholesale slaughter of her kinsmen, the Beauforts and their allies.

The countess had apparently been talking quietly to Sir John, Guido and Squire Lambert. All three rose as Urswicke entered. The two clerks assured them that all was well, at least for the moment. Urswicke then politely opened the door for all three guests to leave. Once they had, Urswicke and Bray settled in their chairs. Margaret lifted the ave beads wrapped around her gloved hand. She kissed the ivory cross then turned to Urswicke.

'So?'

'Nothing, my Lady. A great deal of smoke but, in truth, very little fire. I cannot understand what's happening. When I first opened the water-gate, for a few heartbeats, I am sure I glimpsed through the murk at least two war barges; they were moored either side of the jetty, kept steady with ropes lashed to its pillars, an easy enough task.'

'And how many men in each barge?'

'My Lady, I cannot say, but such craft can contain about twelve men a-piece. Six oarsmen and usually about six archers. Yet for what purpose? What was the point of a storm of fire arrows loosed against the night sky? So much energy and cost for little more than a fire show. War barges, oarsmen, archers are not cheap to hire, especially in the dead of winter. So why?'

'Whoever they are,' Bray intervened, 'their intention at this moment in time is simply to frighten, to threaten about what might follow. I agree with you, Christopher, the person who organised tonight's foray must have a great deal of money to launch such an attack.' Bray drummed his fingers on the arm of his chair.

'I'll make enquiries.'

'To whom?'

'Why, Christopher, one of London's most prominent rifflers, that true Prince of Darkness, the Lord Deadly Nightshade.'

'And I shall have words with another prominent gang leader.'

'Your esteemed father?'

'Correct, Reginald. My esteemed father, Sir Thomas Urswicke, Recorder of London and York's most fervent henchman . . .'

Christopher Urswicke pushed his way through the Cheapside throng, his cloak wrapped firmly about him. The clerk walked swiftly, one hand on the hilt of his dagger hanging in its brocaded sheath on his warbelt. The weather was freezing but the sky was clear, the sunlight strengthening as the city came to life. Church bells tolled for the Jesus Mass. Doors and shutters clattered open. Urswicke kept to the middle of the street. He didn't know which posed the greater hazard: the sewer running down the centre of the runnel, crammed with all forms of frozen filth, now melting under the morning warmth, or the rain of slops as households emptied cess buckets and jakes pots, a constant hail of human waste onto the streets below.

Urswicke stared around. Cheapside boasted glorious splendour, cheek by jowl with abject poverty. Rich merchants swathed in furs, their haughty wives also garbed in the best, rubbed shoulders with the Dwellers of the Dark, that legion of city poor who crawled out of their stinking cellars and plague pits to scavenge, beg and steal from many who did not give a whit about their welfare. Mendicant friars moved amongst these denizens of the city's underworld to plead on their behalf. Christopher gave as generously as he could and passed on.

He tried not to be distracted by the different sights and sounds as the crowds surged towards the stalls to buy for larder, pantry and buttery. The season of advent was drawing near and the Cheapside merchants were eager to exploit the demand for food, drink and all the luxuries of the yuletide festivities. The morning air was filled with the smell of perfumes, soaps, incense and candle grease. However, as Urswicke approached the soaring mass of

Newgate Prison, with its formidable iron gates and battlemented walls, the fragrances faded. The air reeked with the stench from the slaughter yards of the Cheapside fleshers and butchers. These merchants of the knife, the club and the hammer were busy slaughtering fowl and beast, chopping the fresh flesh so the breeze constantly carried a blood-tinged spray. The stench was so offensive that Urswicke eagerly bought a pomander just before he reached the great concourse stretching before the prison.

Urswicke always regarded Newgate to be the most miserable place on God's earth. Despite the season and the brightening sun, this day was no different. The execution carts, three in all, draped in red and black leather, were drawn up in a line to receive a host of prisoners for the gallows above Tyburn stream, as well as the great scaffolds at Smithfield's and Tower Hill. The condemned were herded onto the carts by the executioners garbed in black and scarlet, with nightmare masks covering their faces. Some prisoners were praying fervently, making sharp response to the litanies recited by Friars of the Sack. Other prisoners simply slouched, dejected. A few, who had drunk deep on cheap ale, blustered, cursed, cried or just stared unseeingly up at the sky. Further down the concourse, the misery continued, as bailiffs fastened night-walkers and peace-breakers into the stocks. They locked the prisoners in by neck, wrist or foot, before leaving them to the cruelty of spectators who could fling all kinds of filth at them.

Urswicke was glad to break through into the main market. He passed stalls selling everything from the ivory tusks of an elephant to costly fabrics bought in cities along the legendary Silk Road, which lay close to the borders of the Great Cham of Tartary. Everyone seemed to throng here: tinkers and chapmen, eager to buy items for their trays; royal purveyors in their richly embroidered tabards; soldiers and archers from the Tower, and of course a multitude of ordinary citizens who seemed more intent on staring than buying. Bailiffs and beadles, with their sharp white wands, patrolled the market pathways, keen to wield their sharp white canes to clip the head or the hands of the legion of naps, foists and pickpockets who always plagued such places. They were especially vigilant against the tribe of petty thieves – young children, ragged and dirty, who sped like mice, always ready to filch from stalls. In truth the marketplace was a heaving sea of colour, smell and noise. On occasion the clamour was worsened by incidents including the escape of a war dog from its kennel in a nearby mansion. The mastiff savaged two dogs then turned on one of St Anthony's pigs, snouting amongst the cobbles. The screams of the pig echoed shrilly until a Tower archer disposed of both attacker and victim with well-aimed shafts from his war bow. Once both animals lay dead, the dung collectors hastened to collect the corpses. They could sell the pork to some butcher whilst the dog's glossy skin also had a price. Urswicke watched the drama play out; he then made to walk on when he glimpsed movement out of the corner of his eye. He tried to act all nonchalantly, yet he was sure that a Friar of the Sack he'd glimpsed outside Newgate was now standing by a stall. The mendicant acted as if interested in what was on sale as he sifted a large set of ave beads through his mittened fingers.

'What are you doing there?' Urswicke whispered to himself. 'When you have penitents at Newgate waiting to be shrived?' Urswicke walked on until the elaborately carved Guildhall came into sight, its stained-glass windows glinting in the light. Between these ranged row upon row of different coats of arms, a veritable forest of heraldic devices carved and painted in the brickwork. Above the splendid gatehouse, a line of spikes sported a thicket of severed heads, mouldering into decay as crows and ravens plucked at the eyes and whatever soft flesh they could find. A cordon of men-at-arms thronged beneath the gatehouse. Urswicke, however, was immediately recognised, his sealed pass swiftly acknowledged, and he was allowed through into the cobbled courtyard beyond. Here a city scurrier greeted Urswicke before leading him through a doorway, up some steps and into his father's chancery chamber. Sir Thomas Urswicke was busy reading a manuscript. He lifted his head and his smooth, jovial face broke into a smile which Christopher regarded as nothing more than a Judas smirk.

'Beloved son, *pax et bonum*.' Sir Thomas waved to a cushioned chair to the side of his desk. 'Sit, rest yourself, would you like wine, a morning ale perhaps?'

'No thank you, esteemed father.'

Sir Thomas grinned.

'Let me finish this,' the Recorder lifted a beringed hand, 'and then, beloved son, I will be your most devoted listener.'

'Thank you, dearest father.'

The Recorder returned to his reading. Christopher studied his father, whom he regarded as one of the greatest villains in London. A born liar, a womaniser, a lecher, who had driven Christopher's beloved mother to an early grave. A trickster who would sell the shirt off your back, Sir Thomas had risen swiftly to sit high on the secret council of his Yorkist masters. Recently knighted by the King, Urswicke senior positively revelled in the glory and honour bestowed on him. A true fox of a man with his friendly, green eyes and jovial face, his moustache and beard clipped finely, as was his crimped auburn hair. The Recorder, lost in some business, pulled his furred robe closer about him as he read the manuscripts, lips moving soundlessly as he mouthed the words. Christopher watched and wondered, not for the first time, if his father's eyesight was impaired or whether he was simply taking his time and making his beloved son wait. Christopher suspected the latter, so he forced himself to relax, listening to the sounds from the courtyard below.

'Well?' The Recorder folded the manuscript he was reading and pushed it away.

'Urgent business, esteemed father?'

'Very urgent,' he murmured. 'Treachery and treason walk hand in hand, dear son. Plotting and counter-plotting are constant. Intrigue is in the very air we breathe. Danger threatens. Traitors lurk in the shadows. Killers wait to strike. Assassins slope like wolves through the murk and I, beloved son, go hunting all of these. You've seen the heads above the gateway?'

'I have, esteemed father, but never mind that. I do wonder . . .'

'What?'

'I thought, esteemed father, you were to lead an embassy to Rome?'

'Ah.' Urswicke senior shook his head. 'Not any more. Pressing business here. But never mind that.' The Recorder leaned back in his chair, then looked over his shoulder at the hour candle on its stand in the corner. 'The hours flit,' he murmured. 'So, dearest son, what is your business here?'

'Esteemed father, listen carefully.' And Urswicke, in brief, pithy sentences, described what Sir John Stafford had told him before moving on to the more recent attack against Countess Margaret's riverside mansion. The growing sense of danger and the sheer injustice of the defamatory proclamations about the countess posted around the city. The Recorder heard him out, face all serious, gently tapping his fingers on the leather-bound ledger before him. When Christopher finished, Sir Thomas pulled a face.

'All very sad,' he declared. 'All a great nuisance. Yet what has this to do with me?'

'Esteemed father, you are Recorder of this city, a member of the Royal Council. You have a clear responsibility for the safety and security of London. In which case, is it permissible, is it legitimate to tolerate – even permit – such outrages?'

'A display of fire arrows, nothing more, nothing less.'

'And Sir John's account of the attacks on him.'

'Beloved son, Woking is in Surrey, well beyond my jurisdiction.'

'But not that of the Royal Council, whilst the countess and her townhouse are very much in London.'

'Look.' Urswicke senior drew himself up in his chair. 'Let us be blunt. Let us be honest. Let us go to the heart of this matter. In brief, Margaret, Countess of Beaufort, comes from traitorous stock. No, No,' the Recorder held up a hand, 'hear me out, beloved son. The Beauforts fought the Brothers York tooth and nail until God delivered them into our hands at Tewkesbury. The Beauforts and their entire coven were despatched into the dark. They are gone, they are no more. All they left was little Margaret and her sorry son, Henry, now shivering in Brittany. Pathetic though he may be, nevertheless he declared that he is the last legitimate Lancastrian claimant to the English Throne. A spurious challenge from a callow youth and his ill-advised uncle Jasper, who styles himself Lord of Pembroke.'

The Recorder, now in full voice, raised a hand as if taking an oath. 'Beloved son, as I have said, let us go to the very heart of this problem. Attacks have been launched on the countess's good brother Sir John Stafford and his two companions Squire Lambert and Physician Guido. Similar assaults have taken place on the countess's riverside mansion. So first, because of what I said earlier, do you think these attacks are the fault of York, lashing out at its last, pathetic opponent? I assure you it is definitely not! You see, beloved son, the Brothers York are highly intelligent and deeply versed in the art of politic. Naturally we would like to secure the person of the countess's son Henry, but that does not mean we nourish ill designs against his mother the countess. Let me be frank, this is not because we are merciful.' The Recorder laughed and shook his head. 'Oh no, it's a matter of politic. We do not wish to be, or appear to be, persecutors of Countess Margaret. The Beaufort woman is popular and well liked and deeply respected by many of the nobility and commons. The bishops also, both here and abroad, regard her most favourably. She has been generous to Holy Mother Church and of course she also enjoys the favour and protection of the Duke of Buckingham and the entire Stafford brood. Oh, I could go on and mention how the Lady Margaret is so fervently supported by the colleges of Oxford and Cambridge, which she has enriched through generous endowments. So, beloved son, it is not in our interests for the countess to be harmed in any way while she lodges in this kingdom. Of course,' he sighed dramatically, 'the Beauforts had, and still have, powerful opponents. Yorkist zealots who would love to annihilate the Lancastrian cause; hack it out root and branch and extinguish it completely.'

'But surely that is not you, esteemed father? And if the Brothers York wish to be seen as tolerant of the countess, surely they can help her now?'

'I shall certainly make careful enquiries. Moreover, as you may appreciate, beloved son, I cannot post guards around the countess's mansion – that could be misinterpreted as house arrest. His Grace the King would not permit it.' The Recorder rubbed the side of his face and smiled ruefully. 'So much trouble eh, such a tangle! But do you know what, Christopher? I would pay good silver to know whom you really serve?'

'Beloved father, the same person you do.'

'Who is?'

'Myself.'

The Recorder chuckled, rocking backwards and forwards in his chair.

'Very good, very good, my son.' He then leaned forward. 'Rest assured, Christopher, I shall do something, but let me think.'

Christopher glimpsed the sneer which flitted across his father's face, the tightening of lips, eyes abruptly glancing away.

You're lying, Christopher thought; this is all a lie and I am wasting my time. 'I should be gone,' he told his father. 'You're taunting me, playing the cat to my mouse. Your hatred for the countess is greater than any love for your only son. This is futile.'

Urswicke rose and made his farewells. He left the Guildhall and hurried along a maze of narrow streets leading down to the river. He then turned and followed the thoroughfare running along the north bank which would take him back to the countess's mansion. He was so deep in thought, reflecting on his meeting with Lord Mephistopheles, as he called his father, that he'd forgotten about being followed until he glimpsed two Friars of the Sack in their distinctive earth-brown robes and black-and-white striped hoods. Both friars were making their way towards him along the narrow alleyway, a torch-boy hastening before them. The fiery brand that the lad carried created pools of light around both him and his customers. The presence of the torch-boy re-assured Urswicke, until he heard a noise behind him. He abruptly turned, and shadows further down the alleyway quickly moved back into the darkness. Urswicke threw his cloak back. The two friars approaching him were walking faster. Urswicke drew both sword and dagger as the torch-boy abruptly lunged forward, the blazing brand he carried aimed directly at Urswicke's face. The clerk lashed out with his boot, a well-aimed kick which sent the boy staggering back so he collided with the two friars. Urswicke did not wait or turn to confront the enemy behind him, he just lashed out with sword and dagger, forcing the two friars aside, then ran. He reached the mouth of the alleyway leading on to the thoroughfare when screams from behind him made him turn and glance back. However, the alleyway was so dismal, so murky, that all Christopher could make out were jostling shapes and the cries of someone mortally wounded. Urswicke decided not to tarry to find out what was happening.

'Enough is enough,' he whispered to himself. 'Enough evil for one day.'

PART TWO

'Those recruited to the Garduna would be absolved of all wrongdoing.'

Reginald Bray would have heartily agreed with his comrade. Confident that his mistress was secure and protected, Bray had decided to take Bernard's corpse, sheeted in a shroud and fastened to a handcart, down to the public mortuary, the Paradisium, near St Mary Le Bow. He would pay the coffin fee to the Harrower of the Dead, who'd also arrange for three requiems to be chanted for the dead man's soul. Bray just wished he could force his way through the throng clustering around Cheapside's stalls, all eager to buy or to reach the stocks to mock the unfortunates imprisoned there. Advent was fast approaching, and all the preparations for Christmas. The shops and stalls were busier than ever. The fleshers and butchers now deeply immersed in a frenzy of cutting sheep, deer, swans, pigs, chickens, peacocks, porpoises and seals. The many pastry shops were also in a flurry, offering pies, tarts, pastries, sugared delicacies and honeyed wafers. The smell of food, raw or cooked, hung heavy in the air.

Mummers and masquers were also flooding into the city, offering their services to stage advent plays in churches and chapels across London. Some of these mummers now advertised themselves, staging scenes from their masques to provoke the interest of any would-be hirer. King Herod pushed his way through the crowd, his head and face almost hidden by a thick, blood-red beard and wig. He breathed out insults and warnings to his gaily decorated wife who, garbed in bright scarlet, urged her husband on to the slaughter of the Divine Child. Some of the crowd stopped to witness this as well as the arrival of the Magi, all three sharing the same poor hack. Soldiers, wearing the blue and mulberry of York, began to poke fun at the scene. Herod called up his minions and a fight ensued.

Bray cursed. The way forward was blocked, but then he glimpsed

the mouth of Catstail Alleyway which would provide a way out.
Bray pushed his handcart forward, banging other people's legs
and being greeted with a litany of filthy abuse, but at last he was
through. He placed the handcart against the mouldering wall of
the alleyway and, despite the dirt which swilled around his boots,
and the horrid stench that wafted on the cold breeze, he leaned
against the wall until his breathing calmed and the sweat cooled.
Bray glanced back at the crowds which surged past the narrow
mouth of the runnel. He took a deep breath, gripped the handles
of his handcart and began to push it along the rutted ground. He
drew level to the entrance of an ancient alehouse when its battered
door was flung open and a drunk lurched out. The toper stared
blearily around, then staggered across to clutch Bray's arm.

'Where are you going?' he slurred, pointing ahead into the inky
blackness. 'Don't you know the alleyway is blocked off?'

'No, no.' Bray shook off the man's hand. He watched him
stagger away, then pushed the handcart on. He had only gone a
short distance when he stopped and groaned. The drunk had been
correct. A house, much decayed, had collapsed, creating a barrier
across the alleyway. Bray, cursing under his breath, turned the cart
and, as he did, tensed. Just for a fleeting moment he'd glimpsed
movement at the far end of the alleyway. Dark shapes against the
light which quickly flitted back into the shadows. Bray crossed
himself, muttered a prayer and pushed the handcart on. He passed
the alehouse just as two women, whores by the way they swaggered, stepped out. Bray pushed on, but the two ladies of the night
were not to be ignored. In the dim light of the alleyway, they
looked young and wholesome, their olive-skinned faces framed
by perfume-drenched wigs. They both grinned at Bray as they
blocked his path, smiling provocatively, their full breasts straining
at low-cut bodices.

'Monsieur, you wish to rest and play?' They pointed to an
enclave cut deep into the alleyway wall. 'Come now.' The whores
parted to go either side of the cart. Bray had to concede that both
young women were fair and homely, unlike the raddled hags who
usually prowled these dark places.

Bray smiled at the woman on his right, then froze as three
figures abruptly appeared in the mouth of the alleyway. Bray,
confused, dropped the handcart. A voice screamed a warning in

broken English. Bray turned then swerved as the woman who had gone behind him lunged forward with a sickle-shaped dagger. Bray crouched, pushing the cart to block the woman to his right. All was confusion. The whores were also alarmed at the arrival of these three strangers, but they too were trapped. Crossbows clicked, both women were hit, one deep in the throat, the other high in her back as she turned to flee. Bray pulled himself up then drew his own sword and dagger.

'*Pax et bonum*,' a voice called. 'Master Bray, we are not your enemies.'

Hooded, cloaked figures crept forward. They totally ignored Bray as they crouched beside the fallen women, pulling back the head of each to give the mercy cut, a deep slit which opened their throats.

'I think they are dead!' Bray declared sarcastically.

'We have to ensure they remain so,' a voice mocked back.

Bray watched as the women's clothing was searched and items snatched away. Bray used this moment to leave the handcart and stand with his back to the alley wall, sword and dagger ready. The three men grouped around the handcart.

'Who are you?' Bray demanded.

'Friends of Andre Bernard. We saw you leave the countess's house. We guessed you were moving Andre's corpse to the Paradisium, where you have arranged for him to be coffined and given honourable burial.'

'Aye, and to pay for requiems to be sung for his soul.'

'The countess is most gracious, but we shall take Andre's corpse. It is only fitting. How did he die?'

'Poisoned! Poisoned in a waiting chamber at the countess's mansion, though as yet we don't know how, why, or who is responsible.'

One of the men stepped forward, bloodied hands raised in the sign of peace. He pulled down the muffler across his face. Bray was aware of a young, sharp face with searching eyes.

'Is that the truth, Master Bray? Yes, or no?'

'Yes, and who are you?'

'Wait and see, Master Bray, wait and see.'

'And these?' Bray pointed to the corpses of the two women.

'Devils incarnate, Master Bray – the Garduna.'

'Who are they?'

'As I have said, Master Bray, wait and see.' The speaker paused as two street swallows burst into the alleyway and stood gaping at the corpses. They then turned and fled.

'It's time we were gone,' Bray declared, sheathing his sword and dagger. 'The news will be all over Cheapside.' Bray pushed his way past his rescuers, crossed himself and hurried out of the alleyway, determined to put as much distance between himself and the place of slaughter as possible.

Bray threaded his way through the noisy throng. He crossed the Street of Sighs which bordered Whitefriars and the Place of the Tombs, where the shadow-shifters and midnight people lurked. These stayed housed in their miserable cellars until the light faded. Only then would they crawl out, hungry for plunder. During the day the place was as silent as any tomb, yet they still had watchers guarding every twist and turn of the paths: the runnels snaked past crumbling mansions and rotting dwellings, pushed so close together that the houses looked like a line of drunken men. War dogs chained to posts growled and snarled. Voices sang out about the approach of a stranger. Bray replied, shouting out who he was and why he was here. Once again, Bray drew sword and dagger. The voices faded into silence. At last he reached Magpie Lane; halfway down stood a shabby tavern, The Poison Pot. Two rifflers standing guard on the door tried to block his entrance.

'I do not think,' Bray grated, 'that the great Lord Nightshade will be happy that the man who so successfully defended him on a capital charge before King's Bench is now being denied access to him.'

The two rifflers hastened to allow him through into the murky, low-ceilinged taproom, which reeked of spices used to cure the hams hanging in nets from the ceiling. The light was dim, the shutters pulled fast. The room was dark, except for the blaze of light from the fire roaring gustily in the hearth at the far end. The man sitting in the huge quilted box chair rose after one of the rifflers whispered in his ear. Clutching his fur-rimmed robe about him and carefully adjusting his skull cap, Deadly Nightshade, Lord of London's underworld, strode quickly to clasp Bray's outstretched hand. He gripped it warmly and smiled most benevolently at his visitor.

'Reginald, so good to see you.' Nightshade's smile widened. He let go of Bray's hand and stepped back to study his visitor from head to toe. 'You haven't changed, my friend. Come.' Nightshade gestured at the cushioned chair next to his. He insisted that Bray remove his cloak and share a cup of the 'best wine stolen from Bordeaux'. Both men sat down. Nightshade whispered to his henchman. Bray used the opportunity to study this most sinister character, who dressed like a poor curate. Nightshade was garbed in a shabby black gown, except for the silk bands around his throat, tied carefully to hide the noose marks. The riffler chief had been condemned to three different hangings. On each occasion, either a pardon had arrived or Nightshade had been cut down by comrades who stormed the scaffold. A man who had been strangled three times yet still escaped the noose was regarded as a legendary figure throughout the city underworld. The riffler chief was a former cleric who knew enough Latin to claim benefit of clergy, if accused of any crime, though sometimes he found it difficult to prove his clerical status. A strange character, Nightshade was reputed to have a liking for dressing as a woman. He certainly painted his face as generously as any London whore, and insisted on dyeing his long, shaggy hair different colours. Today he had dyed it blue. Deadly Nightshade looked as gruesome as ever, despite the constant smile on his small round face.

'Well.' Nightshade took a deep breath. 'What does Reginald Bray want from me? Information?'

'Perceptive as ever,' Bray murmured in mock astonishment. 'Information, my Lord Nightshade, about events in London.'

'Ah yes, events in London.' Nightshade slurped from his goblet carved in the shape of a skull. He smacked his lips in appreciation. 'I have heard about one event. My street swallows, darling boys, have just reported the killing of two whores. Spanish girls, apparently. Witnesses claim they have never been seen before.' He leaned closer. 'Happened within the last hour. Any knowledge of that, Master Bray?'

'You've been keeping close watch on me and mine?'

'Of course, my friend. Ever since the most recent attack on you. A shower of fire arrows against the water-gate of your noble mistress's townhouse!'

'You know about that?'

'Well that's obvious, my friend, it intrigues me. More importantly, it certainly did not have my permission, sanction or support.
Such an attack should have been brought before me.'

'Do you know who was involved and why?'

'Not yet, but I have two of my most faithful henchmen,
Wormwood and Underhill, scurrying here and there.' Nightshade
supped at his wine. 'I tell you this, my friend, something stirs
deep in the dark.' He refilled his goblet. 'Though, my friend, I
cannot say what, except for rumours about the emergence of
strangers – men and women not of our brotherhood. So, Master
Bray, for the moment that's all I can say. But,' he added, 'before
the vespers bell tomorrow, I am certain we shall both be wiser
men . . .'

Countess Margaret signed and sealed the letter she had dictated
to Sir Thomas Urswicke. The countess had been blunt and forth-
right, bitterly declaring that neither she nor her household were
safe from attack, be it on the river or along the streets of London.
She demanded, as a royal kinswoman, that she and hers be afforded
the Crown's protection, and that those responsible for such
murderous, malicious attacks be unmasked and brought to justice.
The countess sat back in her chair, Bray on her left, whilst Urswicke
hurried out of the chamber to hand the sealed letter to Fleetfoot
for urgent despatch to the Guildhall. Once the courier had left,
Urswicke rejoined the countess. For a while she just sat, fists
clenched in her lap, her narrow face pale and tense.

'My good brother Sir John,' she declared, 'advises me to join
him in Burgundy. He claims it is the safest place for us and our
King would not balk at that. If we fled to join my son in Brittany
or Louis XI in Paris, we could be deemed as traitors consorting
with the enemy. Everything here would be confiscated, forfeit to
the Crown.'

'There is some logic in what Sir John says,' Bray murmured.
'For this cannot go on. These attacks—'

'There's a number of threads,' Urswicke intervened. 'First the
sinister events around Woking. Fire arrows in the dead of night.
Shafts loosed in a forest glade. Caltrops strewn along a path and
other macabre warnings. At first these could be regarded as deeply
threatening, but in the end just a great deal of drama with no real

danger. The second thread are the events here in London. Again, more fire arrows loosed, this time at our water-gate, and once more a great deal of sword clashing but nothing else. The third thread is much more pernicious. Murder and attempted murder. Our visitor Bernard poisoned before we could even meet him. Bernard was murdered but why, how and by whom remain mysteries. The fourth thread. Who are the perpetrators of all this? Those responsible. Is it one individual or a group? Did he or they plan these ambuscades in Woking then follow Sir John Stafford back here to continue their mischief? The fifth thread we have touched upon. The fire arrow attacks both here and Woking pose no danger. However, the assaults on both Bray and myself were truly murderous. Sixthly,' Urswicke paused, 'do we have an enemy within?'

'What do you mean?' Bray demanded.

'Just a thought. It certainly could explain Bernard's murder. And finally,' Urswicke continued, 'there's those filthy proclamations and their horrid allegations.' Urswicke broke off at the sound of shouts and yells below. Footsteps echoed along the gallery followed by a furious knocking on the door which was flung open as Hardyng burst in.

'My Lady, gentlemen,' Hardyng beckoned, 'you must come.'

'Why, what is the matter?' the countess demanded, half rising.

'Lambert has been poisoned. He's retching and vomiting below.'

Urswicke told the countess to stay while he and Bray followed Hardyng down to the scullery. The steward cleared the curious thronging about in the doorway. In the scullery beyond, Lambert sat on a stool by the open garden door, vomiting into a bowl held by Sir John. Guido, crouched on the other side of the squire, was gently urging Lambert not to worry, to relax and let his stomach purge itself. The young man raised his head at Urswicke's approach. He looked ghastly pale, vomit dribbling down his chin. He tried to speak, only to turn away and retch.

'He'll be fine,' Guido murmured. 'I fed him salt and water; his retching will expel the evil humours.'

'How?' Urswicke demanded. 'How did this happen?'

'It would appear,' Bray replied, 'that a local pastry shop sent a tray of honeyed comfits for Sir John, yes Hardyng?'

The steward simply stood shaking his head.

'For God's sake man, calm down and tell us.'

'I was going about my duties,' Hardyng, clearly flustered, replied. 'I heard a knock on the door, and since,' he stammered, 'since the last nasty occurrence . . .'

'You were careful?' Urswicke soothed. 'Naturally you were cautious, we understand that.'

'I answered the door, opening it up on the chain, I peered out. Dusk was falling. Nothing to be afraid of – just a young boy holding a sealed box. He said he'd been sent by the Dulcimers; it's a shop patronised by the countess. The pastry boy said it was a welcoming gift for Sir John.'

Urswicke shrugged.

'I took it and gave it to Lambert,' Hardyng finished.

'And I am sure, when we investigate,' Bray declared, 'we will find that Dulcimers sent no gift. The pastry boy was probably a street swallow hired for a coin.'

'I would agree,' Urswicke declared. 'Any investigation would only reach such a conclusion, which would be totally useless.' Urswicke, who had walked to the door of the scullery, turned and came back. Lambert was now recovering, though he still sat slumped, the bowl full of vomit resting on his lap.

'So what actually happened?' Urswicke crouched beside the victim. 'Tell me.'

'Hardyng gave me the box of sweetmeats.' Lambert gasped, pausing to control his breathing. 'I thought it was a kind gift. I was hungry. I broke the seal and opened the box. The sweetmeats looked truly delicious so I ate one. Within a few heartbeats, my belly began to gripe.'

'He'll recover,' Sir John declared, kneeling down on the other side of Squire Lambert. Stafford gently stroked the young man's hair. He caught Urswicke's questioning look and abruptly removed his hand.

A loud knocking on the main door of the house brought Urswicke to his feet. Hardyng, quietly mouthing curses, hurried to answer it. He came back gesturing at Bray.

'Someone to see you, sir. He rejoices in the name of Wormwood.'

Bray met his visitor in the hallway; he was a small, cheery-faced man, with a mop of unruly hair. He handed Bray a narrow leather sack.

'My friend,' he murmured, Wormwood's voice was scarcely

above a whisper. 'Lord Nightshade sends his regards. My comrade Underwood is busy with me, casting about for the information you need. In the meantime, we collected this from the Standard in Cheapside, one copy amongst many.' Wormwood stood back and bowed. 'Master Reginald, I must be gone.'

Bray closed the door and shook out the contents of the leather sack. He unrolled the parchment and groaned. He glanced over his shoulder at Urswicke who had followed him from the scullery.

'More of the same, my friend, more of the same . . .'

'Read it again, Christopher, please.' The countess fought to keep her voice calm. She stared around the chancery chamber on the ground floor of her mansion. Urswicke and Bray had been joined by Guido and Sir John.

'Mistress.' Urswicke picked up the proclamation. The parchment and the black ink were identical to the first broadsheet he had seen. 'Mistress,' he repeated, 'these are lies. Malicious, hurtful lies.'

'Read,' the countess insisted.

'Know ye,' Urswicke began, mouthing the words carefully, 'know ye that the woman, the self-proclaimed Countess of Richmond, mother of the traitor and false claimant Henry Tudor, kinswoman of Jasper Tudor, as well as other traitors of the House of Beaufort, is a virago who has innocent blood on her hands. Murder is lodged at her mansion. Little wonder strangers perish there whilst those who rightly judge her wrong loose fire arrows as a warning. Margaret of Richmond, the Beaufort Bitch is, for all her crimes, twice as fit for Hell as any sinner. Know ye that . . .'

Urswicke let the proclamation slip from his fingers. 'My Lady, I can read no more of such fetid filth.'

'Leave it, mistress,' Bray counselled.

The countess nodded. She sat for a while, eyes closed, then she sighed noisily, opened her eyes and stared around.

'I have petitioned my father for help,' Urswicke declared, 'and I have sent Fleetfoot with a second request for assistance in which I detailed the poisoning of Squire Lambert. The poor boy is now recovering?'

'Very much so,' Sir John replied. 'Guido gave him a purge then, when his belly quietened, a light sleeping potion.'

'My sweet sister,' Stafford continued briskly. 'I beg you, and those who advise you, to join me and mine in Burgundy.' He lowered his voice. 'Duke Charles is certainly not on the best of terms with York. He would give you and yours, and especially your exiled son, the warmest welcome and safest refuge. You would all enjoy his direct protection. You would be provided with every courtesy. Yes, Brother Guido?'

The physician nodded. 'Too true,' he murmured, 'too true.'

Urswicke studied his mistress. He could see she welcomed Sir John's suggestion, whilst he was tempted to agree. These attacks on the countess were only part of the burden of who she was and what she represented. The countess would never be acceptable to the Brothers York. Danger in all its forms stalked Margaret Beaufort: the silent assassin with a dagger or poison; the arrow loosed from the darkness of some alleyway: an unfortunate accident on land or sea; zealous Yorkists, like the felon who penned that proclamation, always ready to spring an ambuscade along some lonely coffin path. He glanced at Bray who sat, eyes half closed.

'Burgundy is a possibility,' the countess declared. 'A strong possibility.'

Urswicke noticed how both Sir John and Guido welcomed this most warmly.

'However,' the countess continued, 'we are not in Burgundy yet and we must take precautions.'

'One of which,' Sir John intervened, 'could be a swift withdrawal from here to the Burgundian war cog now berthed at Queenhithe, *The Pegasus.*'

'A good worthy cog,' Guido murmured. The physician rose and bowed towards the countess. 'My Lady, if there's nothing else,' he gestured at Sir John, 'we really should return to Squire Lambert.'

The countess replied there was nothing for the moment and the meeting ended.

Urswicke and Bray inspected the manor to ensure all doors, gates, posterns, windows and shutters were secure. Bray declared he was tired and retired for the evening. Urswicke visited the countess and, at her request, joined her in compline, reciting the responses as Margaret murmured the psalm. Urswicke fervently prayed the verses, which compared God to a fortress, a wall of iron, a sure rock of safety.

After the service, Urswicke tried to discuss with the countess what might be the rock which secured her and her household? She just smiled, stroked his arm, and said she must reflect.

Once Urswicke had left, closing the door behind him, Margaret put her face in her hands and wept bitterly, making no attempt to control her quiet sobbing. After a while she felt calmer. She took a cloth from the lavarium and gently dabbed her face. She then walked over to the triptych celebrating St George's victory over the Dragon of Egypt, the Devil, the fiercest of all serpents which, according to legend, moved in a fiery glow as if it was an angel of light. This legend had inspired the painter, who'd depicted the dragon preparing to spread out the coils of sin, to trap souls on their journey to Heaven. The dragon waited for such souls to suffocate on sin, be caught in the coils of guilt and so be consumed. The artist had cleverly crafted this and, in doing so, diverted the attention of anyone staring at the triptych from St George, whose shield and tabard proudly proclaimed the Beaufort arms. Margaret smiled to herself. This was her private memorial to those Beauforts slain in battle or hacked to death on the scaffold of some country town. She crossed herself, whispered a requiem, and returned to her chair before the fire.

'What can I do?' she murmured to the dancing flames. 'Where can I go?'

Margaret let her mind sift the possibilities. Scotland was regarded as hostile by the Brothers York. France? I would be depicted as consorting with the enemy. Brittany? I would be accused of closeting with attainted traitors – my own beloved son Henry and the redoubtable Jasper Tudor. Spain was in tumult, the Catholic states of Castile, Aragon and Leon trying to unite against the forces of Islam. Burgundy would be the most suitable. Duke Charles was no longer a friend of York. The countess paused in her reflections as a random thought caught her attention; she was determined to share this with Urswicke. In the meantime, she had one other path to follow which might prevent attack against her and her household, one not even Urswicke knew. However, for the moment, she must bide her time.

*   *   *

The Basilisk stood on the corner of Snake Alley, well-named for the narrow winding slit of a trackway, no broader than a coffin path. The Basilisk was derelict, the haunt of mice, rats and other vermin. However, on that particular night, lights glowed from its dank cellar, where a man, completely stripped naked except for his loincloth, lay spreadeagled on the muddy floor. The prisoner's ankles and wrists were tied fast to the pegs driven into the squalid dirt. He was surrounded by cowled, visored figures. One of these, their leader, knelt beside the prisoner and pricked him lightly under the chin with the tip of his long dagger.

'So,' the leader whispered in Spanish. 'You are Rafael from Gijon in Galicia. That is what the scrap of parchment, a tavern bill, proclaims you to be. Are you Spanish, Rafael?'

The prisoner just gabbled back in a tongue none of his captors could understand.

'I know you,' the leader whispered. 'And now you must know me. I am François, captain and leading light of the Luciferi. Our chancery is the Secret Chamber, the Cabinet Noir deep in the Palace of the Louvre, home of our most Christian King Louis XI of France. You my friend,' François pricked with his dagger again, 'are a member of the Garduna, that legion of demons housed in secret lairs around Toledo. You are Garduna,' François repeated. 'You are not a master, but what? Are you one of the Chevatos? A Capataz? Or a member of the Floreadores or Ponteadores?' He nipped the prisoner's throat with the dagger point; his swarthy-faced captive simply struggled against his bonds, eyes glaring with malice.

'Why are you here?' François demanded. 'Where are the rest of your rat horde? Where did you land?'

The prisoner again gabbled back in the language nobody there could understand.

'Very well.' François rose to his feet. 'Armand,' he turned to his henchman, 'you have the funnel?'

'Of course.' Armand held up the leather tube with long straps on one end.

'Fasten it around our guest,' François ordered.

Armand did so, with the help of comrades, shifting and shoving until the open end of the funnel rested firmly against the right side of the prisoner's body, just below the chest.

'And the rat?' Armand went into the dark and returned holding a rusty cage. The rat it contained was a fully mature rodent, starved and confused. The rat beat its snout time and again against the cage, its clawed feet scrabbling furiously, desperate to escape. François, gingerly holding the cage, forced his prisoner to stare at the rat beating itself against the wire.

'See my friend,' François murmured, 'something we learned from our English hosts, to make people more amenable. Look!' he pointed back over his shoulder at Armand, who drew closer holding a flaming cresset, 'yes, yes, let me explain. We are here in this disgusting cellar. No one knows we are here, no one really cares, no one will see or hear anything. We are all alone. Now brother rat here is desperate to escape. Even more desperate to eat. We intend to slip the rat into that funnel, now fastened so close to you. Armand will then start a fire at the other end of the funnel, forcing the rat up against your body. Desperate and terrified, the rat has no other way out except to gnaw his way through you. I assure you it is a cruel, horrid death. You will die screaming, an agonising end to your wicked life.' François paused. 'We know you are of the Garduna. You were with those two Cobertas who attacked the countess's men. You were your comrades' dagger man, their guard, their protector, yes? All of you are Garduna. Yes?'

Once more the prisoner spat back in a tongue no one present could understand.

'Ah well.' François rose to his feet. 'Armand, proceed.' The cage was thrust next to the funnel's opening, the bolts across the lid removed so the small wire-mesh door could be lifted. The rat lunged forward, snout and paws scrabbling at naked flesh. Armand lit the pile of oil-soaked chippings, using his dagger to push the small fiery bundle up against the open end of the funnel. Again the rat lunged forward; this time it bit and the prisoner screamed.

'Very well, very well,' he shouted.

'So, my friend, you do speak.'

'Release me,' the prisoner pleaded. 'Release me and I will talk. I am, as you say, a Capataz . . .' He broke off screaming as the rat bit again.

Using their daggers, François and Armand forced the rat back into its cage and clasped the small door shut. The cage was taken away, the funnel unstrapped and the prisoner's bonds cut. François ordered wine to be splashed over the rat bites, then crouched beside the prisoner, who was now massaging his arms and tugging at the cuff of his loincloth. François realised something was wrong, even as the prisoner, who'd secretly taken the pellets from the hem of the linen cloth, thrust them into his mouth and swallowed immediately. François lunged forward, and his comrades hastened to help, but the prisoner just grinned in a display of yellow, broken teeth.

'The Garduna,' he whispered, even as he began to tremble, 'the Garduna will avenge me.' He then fell back, jerking and thrashing about in a fatal fit.

François could only watch his prisoner die. At last the Garduna lay still, eyes popping, mouth dribbling a dirty yellow froth.

'He was certainly Garduna,' François declared. He crossed himself as he got to his feet. 'And we learnt nothing. We are certainly no wiser. We know the Garduna are in London. We recognise they are implacably opposed to our saintly King and the countess. But who hired them, God knows? And where do these vermin lurk? Again, that's a secret.' He beckoned his comrades closer. 'I suspect,' he declared, 'we are facing an entire battle group under a senior captain. They are well armed and most proficient. But how did they get here? Where are they hiding? What do they intend? We suspect they have designs against Countess Margaret and her household. The comrades I despatched to Woking have reported strange occurrences and the same here in London.' He picked up a wineskin and took a generous mouthful before passing it around. 'We tried to meet with the countess; poor Andre went into her house only to be poisoned. So the Garduna must have their people either in or close to the countess's household. In a word, we cannot trust anyone around her.'

'Bray and Urswicke were attacked,' Armand declared. 'They are reputed to be the countess's most loyal henchmen.'

'But are they truly? Urswicke's father is an ardent Yorkist, a member of the Royal Council, their nominee as Recorder of London. Urswicke senior, along with others, belongs to the war party, urging King Edward to strike at France. Oh no, we are still in the dark here, stumbling about looking for a door to open. We cannot really trust anyone.' François paced up and down the cellar.

'What,' he exclaimed, 'did our comrade Lucien mean before he had his throat cut in a tavern along the road to Paris?'

'François?'

'Lucien wrote me a cryptic message saying he was to meet an informant at The Salamander, an auberge on the road between Paris and Provins. We do not know who this was, but Lucien claimed that the man he was to meet had information about something which could prove most injurious to the House of Lancaster and the kingdom of France. Now we do not know the slightest thing about what that could be. Lucien and the man he was going to meet were murdered. Just scraps,' he whispered, 'about harm to be done.' He clicked his tongue. 'Two of ours were murdered and the auberge they died in burnt to the ground.'

'The Garduna?'

'Undoubtedly!'

François picked up his warbelt, which lay close to the dead man. He buckled this on and pointed to the corpse. 'A Garduna to the end. Loyal and ruthless, I should have searched him more thoroughly.'

'François, he still would not have confessed.'

'Well, his soul has gone to judgement. Now bury his corpse.'

'Where?'

'Why here. Then let's be gone.' François walked to the door and turned. 'So far we have killed at least five Garduna along the narrow alleyways of London. The Garduna will learn about their losses and come hunting us. If we could only find their nest, their lair.'

'Have you heard from Baptiste and Corneille?'

'No, Armand, I have not. Both men are skilled verderers, or were, before they joined the Cabinet Noir. I have ordered them to search around the countess's manor in Woking, to blend in with the forest people and discover what they can. Who knows what they might find.'

The Master was also holding a meeting in the taproom of The Chasuble, which lay deep in the close, wet greenness of Woking Forest. He and his battle group – or phalanx, as they were sometimes called – had settled in comfortably enough, swallowed up by the dark, spacious tavern they had seized. The hostelry's former occupants had now disappeared, buried deep in the woodland morass only a short walk away. The freezing weather, the icy rain and bitter winds kept the forest paths clear, though the tavern would entertain the travelling chapman, tinker or itinerant priest. On such occasions, members of the Garduna would simply melt back into the tavern's many chambers, and the suspicions of the travellers were never roused. They would leave the tavern fully rested and well fed. The Master had now summoned his entire cohort together. He needed to reassure them to keep matters as simple and as quiet as they were now. He climbed onto a barrel and his followers fell silent. The Master's power was absolute. The legal axiom, 'that the will of the ruler has force of law' certainly applied to the Garduna.

'I have news of our comrades,' the Master proclaimed. 'Some good, some bad. Beatrice and Julia have been killed.' He raised a hand, shaking his head. 'No, no, do not question me. Rafael was taken prisoner and is most certainly dead, if not at the hands of our enemies, then certainly by his own. Rafael would never talk. We may have lost two more!' He paused as his battle group whispered amongst themselves, nodding in agreement at his words. 'However,' the Master again lifted a warning hand, 'we and our allies, or should I say those who wish us well, have our successes. We have attacked the countess's mansion; we have learned that the Luciferi lost a man there. We have caused chaos around her manor and put the fear of death into the countess's two henchmen, Urswicke and Bray, though they do seem difficult to kill. Nevertheless, we press on. We might attack Woking Manor; the plunder there would be rich and plentiful. Anyway, take courage. I appreciate we are in a foreign land, amongst strangers and with enemies all about us, but we are the Garduna. We fear nobody, we go where we will, we do what we want.' He spread his hands. 'Do not worry about us being trapped or cut off. You know how we arrived here, and that same smooth passage is our way home.' The Master fell silent as the tavern door opened and two of the watchmen hurried in to genuflect before their leader.

'Master,' one of them gasped. 'We hastened as fast as we could.'
'What is it?'
'Strangers, travellers,' the second watchman replied. 'Ostensibly verderers, but we followed them, keeping to the forest edge. At

first nothing suspicious – they gabbled in English, but then one of them slipped, made a mistake. For a short while they spoke in French, fluently and fast, before lapsing back into English.'

'Luciferi?' Alfonso demanded. 'Scouts despatched to discover us. Master, what should we do?'

'Give them a warm welcome,' the leader replied, climbing down from the barrel. 'Greet them cordially, then cut their throats.'

'The countess asked me the same question,' Urswicke murmured as he and Bray entered the tangle of alleyways and coffin paths stretching through Whitefriars. Both men had drawn sword and dagger, a stark warning to those human wolves sloping through the dark either side of them. Bray abruptly paused and clutched Urswicke's arm.

'Are you sure of that?' he demanded. 'That the countess asked what would our enemies want her to do now? But that's like speculating on how many angels can sit on the point of a pin?'

'Well, that's what she said,' Urswicke replied. 'And I'm beginning to reflect on the same, my friend. Reginald, something about all this truly reeks, but for the life of me I cannot say where the stench originates. Ah well. Let's discover what Lord Nightshade has found for us.'

They turned into the alleyway leading down to The Poison Pot and abruptly stopped. The entrance to the tavern blazed with light. So many torches glowed that it seemed as if a bonfire was merrily burning. Close by clustered a host of armed men, buckled and harnessed for battle. They thronged on the cobbles, guarding every door and window.

Muttering under his breath, Bray led Urswicke into the mass of armed men. They would have been denied entrance except for a voice bellowing that the visitors were Bray and Urswicke, whom the Lord Nightshade was expecting. They were allowed through into the taproom and Bray gasped in astonishment. More armed men thronged here, occupying every table and overturned barrel. Lord Nightshade sat before the fire, toasting a succulent piece of chicken over the flames. He drew this out, put it on a platter, then rose to his feet and bowed at Bray and Urswicke. He led them across to a window embrasure, a comfortable enclave with cushioned seats, a fine table and sparkling braziers, which exuded heat and fragrant puffs of smoke. Once settled, Nightshade drew a deep breath.

'I'll not offer you any drink,' he slurred, patting his yellow-coloured hair, 'but at least I'll tell you the reason.' He pointed at Urswicke. 'Oh, by the way, Master Christopher, I know who you are. I believe you share your father's name but not his nature, and that is good, otherwise I wouldn't entertain you. So, gentlemen, let's get to business. Foxglove,' he bellowed across the taproom, 'bring me that barrel.' A thin, waspish young man hurried forward holding a cask, which he placed on the table. Nightshade leaned across, removed the lid and, wrinkling his nose at the sour stench, took out the two heads severed cleanly at the neck. Bray did not recognise the first, a narrow face almost hidden by black bushy hair, the heavy-lidded eyes half closed. However, he certainly recognised the second: Wormwood, his round, wizened face now crumpled in death. Both heads had been cauterised, the severed necks coated with tar and pitch. Nightshade toasted both of these gruesome remains with his goblet, put the heads back in the barrel and gestured at Foxglove to remove it.

'I'll be blunt,' he whispered. 'These heads are a warning to me. Nevertheless, I know who are responsible. Let me add, I know little about them, but I understand the Garduna are prowling through London. They are on the hunt, and the likes of me should leave them well alone.'

'Garduna?'

'Garduna, Master Bray. As I have said, I know little about them but what I do . . .' He gestured across the taproom. 'Compared to them, we are angels.' He leaned across, his black-ringed eyes full of fear. 'The Garduna,' he hissed, 'are a guild of professional assassins, skilled in killing and utterly ruthless. Rumour has it that an entire battle group is loose in the city.'

'Against whom?'

'It would seem against your mistress, the countess.'

'Why?'

'Heaven only knows, Master Bray, but now you must be gone.' He lowered his voice even further. 'I shall shout so as to convince the spies, the informants, whom the Garduna have certainly placed in and around this tavern. So let us proceed. Foxglove!' Nightshade staggered to his feet, pointing at Bray and Urswicke. 'Show our guests out. I cannot help them so there is no need for them to return.'

Urswicke and Bray, each lost in their own thoughts, left the tavern and walked quickly back to the countess's mansion. Hardyng – all breathless – was waiting for them. The steward apologised that he'd been distracted by saying farewell to a visiting Benedictine who, just after Urswicke and Bray arrived, slipped through the door all cowled and cloaked in his black robes. Apparently the monk had sought audience with the countess, who now wanted Urswicke and Bray, immediately on their return, to join her. Hardyng led them down to the chancery, knocked on the door and ushered them inside. The countess sat in a high-backed chair, two strangers either side of her. Both men rose to greet them.

'My name is Eglantine,' the younger one declared. 'I am a senior clerk in the chancery of the Secret Seal and this,' he turned to his companion, 'is Clairvaux, my henchman.'

Urswicke and Bray clasped hands with their visitors, Christopher using the distraction of the courtesies to study both men. Eglantine was narrow-faced, clean-shaven, his bright blond hair cropped close on top but completely shaved on all three sides. Clairvaux was smaller, thick-set, with night-black hair cut close, an elegant and neatly trimmed moustache and beard. Both men were dressed in the sober but costly garb of well-placed clerks, their long jerkins and thick hose of the purest wool. They had taken off their hooded cloaks which, together with their warbelts, hung from wall pegs just within the door. Each of the clerks wore a chancery belt and sported the much-coveted Secret Chancery ring on the little finger of their right hand. Once the introductions were over and they had taken their seats, the countess pushed across a document for Urswicke and Bray to read. It was a letter from Urswicke's father, introducing the clerks and assigning them to Countess Margaret, 'to resolve all the problems and challenges facing her'. The Recorder concluded by saying he had the fullest confidence in these two officials, who would use their skill and expertise to bring matters to a satisfactory conclusion. The letter bore the royal signet seal, demonstrating that the two clerks had the full support of the King.

'It is good of my father,' Urswicke smiled as he pushed the letter back, 'and of you too. We need every comfort and support but, tell me, how do you intend to help?'

'Well, as I informed the countess before your arrival,' Eglantine retorted, 'we would be grateful to share a bedchamber here and, if the countess agrees, we would like to question everyone, including your good selves.'

The day was drawing to a close. The mist swirled like a host of ghosts along the coffin path leading up to the dark mass of Chertsey Abbey. This truly was the hour of twilight, the time of the bat, that sliver of time between dusk and darkness. The great bell of Chertsey had just boomed out the end of vespers. The beacon lights, huge lanternhorns, had been fired in the abbey towers to glow through the gathering murk. The shimmering light was a welcome sight to the three pilgrims, as they proclaimed themselves, who had left London before dawn and were now within reach of their destination: Jasper Biscop, his wife Katarina and their son Henry, or so they called themselves. They all now sat slumped on the three poor hacks they'd bought from a stable near Queenhithe along the Thames. The same quayside where they had disembarked from the Hainault cog. It had been a long hard ride from the riverside. Now they had safely reached this ancient Benedictine house and the secrets it contained. Katarina, who led the other two, pushed her mount as close as possible towards the abbey postern gate. She then leaned over and tugged at the door rope. The bell echoed, harsh and hollow. The postern gate creaked open. An ancient Benedictine lay brother, lantern aloft, slipped through the gate and smiled up at them in an open display of gums and one solitary tooth.

'I am Katarina Biscop,' the woman declared. 'This is my husband, Jasper, and our son Henry. We carry letters signed and sealed, proving our worth. We seek refuge and rest here.' The lay brother, still grinning like a jackanapes, nodded in agreement. The gate was pulled further open and they clattered into the great cobbled stable yard. Ostlers hastened to take their horses, quietly mocking the poor state of the three tired old hacks. Katarina, however, just brushed through them like a queen, Jasper and Henry trailing behind, as they followed the porter across the cobbles to the well-endowed, comfortable guest house. Their guide placed them in the small lodge just inside the door. He lit candles, fired a brazier, then scurried away, chomping on his gums, loudly re-assuring them that he would inform Abbot John May of their arrival.

'Make yourself comfortable,' Katarina declared. She glanced at Jasper, his long-jawed face and deep-set eyes almost hidden by thick grey hair, moustache and beard, which desperately needed to be shorn. Jasper grinned at Katarina.

'I confess I am a sight,' he grated as he tried to hide the Welsh lilt in his voice. 'But it's best if I stay like this, at least for the journey. And the same goes for you, boy.' He pointed at Henry, slouched on a wall bench. 'Remember!'

'He will remember.' Katarina went across and gently caressed the young man's thick auburn hair. Katarina's lovely face creased into a sweet smile. 'Remember, Henry Tudor, you are no longer a prince, a King in waiting, you are a pilgrim. You have a speech defect, a tangle of the tongue, and we have brought you to Chertsey to pray for the help of the saintly King Henry, the last legitimate Lancastrian King. The glorious martyr of our house foully murdered by the Yorkist lords. We are here on pilgrimage to seek King Henry's help and to pray over his remains which lie buried in the abbey church. No.' Katarina pressed a finger against Henry's lips. 'Not a word. Not now. Not here. Remember what I said. You must always act as if the very walls, even of this new, strange place, have both eyes and ears. We walk in the light but all around us stretches a darkness where monsters lurk.' She fell silent at the sound of sandalled feet outside, followed by a knock on the door. Jasper answered it and Abbot John May swept in. He closed and bolted the door behind him. For a few heartbeats he leaned against it, eyes closed, then he smiled at his three visitors, who immediately knelt to receive his blessing. The abbot hastily sketched this before exchanging the kiss of peace with each of them. Once they had taken their seats, the abbot squatted on a stool and leaned forward. He scratched his scrawny hair, his gaunt face now all serious, his sharp eyes narrowed in concern.

'I expected you earlier,' he murmured.

'Father, the Narrow Seas were all in a tumult. You will let the countess know?'

'Of course. I will despatch one of the brothers at first light. Now, I know why you are here! We are all involved in the secret known only to the countess and possibly her two henchmen, Masters Urswicke and Bray. However, that doesn't mean our secret is safe. Oh no. There is a great deal of curiosity about Chertsey.'

'By whom?'

'The Lords of the Night, those who deal in power.'

'Such as?'

'Well, the saintly Henry is said to lie buried beneath a slab in our lady chapel: his remains were brought here for honourable burial. Shortly afterwards, King Edward wrote to the abbey saying a hermit calling himself Cornelius wished to occupy the anker-hold, now standing empty in the north transept of our abbey church. A comfortable enough chamber, which provides a very clear view of the blessed Henry's tomb in the lady chapel.'

'And you think Cornelius is a Yorkist spy?'

'Lady Katarina, that is very possible. Indeed, the King has made it very clear that if Cornelius should die or leave, the Crown holds the rights of advowson, the power to appoint another.'

'So,' Katarina declared, 'the tomb and all who honour it are under constant watch? I am sure this anchorite keeps a faithful record of who visits the tomb, who they are and what danger they might pose. However, to cut to the quick: anyone who visits the tomb and prays before it must have sympathies for the House of Lancaster.'

'Precisely, which is why I should take you now so you can view it and act as simple pilgrims, the parts you have assumed. There's something else.' Abbot John shook his head. 'About a month ago we had a Spanish visitor. A young man claiming to be preparing for the priesthood, with a special devotion to the Benedictine Order. He stayed for a while as a guest, diligently participating in the abbey horarium. He joined us in the choir to pray and chant. He attended Mass then he left.' The abbot shrugged. 'After he'd gone, I never gave him a second thought. Then a week ago, two more visitors arrived, both Spaniards, allegedly husband and wife from Toledo. They claimed to be pilgrims beseeching heaven so the lady would conceive a child. They were well dressed and prosperous looking, their command of English was good. They maintained they had visited Santiago Compostella and intended to visit St Edmunds, Canterbury, and, above all, the shrine of Our Lady at Walsingham.'

'And they too claimed to be seeking the help of the sainted Henry?'

'Of course.' The abbot blew his cheeks out. 'They have gone

now,' he declared. 'But, my friends I assure you, I have never seen such visitors so keen to walk the abbey, as if they wished to closely memorise its extent, count the number of buildings, the thickness of its walls, the strength of our gates, and the rest. They claimed to be fascinated by Chertsey Abbey and so they appeared to be.'

'But you think they were here for something else?'

'Yes, Katarina. I have no proof of this, but the young man from Spain, the married couple from Toledo a mere coincidence? I just entertain this suspicion that they were spies despatched to survey our abbey, but for what purpose, I cannot say. Anyway, as far as your stay here is concerned,' Abbot John smiled thinly, 'you must be gone just before daylight tomorrow morning.'

'What!'

'Katarina, listen and act on what I say. Tonight I will take you to the shrine, the tomb of the blessed Henry. Our abbey church will be deserted and cloaked in shadows. However, do remember our self-invited anchorite. He will be there and he will be most curious. However, as I have said, act your parts, pray, genuflect and cross yourselves. Tomorrow, just after dawn, leave on foot. We will look after your sorry hacks. But then come back in a different guise as the abbey bells toll just before High Mass. Return to the same narrow postern door through which I shall usher you out. Once you have returned, I shall take you to a small derelict storeroom, where I will make preparations. Jasper, you must shave your head, moustache and beard. You will emerge as a new lay brother, Simon by name. Katarina, we need women to clean and wash. You will be given a bed loft in one of the stables.' The abbot grinned. 'Don't worry, you will be comfortable and warm enough. You must assume the name Miriam. Henry, my boy, you will be Bodkin, a grease-covered kitchen scullion, a spit-boy with a serious speech defect. All three of you will be given clean, warm lodgings and eat and drink merrily enough in our refectory or buttery.'

'But why all this?' Katarina asked. 'The countess wanted us to stay here as pilgrims.' She laughed sharply. 'Not become members of your community.'

'The countess has in fact ordered this. She and I communicate, but not by letter or her courier Fleetfoot, but through a trusted member of our community. He takes messages, written in a secret cipher, backwards and forwards. Lady Margaret and I also meet whenever we can. The countess claims she faces hideous though secret threats. She needs to visit Chertsey without provoking suspicion. Of course, she fully intends to meet with you three . . .'

'What danger threatens her?' Jasper rasped.

'I don't know. I am not privy to that. So, you will do what I say, yes? I need your solemn word. All this is best for you, the countess and myself.'

'You have our word,' Katarina assured him.

'Good.' The abbot got to his feet. 'You came here to visit the blessed Henry's tomb and so you shall, but be wary, watchful and wise. Follow me.'

Abbot John led them out into the cold hollowed passageways and galleries. Places of shifting shadows where the sconce torches spluttered and crackled against the windswept darkness. Now and again they would glimpse Black Robes hurrying past them, cowls pulled up to hide faces, hands deep in the sleeves of their robes. Tongues of candlelight kissed the darkness; these shed a golden glow around the carved, saintly faces of angels, as well as the grotesque features of monkeys, demons and devils, who glared down as if impatient to break free of the stone, to creep and crawl along these ghostly corridors. They left the buildings, going out into the freezing cold cloisters; the garth grass was already white under a tightening frost.

They reached the abbey church, with its tower pointing like a warning finger up at the sky. Abbot John led them through the Devil's door into the north transept. An occasional cresset torch flamed, flared and spluttered, casting shadow as well as light. The torches were placed so as to bring to vivid life the different wall paintings, brilliantly hued scenes from the scriptures. All of these were dramatic, be it David lifting Goliath's severed head or Christ expelling a legion of orange-skinned, monkey-faced devils from the Gerasene demoniac. Abbot John raised a hand, whispering that they stay as he pointed down the transept to a broad pool of light thrown by candles blazing on their spigots.

'A favourite trick of our anchorite,' he murmured. 'He lights tapers around King Henry's tomb so he can see whoever visits, even at night. So let us go up but do not be distracted by the anchorite, keep your backs to him.' Abbot John abruptly paused as he sighed noisily.

'Why should I?' he whispered. 'Why all this mummery, this pretence?'

'Father Abbot?' Katarina, now alarmed, demanded: 'What is the matter?'

'Let us leave this,' the abbot whispered. 'Katarina, you and yours must not endanger yourselves over a sham, a mockery.'

'What do you mean?'

'Henry is not buried in the chapel but somewhere out in God's acre.'

'Never!'

'A secret,' the abbot retorted, 'known only to the countess and her two henchmen Urswicke and Bray.'

Over the next few days following their arrival, both Eglantine and Clairvaux made themselves at home in the countess's mansion. They were given a spacious, very well-furnished chamber and were invited to have their meals with the rest of the household in the buttery or refectory. For the rest, Urswicke and Bray left both clerks to the care of Hardyng. The steward was now deeply disturbed by what had happened, eager to inform Eglantine and Clairvaux about Bernard's mysterious murder. The two chancery clerks promised they would question the steward as they would all of the countess's retainers. Bray and Urswicke decided not to interfere. Advent was approaching and both the countess's henchmen were swept up in what the countess called the 'tedious round' of court celebrations, which Edward and his coven used to proclaim and enhance the power of York. Westminster Palace became the heart and home of all this mummery, with pageants being staged to venerate the girdle and ring of the Blessed Virgin, two of the abbey's most precious relics. Carpenters and craftsmen laboured all the hours to set up the different stages of the masques in a blaze of colour and finery, be it a shimmering vermilion or pints of pink dye. Lifelike effigies of individuals mentioned in the nativity story were arranged around the palace. Choirs rehearsed. Musicians set up a stage or occupied the abbey's different lofts and galleries. Whatever the theme, it was all dedicated to extolling and celebrating the power of York.

An array of rich hangings, coverlets, carpets, turkey rugs, shields, curtains and livery proclaimed the glorious suns and gorgeous roses of the ruling house. The countess and her henchmen had no choice but to witness all this. They also had to listen to the list of precious gifts exchanged between the different Yorkists lords and ladies, be it costly reliquaries or a cross fashioned out of gold and silver hanging on cords of pure silk. The countess was invited to such festivities and had to attend, though she and her retinue left as soon as they could.

In the main the countess kept to her mansion, entertaining her guests. Urswicke and Bray joined these occasions, reminiscing over the past, planning a possible move to Woking Manor or even across the Narrow Seas to Burgundy. They were gathered in such a meeting on the fifth day after the arrival of Eglantine and Clairvaux when they were interrupted by a highly nervous Hardyng.

'What is it?' Urswicke snapped, now tired of the steward's constant nervousness. 'For goodness' sake, man, you look as if you've seen a ghost.'

'Perhaps I have,' Hardyng wailed. 'But sir, I was with the rest of the household at the front door. There's a mummer's troupe performing a masque there. They call themselves "The Clerks of Oxford". Anyway, I decided to go to the jakes cupboard. I went along the gallery.' Hardyng turned and pointed back. 'Sirs, you must see this.'

The two henchmen rose. Bray told the countess and her guests to stay. Urswicke gripped Hardyng by the shoulder and made the steward turn to face him.

'I bring bad news,' Hardyng whimpered. 'I do so again. Come sir, I will show you.'

Urswicke and Bray left the room and followed Hardyng down to the chamber on the first gallery occupied by Eglantine and Clairvaux.

'I have been outside,' Hardyng mumbled. 'The shutters are pulled fast, which means the window must be locked. I knocked on the door as soon as I saw it.'

'Saw what?'

'Master Bray, I saw that.' Hardyng stopped outside the guest chamber and pointed at the polished floor.

'In sweet Heaven's name,' Urswicke breathed, crouching to stare at the thin worm of blood seeping out from beneath the door. Urswicke rose to his feet.

'You have a second key?'

Hardyng unclipped the heavy ring crammed with different keys from the hook on his broad working belt.

'I have it here,' he retorted. 'But what is the use? The key on the inside is turned and I think the bolts are drawn across.'

Urswicke pounded on the door, shouting questions. Sir John and his two companions joined them, along with a gaggle of cowed, terror-struck servants. Urswicke quietly cursed. Hardyng was not alone. If they were not careful, the countess's mansion would soon acquire a sinister, macabre reputation. Servitors, maids and the rest would soon find excuse to leave . . . but that would have to wait. Urswicke snapped his fingers. 'Hardyng, you and five others break down the door.'

The steward hurriedly agreed and the loud banging echoed through the house. The countess, her face ashen and drawn, came down wrapped in a winter cloak. She had to stand and watch the fine door of one of her principal chambers be pounded until it splintered, cracked and fell away. Urswicke grabbed a lanternhorn, telling Bray to keep everyone out.

He entered the chamber. It smelled fragrant, and the leaping tongues of flame from a host of beeswax candles provided light, as did the fire, the logs crackling merrily in the heat. The chamber lay undisturbed, the chancery desk strewn with scraps of parchment, quills and other writing implements. The two box beds were neatly made up; the curtains at the large window pulled across. Everything was in order, be it the lavarium, coffers and caskets; nothing looked disturbed. Urswicke lifted the lantern and went to kneel at the threshold. He stared down at the two severed little fingers trailing a thin line of drying blood. On each winked a Secret Chancery ring. 'Bray,' he hissed hoarsely, 'fetch me a sheet of vellum.' His colleague brushed by him towards the desk. He handed a square of parchment to Urswicke. He delicately lifted both fingers onto it, folded the parchment into a small parcel and placed it on the desk. He then shouted at the others to leave, not to wait, urging Bray to take the countess and her guests back to their rooms.

Once they had gone, Urswicke closely inspected the chamber floor, its walls, ceiling and window. He found nothing amiss, no secret hatch, door or enclave. The window was secured by an inside clasp. The shutters likewise, the bar across them held securely in its clasps. Urswicke crossed to the door and examined the fractured lock with its key inside, as well as the ruptured bolts at top and bottom. Urswicke lifted the lanternhorn and placed it on the desk. He scrutinised everything, sifting through the narrow memorandum ledger where Eglantine had described the information he'd received from all those he had questioned. Eglantine had written his entries in a fine cursive script. Urswicke found this easy to follow yet, even after a superficial look, there was nothing contained in the notes which Urswicke didn't know already.

'The countess is waiting for you, Christopher.'

Bray, warbelt strapped on, stood in the doorway.

'In God's name,' he added. 'What is happening here?'

'Heaven knows.' Urswicke got to his feet and picked up a chancery bag: he thrust into it Eglantine's papers, as well as the macabre parchment parcel containing the severed fingers. He and Bray then joined the others in the countess's chancery chamber. For a while Urswicke just sat, staring down at the table top, rubbing its shiny surface with his right hand.

'Christopher?'

'Mistress.' Urswicke lifted his head. 'I do not know what to say. For the life of me I cannot explain what's going on. We have,' he lifted his hands, 'a secure locked chamber. No sign of any other entrance or secret hatch. Only that heavy door, locked and bolted from within. Yes, Master Bray?'

His colleague nodded in agreement.

'Inside that chamber,' Urswicke continued, 'are two mailed clerks, young men skilled in chancery matters but, I would wager, also experienced in sword- and dagger-play. These mailed clerks are comfortable, secure and protected. Nevertheless, silently, and without any sign of resistance or defence, something or someone entered that chamber. The two clerks were slaughtered, their fingers bearing the chancery rings severed and left.'

'You say slaughtered?' Guido intervened.

'They must have been,' Bray replied.

'Two mailed clerks like our visitors wouldn't just offer their hands for mutilation, which means they must have been killed,' Urswicke insisted. 'Though how and why is a mystery, and the same applies to the whereabouts of their corpses. I mean, what happened to them? They weren't thrown out of the window or carried through this building. Why weren't they just left? I have rarely heard of someone being murdered, their bodies mutilated and then removed. Why not leave the entire corpse for people to view?'

'And the ring fingers being severed and left there.' Guido gestured around. 'Why do that?'

'A mark of contempt, perhaps?' Urswicke answered. 'A gruesome act permeated with malicious hatred. The message is clear enough. Two royal clerks slaughtered, their fingers left as a sign that they had failed, horribly so, in what they were supposed to do!'

'The King will not be pleased,' Countess Margaret declared. 'Two royal clerks, senior officials in the Secret Chancery, have been murdered. Even if somehow they were still alive, they were certainly assaulted in the most cruel way, whilst under my protection in my house.' She breathed in deeply. 'Reginald, Christopher, question the servants closely, ask them if they saw or heard anything untoward.' The countess paused as the tocsin began to toll.

Cursing loudly, Urswicke sprang to his feet. Along with Bray, he strapped on his warbelt and hurried out into the passageway. Hardyng, openly weeping, couldn't speak, but just pointed towards the front of the house from which servants were now fleeing, milling about in the gallery beyond the hallway. Urswicke ordered Hardyng to join them, then hurried towards the main door. Most of the windows on that side of the house were closed and shuttered, though the noise of arrows smacking into the woodwork was clear enough. Indeed, one fire arrow had smashed through an upper window next to the main door. The arrow clattered along the polished floor until Bray stamped out the flames.

Bray hurried to the armoury and brought back two long kite shields. Urswicke took his, locking it close to Bray's. A brave servitor, a turnspit boy, opened the door. Urswicke and Bray, shields up, edged out in front of the house; the path leading up to the main entrance was always well lit with cresset torches lashed to poles. These now illuminated the path, as well as the six archers who knelt, bows bent, a small pot of fire blazing before each of them. The bows swung up together.

'Back,' Urswicke shouted.

They hurriedly retreated, slamming the doors shut even as the arrows thudded into them. Bray and Urswicke crouched, listening keenly into the silence. They were joined by Sir John, Guido and Squire Lambert, as well as the more courageous among the servants. Squire Lambert, showing no sign of his recent sickness, volunteered, even insisted, on going out to see what was happening. Urswicke reluctantly agreed. Lambert slipped through the main door then waited at a crouch, glancing back at Urswicke, who peered through the slit ready to throw the door open at the first hint of danger. Lambert continued to crouch on the top step, peering into the dark.

'Nothing,' he declared over his shoulder. 'Nothing at all, Master Christopher.'

Urswicke joined him on the steps, Bray and the others following him.

'Well,' Urswicke declared. 'Send out some men, though I doubt if they will discover anything.'

Urswicke and the others rejoined the countess, where Urswicke delivered a pithy description of what had happened. The countess heard him out then grasped her set of ivory ave beads, threading them quickly through her fingers, a mannerism which betrayed her deep agitation. Urswicke knew his iron-willed mistress would calm the seething fears within her. To distract himself, he emptied the chancery satchel and pulled out that gruesome parcel. He opened it and peered at the two severed, blood-encrusted fingers. He turned them carefully then scrutinised the rings. He was convinced that these had been cut from those clerks, though everything else about their deaths was cloaked in deep mystery.

'Christopher,' the countess ordered, 'take those damnable remains to your father. Leave them with one of his henchmen, then come back here. First however, you and Bray must reassure the servants, whilst I will have words with our guests.'

Urswicke promised he would send the gruesome parcel to his father, then left to meet the servants, but it was a futile exercise. Most of them had already fled. Hardyng openly admitted that the house was becoming quite deserted and, by the same hour tomorrow, only a few, including himself, would remain. Urswicke and Bray quietly agreed with the steward and told him to try and hide his fear. Urswicke then left for the Guildhall.

On arrival he was informed that his father was deep in council with the King and his brothers. Urswicke decided not to stay. He handed over to one of his father's officials the gruesome parcel, together with a letter penned by himself explaining the circumstances behind this macabre development. Once back in the countess's mansion, Urswicke predicted that they would receive a swift response from Sir Thomas and his masters. He was not disappointed. The following morning – just after the market horn shrilled its response to the last bell for the Jesus Mass – a haughty courier, garbed in the glorious royal livery, delivered a summons to the countess and her henchmen. They were to present themselves at the Guildhall council chamber at noon on that same day.

PART THREE

'At the head of the Garduna was the Great Brother or the Grand Master!'

K atarina wiped the sweat from her brow on the back of her wrist before returning to scrubbing the wooden platters in the corner of the abbey's great kitchen, a warm, steam-filled chamber with its cavernous roof and long, arrow-slit windows. Days had passed since her arrival. Abbot John's plan had been most successful. Katarina and her companions had left the abbey, then quietly slipped back to blend in with the rest of the community. She now worked as a scullery maid and laundry woman. Jasper – hair, moustache and beard all shorn – had successfully assumed the guise of a lay brother. He had a special responsibility for the stables where their horses were still housed. Katarina certainly felt protected from without. Chertsey was a most secure fortified place. Sacked twice by the Northmen, the abbey had developed like a fortress with deep moats, broad ditches, not to mention sluices and water-gates, as the building stood close to the abbey river, an offshoot of the Thames which regularly flooded the water meadows to the east of the abbey. More importantly, the countess's manor of Woking lay only seven miles to the south of this embattled house of prayer.

On her arrival, Katarina had felt secure enough, though this had begun to seep away under a deepening unease which she couldn't explain. Certainly something was happening outside. She had listened very carefully to visitors to Chertsey. Even though there were few due to the harsh winter weather, verderers and forest people came to barter for food or sell items to the good brothers. All of these whispered about a presence, a malicious one, prowling the forests beyond the abbey walls. Nothing certain, definite or distinct, just shadows flitting amongst the trees, of horsemen merging in and out of the mist or an abrupt disturbance of wildlife. Now and again, woodsmen commented on eerie calls swirling through the green, misty darkness, to be answered by others. Katarina recalled the abbot saying the countess believed she was confronting real danger. Was this just in London, Katarina wondered, or here as well? She felt tempted to confide in Jasper but that was too dangerous. Chertsey lay close to Woking Manor. The countess's affairs would be carefully scrutinised and Katarina was determined that no one would discover a connection between herself and young Henry's mother. Moreover, the abbey itself must have watchers; the walls would have both eyes and ears. People were curious. A group of Dominicans, in their distinctive black-and-white robes, had lodged at Chertsey for a day and Katarina had noticed how closely they studied her as she moved around the refectory.

The Dominicans, however, were perhaps just curious. Katarina was growing aware of a more imminent danger. The self-styled anchorite from the abbey church, Cornelius, was undoubtedly interested in her. Yet that puzzled her. She was certain Cornelius did not know her, nor could he have glimpsed her face or form during their brief, nocturnal visit to the abbey church. However, Cornelius had the right to come into the kitchen, buttery and refectory. Since her arrival, he had begun to do so daily, perched on a corner stool, as he was now, eating from a bowl while he constantly watched her. If Katarina caught his gaze, he would smile in a display of yellow, broken teeth. Katarina had come to hate the sight of Cornelius, with his long straggly hair and deep-set glittering eyes. She knew what he wanted. She'd caught the lechery in his sly grimaces. Amongst her own people, Katarina was regarded as a beauty, and many a man had paid court to her. The same was true of the castle in Brittany where she, Henry and Jasper sheltered from the murderous anger of the House of York. Katarina knew the world and ways of men, their lusts and their lies. Cornelius was no different, just uglier. Katarina tensed as the anchorite, licking his lips clean of crumbs, sauntered over in a gust of sweaty smells.

'Good-day mistress, I have been watching you.'

'So you have, and I have been watching you.' Katarina deliberately let slip a wooden platter into the barrel, so the hot, soapy water splashed over herself and her unwanted visitor. He cursed, flicking at the drops. He stepped closer; his hand darted beneath

Katarina's outstretched arm to stroke her breast. She knocked his hand away and turned to confront him but he stepped even closer, head forward, face all serious.

'I was there in the church,' he hissed. 'The night Father Abbot brought you in.'

'No, you were in your anker-hold.'

'Wrong, mistress, I left my cell when I heard your footsteps outside the church. I was just across the nave in the shadow of the south transept. I believe I heard some rather interesting items.'

'Such as? What interesting items?' Katarina mocked back.

'Well, what has happened to the boy? That young man who was with you. I am certain I glimpsed him in the kitchens. And the man?' Cornelius edged even closer, scratching a dribble of saliva on his grubby chin. 'Isn't he the new lay brother? The one who has had all his head and face shorn? So my plump, beddable wench. Who are you really? Why are you here?'

'What do you want?'

'To play with you, mistress.' Cornelius opened his ragged robe and tapped his codpiece. 'Come back to my cell and let me play with your full, plump breasts, and go between your long legs.'

Katarina stared at him, heart racing. She must not make a mistake: this anchorite was a truly dangerous man.

'Not in the abbey,' she whispered. 'Not within the sacred precincts, but some lonely place. Now there is an old storeroom, close to a disused well, just a walk away from here, beyond the kitchen yard. Go there and I'll come. I'll meet you. But once you have played with me, no more!'

'Oh yes, no more.' Cornelius almost gabbled, so excited he could barely stand still, moving from foot to foot as he clawed at his codpiece. 'But you come,' he warned. 'No games.' He plucked at her gown. 'I'll have this off you in a trice. I am going to enjoy you; it's been so long.'

'I'll come,' Katarina declared, 'one question!'

'What's that?'

'You're no anchorite,' Katarina taunted. 'You're no holy man. You fully believe in the World, the Flesh and the Devil. So what are you doing here, skulking in an anchorite cell?' Katarina caught herself just in time; it would be a mistake to mention the royal tomb. Let this lecherous rogue tell her himself. She watched

Cornelius and caught the knowing look in his eyes. He pushed his face closer, hot smelly breath on her face.

'What is it you want, mistress?'

'Very simple, I want to know who you are. I think that's reasonable.' She cupped her breast in her hand. 'And then these are all yours. If you don't answer my question, how can you come to me? I want to know who you are, that's all.'

'I am a scurrier, a stable clerk in the Secret Chancery. I was convicted for theft of a haberdashery in Cheapside. Sentenced to hang. I received a royal pardon and readmission to the Secret Chancery.'

'But there was a condition?'

'Of course, mistress,' he snorted with laughter, 'there's always a condition, isn't there? Even me playing with you. Anyway, I was assigned to be anchorite here at Chertsey. My task is to keep visitors under constant scrutiny, especially those who visit the tomb of the so-called blessed Henry. And I do that. Of course, most of the pilgrims are stupid peasants who know no different. My master in London—'

'Which master?'

'No less a person than Sir Thomas Urswicke, Recorder of the city and a member of the Royal Council. He wants me to keep a sharp eye on any prominent Lancastrian, any supporter of that treacherous house, who comes to pray before the tomb of their master.'

'And have they?'

'Not yet, but I live in hope. Now, mistress, I am impatient, it's time to tumble.'

'Then you must go.'

'And you must follow,' Cornelius warned. 'Be there or be sorry.' He turned on his heel and shuffled from the kitchen. Katarina watched him go. She knew what she must do. She picked up a long, wicked-looking fleshing knife. Hiding the weapon beneath her cloak, Katarina left the kitchen and made her way across the mist-bound abbey grounds. The line of buildings with their fine carved stonework gave way to common land, which stretched to the curtain wall of the abbey. Beyond that lay ditches, quagmires, and a thick, spiky gorse which fringed the forest. The derelict storeroom stood in a long line of much-decayed buildings. Cornelius was standing in the doorway. Katarina paused to take a deep breath and clutched the knife more tightly. She was about to walk forward when she heard a sound behind her as if a boot had slithered on freezing mud. She glanced over her shoulder, but she could detect nothing but the swirling mist.

'I am waiting, woman.'

Katarina turned back, smiled and walked towards him. Cornelius grasped her shoulders, pulling her deeper into the warm darkness. He tried to lift her smock but then began to fumble at the buttons on its high collar. He was breathing quickly, muttering to himself as he tugged at the buttons, then stopped to squeeze her generous breasts.

'Soft and sweet, aren't you. Come closer. I think you'll make a merry tumble.'

Katarina tried to hide her disgust. Cornelius's breath smelt sour whilst his clothes reeked of stale sweat and dried urine. She smiled at him.

'I have a surprise!'

He stopped and stared, open-mouthed, as Katarina struck: a blow directly to the left of his chest, a killing thrust. The knife digging deep, straight to the heart. Cornelius staggered back, mouth spurting blood. He tried to speak but then his eyes rolled back and he collapsed to the ground, where he jerked and quivered before lying still. Katarina dropped the knife and crouched down beside him. She went quickly through his pockets and pouches but there was very little to take.

'You killed him, good!'

Katarina whirled round, darting for the knife, but one of the strangers, who had emerged from the mist, just kicked the weapon out of her reach.

'You don't need that mistress, not now.' The man and his companions crouched beside her. They pulled their hoods back and smiled at her. Katarina stared hard and for the first time noticed the colour of their robes.

'You're the Dominicans,' she whispered. 'You wear the black and white.' Katarina took a deep breath. She was still nervous after her deadly confrontation with Cornelius. 'You mean me well, but you prove the old adage: the cowl doesn't make the monk.'

One of the strangers laughed softly. 'You could,' he murmured, 'say the same about your dead friend here.'

'He's not my friend and never was.'

'Apparently.'

Katarina caught the man's accent. French, though skilled in the English tongue.

'You're not Dominicans?'

'Of course not.'

'So who are you?'

The man tapped his chest.

'I am François; this is my henchman, Armand.' He fished into the pockets of his robe and drew out a small candle coloured a deep blue and gold. 'We are the Luciferi, despatched from the Cabinet Noir by no less a person than our august prince, King Louis of France. We work in what you would call the Secret Chancery, our King's own private chamber. The Luciferi take an oath of loyalty to the King and no one else. In our eyes, whatever he wills has force of law.'

'And why are you here?' François glanced at his comrade who nodded imperceptibly.

'In brief,' the French man continued, 'we are hunting the Garduna. No,' François shook his head, 'I cannot explain fully. Time is passing. The hour candle burns quickly. The rings of time disappear! Mistress, I assure you the Garduna are from hell. They have no love for France nor, so we have learnt, for the House of Lancaster. In truth their enemy now becomes our friend and ally.' He smiled, his handsome face crinkling in amusement. 'Mistress, again I assure you, I will take an oath with my hand over the sacrament. The Luciferi have no quarrel with the House of Lancaster, far from it. Our quarrel is with the Garduna and certain members of the English Royal Council. Now we believe – in fact we know – that the Garduna have fielded a battle group here in England. It will only have one purpose: to wreak as much murderous mischief as possible. However, we don't know what this is, how it will manifest itself, what is its purpose or what will be the consequences. We stumble about. Now we do know that the Garduna are busy in London. They may well be responsible for the attacks on the countess's house and her henchmen.' François paused at the harsh screeching of the crows circling above the old storeroom.

'Something,' Armand spoke up, 'something murderous is being

plotted against the countess. We have watched her house in London where strange things have occurred.'

'What strange things?'

'Well, the murder of one of our brothers for a start, but,' Armand shrugged, 'we do not have time to tell you more.'

'But why are you here? Why do you follow me?'

'Logic,' François replied. 'The countess has her city mansion but she also owns the great manor of Woking, only seven or so miles to the north, within easy riding distance of Chertsey. Of course we know that Father Abbot John May was, and still is, a close friend, fervent ally and trusted confidant of the countess. He is also the keeper of the shrine which houses the mortal remains of the saintly Henry VI, usurped and murdered by York. Now, if the Garduna intend mischief against Margaret of Richmond and the entire House of Lancaster, it was only a matter of time before they showed their hand in London, which they have done, then in Woking, which is now a matter of record . . .'

'And finally in Chertsey?'

'Yes mistress, finally Chertsey. We think the Garduna, those soldiers from hell, must be very close, perhaps even closer than we think.'

'Where?'

'We don't know, but the forests between Chertsey and Woking are dense, lonely places. You could hide an army there and it would remain concealed for months. Moreover, King Winter rules. Trying to thread your way through that forest would be a labour worthy of Hercules. Nevertheless, we believe the Garduna lurk there. Eerie events have occurred around the manor, mysterious attacks. More importantly,' François rose and stretched, 'two of our brethren have disappeared.'

'And me? Why your interest in me?'

'Ahh.' Clement smiled, scratching his rich black hair. 'We've kept Chertsey under very close watch. We saw a man, woman and boy enter. We watched the same leave and then return just as clandestinely.'

'Pray God the Garduna didn't do the same.'

'No mistress, as yet they have not cast their nets so far.'

'Do you know what they hunt, do you know what they want?'

'As I have said, mistress, we can only speculate. They intend murderous mischief against the House of Lancaster and the Crown of France.'

Katarina closed her eyes and breathed in deeply, before stretching out and touching François on the wrist.

'I know you mean me well, monsieur, but you must also suspect who we really are. Me, the man, the boy?'

'Let me assure you, mistress, I do suspect, but that is not our business, that is not part of our mission. We hold no grievance against the House of Lancaster. Why should we? Indeed, we want the opposite. The Brothers York are warlike. They have crushed opposition at home and Edward styles himself the great conqueror, the victorious general. We do not want York landing an army at Calais and following the roads into Normandy. We want the English to stay where they are, beyond the Narrow Seas. We will support, we will cherish any who oppose York. Don't you see, mistress, if the House of Lancaster disappeared, who else could oppose Edward and his warriors? So rest assured we intend no ill to you and yours. Indeed, the opposite.'

'But you must suspect what the Garduna really want?'

François just shook his head. 'That's the mystery, mistress, that's what we have to discover, but in truth we don't really know. Now,' François kicked the corpse, 'do not worry about this, leave it to us.' The Frenchman shrugged. 'There are pools, marshes, morasses and plenty of water-soaked ground to hide a corpse until the final resurrection.' François raised a hand in the sign of peace. 'Mistress, it is best if you go but, never forget, the Garduna are on the prowl. They will come when you least expect it, like thieves in the night. I suspect, indeed I am sure, they have business with Chertsey. Pray God when they show their hand we are ready. Take care, mistress, we shall return.'

The countess, her three guests, together with Urswicke and Bray, arranged themselves down one side of the long table which stretched in front of the judges' thrones in the council chamber of London's magnificent Guildhall. Edward the King sat in the centre; his long blond hair, parted down the middle, was now shoulder length. The King looked as if he fully deserved the title of being the handsomest man in England, with his tawny skin and golden moustache and beard. Edward sported a beautiful jewel clasp in his left earlobe, and gorgeous rings on his fingers shimmered in a glow of flashing light. Garbed in a blue and gold tabard, Edward looked every inch the powerful prince – and, Urswicke sensed, a very angry one as well. Indeed, as soon as they'd entered the chamber, Edward's anger was manifest in the way he had sat and glared at those he'd summoned before him. The King's brothers, who sat either side of him, looked equally stony faced. Richard of Gloucester simply stared down the chamber, as if deeply interested in something on the far wall. Now and again Gloucester would lift a hand to rub his white narrow face or pat his long dark red hair, eyes blinking, lips moving soundlessly as if lost in his own world. George of Clarence, Richard's elder brother, looked his usual blustery self, with his mop of unruly golden hair, his handsome face flushed and fat from too many goblets of Bordeaux. Next to Clarence sat two men Urswicke regarded as the most dangerous in the kingdom: his own father, Sir Thomas Urswicke, and Clarence's henchman, Mauclerc. Urswicke regarded Mauclerc as a wolf in wolf's clothing, with his shaven head and face, pitted skin and sharp, narrow eyes. Mauclerc was a killer to the very bone, a true blood drinker who hated the countess with a passion beyond understanding. Clarence was no different: he had betrayed his own family and cause. For a while he had sided with Lancaster, even swearing an oath of allegiance to the late lamented Henry. Above all, Clarence had consorted with the Beauforts, who'd welcomed him as one of their own. All of this died at Tewkesbury. The Beauforts had been annihilated and Christopher truly believed Clarence would not settle until every Beaufort, who reminded him of his former life, was dead and gone.

'Your Grace.' The countess decided to break the menacing silence. 'Why have we been summoned here?'

'My Lady,' Sir Thomas Urswicke barked, 'it is not your place to question the King.' He banged his fist on the table. 'You are the one to answer questions. Our questions.'

'Hush, hush.' The King smiled bleakly at his guests. 'Sir John, Master Guido, I understand you and your squire,' he gestured at Lambert, 'have suffered grievously. And so have you, my Lady, be it at Woking or in London. Here in this city your house has been attacked, a visitor poisoned and now this, the disappearance of two royal clerks, officials high in my service. Men of good family, skilled and educated.' The King's voice trailed away. Urswicke glanced quickly at his father and tensed. Just for a brief passing moment, he glimpsed his father's sly smirk, as if the Recorder was thoroughly enjoying the proceedings, savouring them as a wolf would a blood-strewn feast. Something was very wrong here: was this all a sham?

'My lady.' Richard of Gloucester looked sadly at the countess. 'My brother the King and myself . . .'

'Not to forget me,' Clarence slurred, already deep in his cups.

'We believe,' Richard continued flatly, 'that London is not safe for you. I repeat. Whilst you live here, be it in the city or elsewhere in this kingdom, you are not safe.'

'And I cannot give you any assurance to the contrary,' Edward broke in. 'I simply cannot promise that you will be safe. If I put a guard on your house, will that stop the proclamations being posted at the Standard in Cheapside or the Cross in St Paul's Churchyard? No.' The King shook his golden head. 'My Lady, I cannot be falsely depicted as your gaoler, nor can I allow anything to happen to you for the very selfish reason that I would be blamed. You know that and I know that, so let us not fence or play with words. I cannot keep you as a prisoner, yet I have a duty to protect a leading noblewoman.'

'Your Grace is correct,' the countess replied. 'Sir Thomas.' She glanced at Urswicke senior. 'What do you suggest?'

'What I suggest, madam,' the King snapped, 'what I suggest,' he repeated, emphasising every word, 'is that at least for the season, you leave London and lodge in your manor at Woking. Once there, I urge you to reflect on whether you would be safer abroad.'

'And where is safer abroad?' the countess asked caustically.

'Brittany is unacceptable,' Clarence barked. 'You know that. We cannot have you sheltering with traitors.'

'You mean my blood son and my good brother-in-law, Lord Jasper Tudor?'

'For them I don't give a fig.' Clarence chewed the corner of his lip as he leaned forward, glaring at the countess.

'Peace, peace,' Gloucester declared. 'Madam, you cannot go to Brittany . . . well, you could, but there would be consequences.'

'Being proclaimed as a traitor,' Christopher retorted. 'Being accused of consorting with traitors. Once that happens, the count-ess's lands and possessions would be fully forfeit to the Crown.'

'There are always consequences,' Urswicke's father almost yelled.

'So where do you suggest we go?' Christopher demanded.

'France is our enemy, so,' the King waved his hand, 'your good brother John and Master Guido now reside in Burgundy. Mistress, my dear countess, I would give you permission, letters and licences, so you could join them and lodge safely in Burgundy.' The King shrugged. 'The choice is yours. Look, I have made my wishes known. My lady, we are finished here . . .'

Urswicke sat at the writing desk in the countess's chamber. He leaned back in the cushioned chair and carefully sharpened the expensive quill pen. He glanced across at his mistress who, with Bray on her left, was warming herself before the crackling fire. The countess and her retinue had returned without incident from the Guildhall. Once home, Sir John and Physician Guido had immediately pressed their view. The Brothers York were correct. London was not safe and they should all adjourn to Woking Manor.

'From there,' Sir John argued, 'we could plan leaving this benighted kingdom and shelter at the court of Duke Charles.'

'My lady,' Guido had pleaded, 'once there you will be accorded every honour and privilege. You will be given the richest lodgings. Times have changed, alliances too. Burgundy has little love for Edward of England and his coven. Duke Charles and his courtiers would be most welcoming. They will give you, your son and the House of Lancaster their unstinting support. Once there, your beloved son, sheltering in Brittany, could safely join you. Duke Charles's court could become a rallying point for all Lancastrians. It would mark the emergence of a court abroad bitterly opposed to York and his policies.' Guido was about to provide a more detailed description of the Burgundian court when the countess rose and walked towards them.

'My friends,' she smiled, 'we shall think. We shall reflect, and what you suggest may well happen. For the moment, however, I must take close counsel with my henchmen here. I need their advice.'

Once her guests had left, the countess almost crumpled back into her chair.

'Burgundy,' she murmured, 'has it come to that? Yet my good brother and Guido are correct.' She glanced up and gestured at Urswicke. 'Come, my friend, what do you advise?'

'Never give in, give up, give out or give way. You must plot,' Urswicke declared, sitting down at the chancery desk. 'You must remain keen and sharp. There was something very wrong with that meeting in the Guildhall. I experienced a sense of real danger, something malignant. Indeed, I think it was all a sinister sham, deep deception.'

'What do you mean?'

'My father was smirking.'

'He always does.'

'Look,' Urswicke put the quill pen down. 'We were summoned to an important meeting with the King and his noble brothers, not to mention my august father and Clarence's creature Mauclerc.'

'Christopher, we know that.'

'But why?' Urswicke retorted.

'Because allegedly, two royal clerks, high-ranking members of the Secret Chancery, have been kidnapped, certainly murdered, their chancery fingers severed and left as a gesture of contempt and defiance.'

'What is this?' Reginald murmured.

'Ah, I see where you're going.' The countess's face had changed. She was more relaxed, no longer anxious but half smiling. 'Go on, Christopher,' she urged, 'tell us what you think.'

'Well, we aren't asked about what could have happened; we are not told to investigate, though never mind that! Shouldn't the Secret Chancery be visiting us, asking questions, searching for answers? Reginald, you have informants all over London. Ask them what they know about the disappearance of these two clerks. Make diligent search for their corpses. Eglantine and Clairvaux were sent to investigate. I think we should return the favour because,' Urswicke drummed his fingers on the desktop, 'there's something rotten here, truly malignant. Moreover, I believe my father is deeply involved in this murderous masque. Nevertheless, he has made the most dreadful mistake: why isn't there a thorough search for these two missing clerks?'

'So what do we do?' Bray demanded.

'Leave that for a while and draw close.' The countess beckoned them nearer. 'Come,' she repeated. 'Reginald, this chamber has no eyelets or listening holes?'

'Mistress, I have already assured you of that. Every inch of this chamber has been scrutinised.'

'Then make sure the gallery outside is deserted.'

Bray did so and returned to the chair that Urswicke had drawn up as close to the countess as he could.

'I have news for you,' she whispered. 'Known only to me and Abbot John May of Chertsey Abbey. My son Henry, his uncle Jasper and the latter's half-sister Katarina are in England, sheltering in disguise at Chertsey.'

'Mistress!'

'No, Christopher, I dared not tell anyone – not even you – until it was done. All three now shelter safely under Abbot John's protection.'

'Why have they come?'

'Christopher, you loved your mother. You watched her die. I was with you because your benighted father couldn't give a fig about her or indeed anyone else. I mean no offence, but your father has no soul. He cares for no one except himself. You are different, I am different. I love my only son passionately.'

The countess's eyes filled with tears and her voice broke. Urswicke stretched out and grasped her hand: it was ice-cold. He pressed firmly and let go.

'So,' the countess declared, 'what I say here is a matter for the confessional. The shriving pew under the sign of the five-petalled rose, the symbol for what is said beneath it to be secret and to remain so. Henry,' she continued, 'loves me in return, but there is more to his life than that. He is little more than a boy, an innocent boy, but the true claimant to the English Throne. To achieve that he, who is as gentle as a lamb, must survive this season of the wolf. So,' the countess's voice grew stronger, 'I need to meet Henry to talk to him.'

'But why? I mean why now?'

'Christopher, I just need to because of who he is and what I am. Secondly, Jasper talks of moving to a safer refuge than their castle at Vannes in Brittany. Henry faces the same threat as we do. Where should we hide? Where should we take refuge? Thirdly, I need to speak with Abbot John May. He has this morning sent me a message about revelations from Saint Vedaste Abbey in Arras.'

'That lies at the heart of Duke Charles's lands and territories.'

'Yes, yes it does, and that's what surprises me. However, Abbot John is insistent. Apparently he has a spy in Saint Vedaste, which is a Benedictine abbey under the same rule as Chertsey. As you know, Christopher, Benedictines are a law unto themselves. They have houses in every kingdom under the sun. They do not acknowledge borders, territories and fiefdoms. They move with impunity, and garner information with the same ease. What I can say for the moment is that Abbot John was deeply surprised at what he so recently learnt and insists he should share it with me. So, Henry or not, we are for Chertsey.' She smiled thinly. 'Now, I take counsel with you. I treasure your advice. But,' Countess Margaret folded back the silk cuffs of her pure wool gown, 'on this I am decided, and you must follow. We shall journey to Woking and, when we can, slip quietly into Chertsey.'

'Is Henry safe?'

'Christopher, as you know, Abbot John is my man, body and soul, in peace and war. Jasper,' she grinned, 'well, Jasper is Jasper. A born warrior and soldier. However, Katarina, his half-sister, has the heart, mind and wit for such a venture. She is courageous, fierce, yet cunning. She and I are one. She would lay her life down for me and for Henry.'

'Then let us pray she doesn't have to.'

'Amen to that, Christopher. Now look, Reginald, go to Queenhithe. You'll find a Flemish cog, lately returned from the Narrow Seas.'

'Its name?'

'*The Holy Angel*. Now, its master always waits for my signal to sail again. Seek him out. Tell him to wait even longer and he will have three more crew members on his journey back to Dordrecht.'

'And me?' Christopher declared. 'Mistress, I have urgent business in the city.'

'Then tend to it and we shall continue to thread our way through this morass of murder. Gentlemen, thank you.'

*   *   *

Christopher Urswicke wearily climbed King's Steps, which led from the quayside up to the sacred precincts of Westminster Abbey. It was a bitterly cold evening, a razor-sharp breeze ruffling the Thames with a bitter salt tang to blight the skin and sting the eyes. Urswicke was grateful to disembark. The river journey had been calm enough, yet he was eager to escape the harsh weather. He walked quickly, his cloak gathered close, one gauntleted hand free, the other close to his dagger sheath. Above him loomed the soaring abbey buildings, their cornices, carvings, sills and ledgings still coated with a grim hoar frost. Pools of light glowed at different windows and in various doorways. He heard the faint cadence of plainchant from a choir deep in the abbey church. Dark shapes flitted across his path, Black Robes busy on a variety of tasks. Clerks, scriveners and other royal officials had now left their offices, desperate either to get home or to enjoy the warm cheer of the countless taverns and alehouses along the winding runnels of Westminster. Eventually Urswicke left the abbey buildings, following a path across the royal precincts to the lofty mansions which housed the great offices of state, the Exchequer, the Wardrobe, or the one Urswicke now entered, the Royal Chancery.

He was immediately stopped by guards, who scrutinised the passes, signed and sealed by Countess Margaret. They stepped back and allowed him through. Urswicke went deeper into the darkness, along stone-paved corridors where torches flared in the seeping breeze. Urswicke walked alone, yet he knew he was being watched and scrutinised by the Chancery guards deep in the enclaves on either side. He reached a double gateway, where torches burned and braziers glowed. Again more guards, who examined his passes and allowed him through into the sanctuary of the Secret Chancery, a long, cavernous corridor with a row of chambers on either side. Urswicke was taken into one of these, now vacated as the day's business was done. All around the chamber walls stood carrels where the clerks worked. Urswicke smiled to himself. The room brought back memories, with its smell of vellum, rubbed parchment, soft leather, ink and perfumed sand. Quills and inkpots had been carefully secured. Some of the carrels still had parchments stretched out under small weights ready for the clerks the following morning. A few of these had inscribed their names across the top of their manuscripts, a long cursive script in a night-black ink. Urswicke stared down at the floor, eyes half closed. This chamber provoked other memories though, for the moment, he couldn't place them.

'Christopher, so good to see you.'

Urswicke spun round and smiled at 'Nondescript', once principal clerk in the Secret Chancery and Urswicke's former mentor. A highly skilled clerk, Matthew Murdoch had been given his nickname because of his appearance. He constantly dressed in the simple, earth-brown robe of a Franciscan, a white cincture around his waist, a black hood framing his round, rubicund face with its innocent eyes, sharp nose and smiling lips. Appearances could be deceptive, and this was true of Nondescript. Urswicke knew the former chief clerk had a razor-sharp wit and the keenest of intellects. A clerk fluent in many tongues and a master of the most intricate ciphers.

'Christopher, you are staring at me. Lost in wonderment?' Nondescript laughed. 'I was hoping to hear from you, Christopher, so I was happy to receive your message. Remember you are always welcome here. Now, how is your mistress the countess?' He waved Urswicke to a stool near one of the carrels before pulling one up for himself. For a brief while they exchanged pleasantries, then Nondescript leaned forward and touched Christopher gently on the back of his hand. 'As I said, good to see you, my friend. But why are you here?'

'Two clerks from the Secret Chancery, Eglantine and his henchman Clairvaux?'

'Never heard of them. So what's your intent?'

Urswicke told him and Nondescript whistled under his breath.

'Angels be my witness; I have never heard of them or indeed those two names.' He raised a warning hand. 'Though you must remember, Christopher, Secret Chancery clerks often change their names.' He grinned. 'Be it for amusement or because of the business they have to deal with. But look, give me their descriptions.'

Nondescript rose and took a writing tray with its sheets of parchment, together with inkpot and quill pen. He smoothed out the cream-coloured vellum and, as Urswicke haltingly provided information, wrote out in secret cipher the description of Eglantine and Clairvaux. Now and again Nondescript would break off to shake his head, adding that he knew nothing of either clerk or what might have happened to them.

'There again,' he mused, 'this is the Secret Chancery, where no one is supposed to know anything about the people or the work they do here.' He continued writing.

Urswicke, as he watched Nondescript's firm night-black script, wondered why it sparked memories he couldn't for the moment place. At last they were finished. Nondescript studied what he had copied and again shook his head.

'Never seen them,' he murmured. 'Now I am intrigued. Ah well.' He put the writing tray down. 'What else, Christopher?'

'You have heard of the Luciferi?'

'Of course, the Light-Bearers: the French King's secret agents, controlled by the Cabinet Noir in the Louvre. Over the years I have crossed swords with them. They spy on us as we spy on them. They are skilled, mailed clerks who take an oath of personal loyalty to the French Crown. They are cunning and, under their present King, very busy and, at times, most successful. They flock to this country because King Louis fears that Edward of York will lead an army across the Narrow Seas to repeat the triumphs of Crecy, Poitiers and Agincourt. They are self-sufficient and usually hide out in some derelict building.' Nondescript grinned. 'We know they are in England because, strange upon strange, French merchant cogs and war galleys are moored in the Thames. They, of course, are full of supplies, weapons and, if needed, fighting men. We have the same in King Louis's territories. King Edward does not regard them as a threat; they are allowed to run through his corn-field as long as they don't turn on him.'

'And the Garduna?'

'Ah yes, you mentioned these in your letter asking for a meeting. I have done some research. In some ways the Garduna are like the Luciferi, except they have no prince. They acknowledge no ruler. In truth, the Garduna are a secret society and a most malignant one. They are true children of the night, sons and daughters of the darkness.'

'Why?'

'They are assassins, kidnappers, rapists, smugglers, and any other malignant enterprise which might entice them. In brief they are skilled killers, merciless and unrelenting. The Garduna originated in the city of Toledo and have developed over the decades. They are extremely well organised, trained and equipped for every kind of warfare. The Garduna regard themselves as a race set apart. They are the sacred ones, infinitely superior to anyone else. To them we are simply fodder for the slaughterhouse. They can be hired for whatever mischief you want perpetrated. However, the Garduna charge a high price for their services because they are invariably successful in any enterprise they accept.'

'And their organisation?'

'They have formed into cohorts, war bands, battle groups. The Garduna swear loyalty to both the group and to their leader, the Master.' Nondescript paused. 'The Garduna emerged in Spain,' he declared, 'during the wars against Islam. They are still used both by the Inquisition and, most secretly, by the Spanish Court.'

'You said they were hierarchical.'

'Oh yes, more rigid than Church or State. Each battle group has a Master in command. At the bottom, the Chivorts or Goats; these are new members recently initiated. They perform menial tasks. Next, the Cobertas, loose women used to entice men into ambush. Above these, the Serenas or Sirens, who exploit their charms to seduce men for whatever purpose, usually to secure information or plan murder. The next rank are the Fuelles or Bellows, those who make friends with potential victims. Going up the Devil's ladder even further are the Capataz or Captains. Then the Floreadores, Muscle Men, trained to break into buildings. Finally, the Ponteadores, warriors skilled in sword- and dagger-play, all trained and harnessed for combat.'

'How do you know this?'

'A good question, Christopher, and a very relevant one. I read and memorised the account of an Englishman, Esme Langton, who served as a knight during John of Gaunt's invasion of Castile to claim the Crown of that country.'

'Gaunt? Edward the Third's son; the founder of the Lancaster dynasty.'

'The same, Christopher. Now listen. About a hundred years ago, Gaunt invaded Spain to seize the Crown of Castile on the grounds that he was, through his marriage to a Spanish princess, the legitimate claimant to the Castilian throne. Gaunt's rival, Pedro the Cruel, was supported by the Garduna. Gaunt learnt of this and put the Garduna under the ban. He unfurled the blood-red banner, which proclaims no prisoners, no ransoms, nothing but utter anni-hilation for any Garduna, be it on the battlefield or elsewhere. According to Langton, Gaunt destroyed five Garduna battle groups and personally hanged the Hermano Majo, their Grand Master. The Garduna responded by invoking the blood feud against Gaunt and all his descendants.'

'Is that why the Garduna are now in London?'

'What?' Nondescript gaped at Urswicke. 'Here?' he spluttered.

'I think so.'

'To wage war on the House of Lancaster?'

'Nonsense,' Urswicke replied drily. 'Why should they? The House of Lancaster is almost destroyed.'

'Except for the countess and her son.'

'True, true, but at the moment their cause is weak, so why should the Garduna meddle here? They are mercenaries, ripe for hiring, and I just wonder who has done this.'

'I agree but, Christopher, are you certain? Do you know how many there are?'

'I suspect a full battle group.'

'Well,' Nondescript sighed, 'that will be very, very costly. Whoever hired them must be rich.'

'York?'

'But why, Christopher? Why hire the Garduna to attack a frail countess whose son is a mere boy hiding in exile? Both of them are survivors of a cause which was truly shattered at Tewkesbury last summer. And where are the great Lancastrian lords now? Henry VI lies murdered, his wife – Margaret of Anjou – is report-edly witless and lodged in the Tower. The Nevilles and, especially the Beauforts, all gone into the dark.'

Urswicke nodded in agreement.

'Nevertheless,' Nondescript continued, 'your countess is in danger. She certainly faces threats, be it from the Garduna or elsewhere. Perhaps that explains the arrival of her good brother, Sir John Stafford, and his jovial companion, Guido the physician. Both soldiers, eh? Veterans deeply interested in the past.'

'Ah yes, the Staffords,' Urswicke absentmindedly replied.

'And they have a keen interest in the House of Lancaster, its lineage from John of Gaunt.'

'Really?'

'Yes, Christopher, really.'

'Tell me,' Urswicke demanded, 'the Luciferi? I suspect they are in London to hunt the Garduna.'

'Oh yes, Christopher, they certainly are. The Garduna hate the House of Valois; they are implacably opposed to the French Crown. They have meddled in France's politics for many a year. They cause strife and division. They weaken the kingdom at a time when it needs to be strong. So where the Garduna go, the Luciferi follow. If the Garduna are your enemy, then the Luciferi are your friends. If the Garduna are your allies, the Luciferi are your foes. Now look, Christopher, I have spoken to you enough. I can see you are deeply distracted. I have the names of those two clerks and their descriptions. I will do a careful search and return to you on this. It is a mystery, a masque, worthy of The Clerks of Oxford.'

'What's that?'

'Oh, a mummers' group. One of the many who come into the city during the festive season. This particular troupe stages a masque based on Chaucer's "The Clerk's Tale". You know the story about the faithful Griselda?'

'Do they now? Ah well.' Urswicke rose. 'I am done. I'd be grateful for any assistance on the matters we've discussed.'

They clasped hands, exchanged the kiss of peace, and Urswicke left. Lost deep in his own thoughts, he made his way down to King's Steps. Only then did he become aware of how dark the day had fallen. How bitterly cold the harsh breeze, even sharper than on his journey here. In addition, a dense river mist had crept in, which blinded sight and deadened all sound.

Urswicke climbed into a stout barge with a canopied stern. Its captain gave Urswicke a pot crammed full of fiery charcoal fragments. Urswicke nursed this as the six oarsmen leaned and strained on the oars to the chant of their captain. In the prow a young boy swung a lanternhorn. Now and again he'd blow lustily on a hunting horn to warn off other craft. The oarsmen wisely kept their barge as close as possible to the riverbank and eventually they arrived safely at Queenhithe. Urswicke disembarked and entered the tangle of streets leading up into Cheapside.

He wondered if any more proclamations had been posted about his mistress. He was tempted to go to the Standard, as well as across to St Paul's, but then shrugged this off. More pressing business demanded his attention. He drew both sword and dagger as he glimpsed the Dark Dwellers, the Night Wraiths, the Sewer Squires and all their felonious comrades. These minions of the night kept well away from this armed man, however, young and vigorous, sword and dagger already drawn. Urswicke would not be easy prey. He was only bothered by the plaintive plea of beggars or the whispered invitations from the many whores thronging in every doorway.

Urswicke turned into Catsnip Alley and immediately became aware of dark shadows either side whilst he felt another closing behind him. He stopped, abruptly sprang forward, then turned, sword and dagger out. He went down in a half-crouch, the classic pose of any experienced street fighter. The dark shapes around him held back. Urswicke watched in silence. One of the shadows stepped forward, holding up a crucifix, the usual symbol of friendship.

'*Pax et bonum*, Christopher Urswicke. I am François, captain of the Luciferi. I come in friendship. I wish to help. Let me assure you, your enemy is our enemy.'

'The Garduna?'

'Of course, Christopher. Now come, come.' François thrust the crucifix back into his warbelt. 'Come to where we lodge – The Basilisk in Snake Alley.' François's voice took a more mocking tone. 'Come and see the luxury we offer.'

'The Basilisk proved to be what Urswicke had suspected. A dingy, dark, desolate tavern where time had swept through and then swept on. As they first approached, Urswicke thought the tavern was deserted, but then he glimpsed the glitter of naked blades and realised armed men, muffled and hooded, stood guarding all the approaches to The Basilisk. Inside more men drank and ate at a long buttery table, their weapons at the ready. François issued a spate of orders at them before leading Urswicke up the stairs to a sparsely furnished, dirty chamber, with its stained, chipped floor and damp, peeling walls. François, his dark handsome face all bearded, apologised for the foulsome surroundings, but promised that the Bordeaux being brought up would compensate. It certainly did. Urswicke sipped at the rich red wine as he watched François make himself comfortable on a three-legged stool before him.

'Christopher, you're drinking the best Bordeaux this city can boast. Now, let us forget where we are and discuss what we do.'

'I know who you are,' Urswicke retorted. 'I also know whom you hunt, the Garduna, though I don't understand their true purpose.'

'And neither do we, Christopher.' François tapped his pewter goblet against Urswicke's. 'All we have learnt is that the Garduna are in England to inflict great hurt on both the Crown of France and the House of Lancaster. For them to come so far means this enterprise must be deeply malicious. We do think the Garduna have fielded an entire battle group under the Hermano Majo, their supreme leader.'

'And where do they lurk?'

'We are trying to discover that and bring them to battle. They will take no prisoners, and neither shall we.'

'But you have only a few men against a battle group.'

'We are more than you think. One of our war cogs is berthed at Dowgate. On board we have our own battle group. We can deploy men, harnessed for war, together with engines and machines for attack.'

'And you are certain about this? I mean the Garduna?'

'I am. One of my best men, Lucien, died trying to discover more. He was the one who learned that the Garduna are intent on wreaking great damage against both France and the House of Lancaster. He stumbled onto this secret and tried to discover more, only to be killed.' François shrugged. 'We pursue them, yet we must be careful. The Garduna have allies in the strangest of places.'

'Including the English Court?'

'Perhaps. Certainly people with enough treasure to hire and finance an entire battle group.'

'So the Garduna must have allies in London.'

'Of course. There are those that are with them as well as those forced to comply like your Lord Nightshade. Oh yes, we heard rumours about what happened. We also know about the attacks on the countess's manor in Woking and her house here in London. And, of course,' he smiled, 'we keep you and Master Bray under constant watch.'

'And I thank you for that.' Urswicke lifted his cup in toast. 'You intervened in attacks on us.'

'We certainly did. We took a Garduna prisoner, but of course he never broke. You might as well ask a wall to sing the "Ave Maria". Believe me, Christopher, the Garduna are something you have never encountered before, which is why we also cast about for friends and allies. We do not know who to trust.'

'Yet you sent Bernard to the countess?'

'Yes, and he was poisoned. How, why and by whom?' François shrugged. 'We asked the same questions of your comrade Master Bray. He couldn't answer us and neither can you. I assure you we meant well. We were trying to warn the countess, but Bernard was poisoned. This may well be the work of someone outside the countess's mansion, not a member of her household or,' he sighed, 'you may have a traitor within and he is responsible for murdering poor Andre. Anyway that's why we did not send anyone else. We did not know whom we could fully trust.' He smiled thinly. 'Now we do: you and Master Bray.'

'So what do you want?'

François didn't reply but rose, opened the door and shouted a name. A short while later a young man, slender as a reed, his face freshly shaven under an unruly mop of red hair, hastened into the chamber.

'This is Malachi.' François patted the stranger on the shoulder. 'He speaks fluent English. We call him Hermes – the messenger of the Gods, fleet as the wind and a most skilled horseman. I ask if he could join the countess's household.'

'Why?'

'Master Christopher, the Cabinet Noir in Paris has given me one simple instruction, nothing more, nothing less.'

'And that is?'

'To discover the whereabouts of the Garduna and utterly anni-hilate them. Now, sooner or later, the Garduna will show their hand. I need to know when and where so I can bring them to battle and totally destroy them. Malachi will assist in this.'

Urswicke returned to the countess's house and closeted himself away. Bray was absent on a number of tasks whilst Hardyng, Fleetfoot and whoever else had remained were preparing for the journey down to Woking. Urswicke quickly and quietly inducted Malachi into the countess's entourage. He assigned him to the stables, where he soon proved to be a great help to the few ostlers who had chosen to stay. For the rest, Urswicke stayed in his chamber, leaving now and again to eat and drink. Urswicke desperately wanted to make sense of what he'd seen, heard and felt during his visit to the Secret Chancery at Westminster. He strove to impose order on his jumbled thoughts.

Early the following morning, Nondescript sent a street courier with a short written message, in which Nondescript declared he had done diligent search on Christopher's behalf. However, he could find no trace of clerks called Eglantine or Clairvaux. Nor did their physical description match anybody in the chancery or those listed on the stipend roll of the Exchequer. For a while Urswicke just sat in his chamber, staring at the wall, until there was a knock at the door, and Bray bustled into the chamber. They exchanged pleasantries. Bray explained how he was busy preparing the household for their journey to Woking. Eventually his voice trailed off. He grinned at Urswicke, then leaned across and ran a finger down his comrade's unshaven chin.

'Christopher, you are distracted. You're not really listening.'

'It's those two clerks, Reginald. Eglantine and Clairvaux. They just don't exist.'

'They certainly did.'

'No, they were mummers, acting out a part.' Urswicke played with the ring on the little finger of his right hand.

'Then answer that.' Bray pointed at Christopher's hand. 'How do you explain the severed fingers?'

Urswicke lifted his hand, slipping the ring off and on then he laughed, shaking his head.

'*Habeo, habeo.*' He shouted gleefully in Latin. 'I have it.'

'Christopher?'

'The severed fingers were not from those two clerks. Eglantine and Clairvaux had very soft skin. I remember that when we met and clasped hands.' He tapped the side of his head. 'My memory is good; it has served me right. Those two severed fingers were coarse, roughened. At the time I noticed it, but I didn't realise the significance. Now I do.'

'God save us Christopher, if you're right, those fingers came from different hands.'

'Our two clerks, Reginald, were mummers playing out a masque. Nondescript mentioned a travel troupe. Look, Reginald, you know the captains of the street swallows. We need to speak to them urgently. In the meantime . . .' Urswicke, now elated by his discovery, almost jumped to his feet.

'And in the meantime what, my friend?'

'I need to visit that chamber where our so-called clerks worked. I want to examine its every clasp and bolt.'

Philip Malpas and Thomas Naseby left The Loose-Coat Tavern and, arms locked, staggered drunkenly down the runnel boasting the same name as the hostelry they had just left. Both men were pleased with life. They had drunk deep and long since they had left the stage which they had hired to present their masque. Both mummers had performed well, supplementing even more the heap of silver they'd earned earlier in the month. Laughing and joking, they rounded a corner and stopped abruptly before two of the night watch, men hooded and visored, though their white canes of office glinted clearly enough in the light of the lanternhorn carried by the taller of the watchmen. He now stepped closer, eyes glaring through the visor covering his face.

'Philip Malpas, Thomas Naseby?'

The two mummers, unsteady on their feet, could only cough and splutter, nodding vigorously when the questions were repeated.

'Both of you are under arrest.'

And, before they could resist, Malpas and Naseby were seized, the watchmen skilfully fastening the manacles around their wrists.

'Where are you taking us?'

'Shut up,' one of the watchmen barked.

'Why are we—?'

'I said shut up.'

The prisoners had no choice but to obey. They stumbled along the runnels until they reached the broad thoroughfare leading to the countess's mansion. They were dragged to the steps stretching up to the main door.

'You've been here before,' one of the watchmen taunted.

Malpas abruptly turned around. 'You're not a watchman. I remember your voice.'

'You are right; we are not watchmen.' Urswicke lowered his

visor, then brought up the small arbalest fully primed from beneath his cloak.

'And you are not,' Urswicke hissed, 'clerks in the Secret Chancery. Now quietly, and I mean most quietly, go up those steps and, at our command, do precisely what we ask.'

The prisoners climbed up to the main door. Urswicke pushed by them and, using his own key, unlocked the postern, which swung open. Urswicke and Bray pushed both their prisoners through to stand blinking in the dimly lit hallway.

Urswicke stared around. The house had settled for the night. The hallway and the galleries leading to it lay silent and deserted. No one knew of their mission except the countess. Urswicke had left strict instructions with Hardyng to keep the postern open and the hallway quiet. Urswicke now grabbed Malpas's arm and Bray did the same with Naseby. They took their prisoners down a narrow side gallery leading to the cellar door. Urswicke opened this, thrusting Malpas down the steps, ignoring the prisoner's curses as he struck against the wall. Once all four men had reached the bottom, Urswicke opened a door, forcing both men into the store-room, ordering them to sit on the wall bench. Urswicke and Bray now took off their visors, pushing back their hoods. They unstrapped their warbelts and sat down, facing their two prisoners who were still firmly manacled.

'Now listen.' Urswicke jabbed a finger. 'Listen very carefully. Refuse to cooperate or try to raise a clamour and you will suffer. On that, take my word. My good friend here, Master Reginald Bray, is a ferocious fighter who would cheerfully slit your throats. Now you may think that because you are in the cellar of a mansion you might be able to escape or persuade others to help you, but that would be a fatal mistake. One disturbance and Master Bray will be down to deal with you.' Urswicke laughed drily. 'We too can cut off fingers, can't we?' The two prisoners just stared back. 'We can cut off fingers, noses, ears and, if necessary, heads.'

'Better still,' Bray declared, 'I have many of the sailing fraternity in my circle of friends and acquaintances. I could easily arrange for you to be taken aboard some cog bound for the slave markets in Algiers. Merchants and their ilk are always looking for good, educated Saxon men, to slave in their mines or, even better, work as a eunuch in some harem.'

Naseby moaned in fear. Malpas's long thin face paled. Urswicke could clearly see the two prisoners were totally terrified.

'You must cooperate with us. You see we know a great deal already.' Urswicke leaned forward. 'I have scrutinised that chamber, the one you used while you were here. On the night you disappeared, someone gave you those severed fingers. You were ordered to transfer the chancery rings to them. Yes? Yes?' he repeated. Naseby nodded, Malpas mumbling his agreement.

'Who gave you that order?' Bray demanded. 'Who was behind all this? Who set up the scenery, allocated the parts, taught you the lines?'

'We don't know,' Naseby wailed. 'Everything was done in the dark.'

'Let us go back to that chamber on that particular afternoon. The day you disappeared.' Urswicke kept his voice soft, his tone more gentle than harsh. 'I suspect you were given the fingers before you locked and bolted the chamber door. You then crossed to the window. You knew you were safe, that you would not be disturbed. The rest of the countess's household, those few who remained, were distracted by a mystery play, a masque being enacted outside the house. That was your company wasn't it, The Clerks of Oxford? The masque was specially hired for that day and at that specific time to distract and divert. Easy enough! Yes? After all, as I have said, the countess's household was greatly depleted and those that remained would be hungry for such a distraction.'

The two men just sat, utterly crestfallen.

'Oh yes, both the day and the hour had been specially chosen. Your accomplices outside brought a ladder and whatever else you needed.'

'I do not know what you are talking about.'

'Yes you do, Malpas. I have checked that chamber from floor to ceiling. Every inch of its walls. But of course I concentrated on the window. You remember that, don't you? It's a door window and, lo and behold, I found it freshly oiled and greased. The door window also hangs slightly loose. Certainly enough for a slit to be created and a dagger to be inserted to bring the catch down to rest in its clasp. You arranged all that during your stay there, didn't you?'

Again the two prisoners nodded.

'The shutters were equally easy to manoeuvre. I noticed that if you slammed them shut, the bar, its hinge freshly oiled, slips down into its clasp. Again, if that needed a little help, a dagger blade could be thrust through the gap to ensure it was fully down. So, when you had to leave, you climbed out of that window, closing both it and the shutter. Down the ladder you went and into the dark. The shutter and window are locked behind you, the chamber is orderly, nothing out of place, nothing disturbed except for those two severed fingers. You posed a real mystery, one we were never supposed to resolve. We now know the truth. We've also learnt a great deal about you. You are former clerks, aren't you? From the Halls of Oxford or Cambridge. True?'

'We were clerks at Stapleton Hall in the Turl at Oxford. We grew tired of the trivium and the quadrivium.' Malpas shook his manacles. 'They were as much a chain as these.'

'So you are trained in Latin and the duties of a chancery clerk. But that does not explain your deception of us. So who was behind it? You must have been hired by someone wealthy enough to provide robes, to arrange the cut of your hair, shave your faces and, above all, provide you with two Secret Chancery rings. Oh no, this is not Everyman, some cunning fellow who lives amongst the Dark Dwellers. No, as I said, someone powerful such as the King, his two brothers or, better still, my beloved father?' Urswicke leaned to the side and drew out his dagger from its sheath. He held this up, inspecting the serrated edge. 'Do you know we were summoned to answer to all of these. We were brought to account over your disappearance and, of course, those two severed fingers.' Christopher laughed sharply. 'Perhaps we should sever both your little fingers and send them to Sir Thomas Urswicke, who, I wager, is behind all this mischief. What do you say?'

The two mummers stared bleakly back.

'Tell us,' Urswicke urged. 'Tell us what happened. What truly happened. Confirm or deny what we've said. Come now, you.' He pointed at Malpas.

'We have formed an excellent acting troupe,' Malpas began haltingly. 'We travel the shires south of the Trent. We came into London before Advent to present our own masques on the public stages ranged around the city, be it Whitefriars, Portsoken near the Tower or Smithfield. On one occasion, when we were staging our play *The Scholars' s Song*, we noticed how an extremely well-dressed official was watching our performances, two or three times in a row. Late one afternoon this official approached us, hood pulled forward, a mask covering the bottom half of his face.'

'My father, Sir Thomas Urswicke?'

'We don't know,' Malpas replied. 'We were told to meet again in some chamber of a Cheapside tavern. Monies were offered to us. We are used to such special private arrangements. We earned a silver piece that afternoon just by talking to him.'

'And the chamber in the Cheapside tavern?' Urswicke demanded.

'We were shown to a room and made to sit before a table where lanterns revealed us but kept those we were dealing with deep in the shadows. In short, we were given good coin to buy suitable clerkly dress and have our hair crimped. Our mysterious stranger then informed us about what was happening in the countess's house as well as at her manor at Woking. We were informed about the poisoning of a visitor. Our task seemed simple enough. We were to act the part of chancery clerks.'

'More specifically, the Secret Chancery?'

'Yes, we were to dress, talk and act like royal clerks. We were told to enter the house, be most diplomatic and tactful and question the countess's retainers, including you, on the strange events which had occurred. Of course, we didn't give a fig about them. It was just like rehearsing a play. We learnt our lines. We knew what expressions to adopt, how to walk, to sit. On no account were we to provoke suspicion. As I said, it was easy enough, no real challenge. We were told that our stay at the countess's mansion would be brief, and so it was.'

'And how was it brought to an end?'

'I left to buy something,' Naseby replied. 'A cowled, masked stranger approached me. He ordered me to prepare to leave immediately. Our masque troupe would perform some mummery outside the countess's house. This would divert those within; we were to slip out during the distraction, leaving everything in order. He then thrust a leather pouch at me. He said it contained two freshly severed fingers. We were to put our chancery rings on each of these and place them close to the door so the blood would seep out.'

'Where were they from?'

'I asked the same. The stranger replied that they'd been freshly cut from the corpses of two forgers hanged outside Newgate. The masked man then insisted that all this was to be done swiftly, certainly within the hour. I returned to the house and we prepared.'

'And the window catch and the clasp on the shutters?'

'Oh, before we ever came, we were told to prepare for such a departure; it presented no problems.' Malpas shrugged. 'Very few windows or shutters are perfectly aligned, there's always a slit or a gap.'

'Oh, so very true, Master Malpas,' Bray declared. 'House breakers are as common as fleas on a mangy dog. Indeed, I wager both of you have tried your hand at that, yes?'

Naseby simply glanced away whilst Malpas just sat back on the bench, staring dully before him.

'Did you ever ask the reason behind all this mummery?'

'Of course,' Malpas replied. 'And we were told to mind our own business. We were clearly threatened, warned that if we ever revealed the secret enterprise, we would be killed, horribly so.'

'Well, well gentlemen.' Urswicke made to rise.

'Sir?' Malpas lifted his hand in a rattle of chains. 'We are sorry for the inconvenience, for the deception, but we thought it was harmless enough. We were assured that the truth would never come out.' He lowered his hand. 'So how did you find us?'

'You're a clerk,' Urswicke answered. 'Simply a matter of logic. The real perpetrator of all this is undoubtedly my father. Cunning and as dangerous as any snake. Rest assured, gentlemen, if he ever discovered what we know, I am not too sure how long you and your companion would survive, but that's a matter for you to worry about. You play a game of hazard. You roll the dice,' Urswicke made a face, 'and the game continues. My father hoped for two things: a mystery which we would never solve, and through that to deepen the confusion and chaos around the countess. Now I prayed, reflected and fasted. I thought of that chamber, all sealed from within. Sheer trickery! Two mailed clerks, quite capable of looking after themselves, had simply disappeared, that was a nonsense! There was only one way you could have left and that was through the window. And sure enough, I found all the preparations you made to achieve that. Secondly, two bloody fingers were left on the floor, squeezed slightly so the blood would seep out. Would anyone give up life and limb so quietly, so serenely? No. So those fingers must have come from somewhere else. Thirdly, strange upon strange, a mummers' group appeared outside the countess's house at the very time you disappeared. So that means that everyone in this house was distracted, which afforded you the time and the space to leave as you planned. Fourthly, I have friends in the Secret Chancery. No one there could recall two such clerks with your names or your likeness. Fifthly, I knew that whoever played your parts must be skilled in such deception. Two men used to donning one mask after another, and you two certainly fit the part. Finally, I met with a captain of the street swallows. You know those urchins, fleet of foot and sharp of wit with the keenest of memories. I paid this captain good silver. I also provided him with a close description of both of you, as well as my suspicion about who you really are and where you might feast and drink. The Lord be praised, the captain came back with the names Naseby and Malpas, who love nothing better than drinking until the chimes of midnight in The Loose-Coat Tavern. And so we have it.' Urswicke got to his feet. 'Come, Master Bray. I would be grateful if you could bring these mummers, these jackanapes some food, some wine and a jakes pot. They will have to manage as they are.'

'What will happen to us?' Naseby whined.

'Now that sir,' Bray leaned down, 'is a matter we have yet to decide.'

Countess Margaret smiled at her two most loyal henchmen, closeted close in her chancery chamber.

'You did so well.' She leaned across and squeezed Urswicke's hand. 'Christopher, you are a veritable lurcher.' She turned to grasp Bray's hand. 'Reginald is just as good. Ah well! So Malpas and Naseby confessed everything?'

'Oh yes.'

'And you think this masque was all your father's work?'

'Undoubtedly. My Lady, you know my father's mind as well as anyone. Devious and cunning, he takes to plotting like a bird to flying.'

'We know he was responsible. We know how it was done,' Bray

retorted. 'But why? Oh, I understand more confusion and chaos both here and at Woking. But why go to such lengths?'

'Yes why?' the countess murmured. 'What devious wicked web has been woven?' she asked. 'Undoubtedly to discomfort us?'

'And what do we do with our mummers?' Bray asked.

'Do you know, Reginald,' Urswicke rose and made to leave, 'I don't really know. My Lady, we are bound for Woking tomorrow?'

'Or the day afterwards at the very latest.'

'Good, good.' Urswicke gathered up his cloak and warbelt. 'I need to think and plot.' He bowed towards the countess. 'I must return to the chancery office at Westminster. I have questions for my friend Nondescript.'

PART FOUR

'The lowest rank in the Garduna was held by the Goats'

Katarina Fitzherbert could only lean against the long refectory wall and stare in horror at what was happening. The entire abbey community, be it monks, lay brothers, servants, as well as the weak and ill, plucked from their beds in the infirmary, had been forced to gather here. Katarina gazed across to where young Henry clustered with the other scullions, stable boys and servitors. He looked dirty and dishevelled, as did Jasper, now all shaved and shorn, standing with the rest of the lay brothers. Everyone in the refectory watched the sinister figure, clothed completely in black from head to toe, who was striding up and down the long hall. Now and again, this eerie figure would pause, as if lost in thought. Katarina realised he was in fact using the silence to deepen the fear of all those present. The great refectory had a number of doors, all guarded by similar macabre, dark-garbed figures. Each of these, like their leader, was harnessed for battle: they carried an arbalest and, when their cloaks slipped open, iron-studded warbelts could be clearly seen.

The nightmare had begun the previous evening. Eight Friars of the Sack, or so it seemed, approached the main gate of the abbey, preceded by a cross bearer and an acolyte carrying a hooded lantern. Such funeral processions were common enough. To all intents and purposes a brother had died and wished, for a wide variety of reasons, to be buried in God's Acre at Chertsey. They had been allowed in and given permission. Jasper, in fact, had been one of the lay brothers who'd helped set up trestles in the sanctuary, where the coffin would be placed and the funeral party keep its requiem vigil, the Night Watch, until the dawn Mass was sung. Katarina had heard about this from the conversations of the others, but she had not given it a second thought. Chertsey was a holy place, built on consecrated ground. The Benedictines had a duty to assist in such sacred rituals. Apparently this was no different, and so the abbey returned to its normal horarium.

Darkness fell and the abbey settled for the night. However, the silence and harmony was shattered by the strident ringing of hand-bells. The alarm was raised and, in accordance with the rule of the abbey, all members of the community were to assemble in the nave of the church. People wearily dragged themselves from their beds, hastily wrapped cloaks about them and hurried down. However, they found the doors of the church locked and a host of armed, hooded and visored men guarding every approach.

Immediately chaos broke out. Two young lay brothers tried to resist and were swiftly cut down, slashing cuts which opened their throats. The invaders seemed to be everywhere. One of their captains shouted orders in English, though his voice was tinged with a strong foreign accent. Katarina suspected these unwelcome guests were Spanish, Castilian or Aragonese. Despite their deep hoods, Katarina glimpsed swarthy faces, skin burned by the sun. They were certainly well organised, demanding that everyone on pain of death should go to the refectory and wait. Anyone who attempted to resist or escape would be slaughtered. Katarina managed to get close to Jasper. He whispered how every gate and postern door was guarded, with a strong armed presence in the stables, so no one could enter or leave. Moaning at the bitter cold and muttering amongst themselves, the community filed into the great refectory. Abbot John and his leading monks, the prior and sub prior, were already there, standing on the dais at the far end. The rest of the community, some seventy souls in all, ranged along the walls on either side. The leader of the mysterious, black-garbed horde kept pacing up and down; his escort stood, arbalests at the ready. Three more occupied the choir loft above the main doorway. Eventually, the cries and clamour subsided into an ominous silence, yet still the leader, head down, continued his pacing.

'Who are you?' Abbot John came to the edge of the dais. 'Who are you?' he repeated. 'How dare you invade these sacred precincts? You are blasphemous intruders. You are guilty of sacrilege and fit for excommunication, damned in every aspect of your lives. Two of my community have been cruelly cut down! Murdered on holy ground! They were innocent and, like Abel, their blood cries to Heaven for vengeance!'

The leader, that nightmare figure, ignored the abbot. He just pulled back his cowl to reveal a swarthy, bearded face, framed by glossy black hair. He lifted a gauntleted hand and murmured something in Spanish. Four of his men hurried across. They gathered around him, nodding at their leader's whispered orders. The leader then crossed to where two old lay brothers, plucked from the infirmary, sat slouched at one of the tables. The leader bowed down and in a clear, carrying voice, asked if they were in pain.

'They are very sick,' the abbot said. 'They bleed from within.'

'Silence!'

The leader turned back to the old men and repeated his question. The ancients grimaced in a show of pink gums, eyes all bleary, unaware of how two of the intruders had silently slipped behind them. Katarina breathed a prayer then bit her lip as the garrotte string was skilfully looped over the ancients' bony, skull-like heads and fastened tight around their scrawny throats. The two victims hardly realised what had happened. The garrotte strings were swiftly tightened, pulled, then twisted violently to one side. Both old men, eyes popping as they fought for breath, died in a matter of heartbeats. Each assassin then loosened the garrottes, allowing both corpses to slide gently to the floor.

'This is sacrilegious murder!' the abbot shouted, stepping off the dais. He strode courageously towards the leader but then stopped as two of the intruders came between the abbot and their master.

'You can protest, my Lord Abbot,' the leader shouted for all to hear, 'but if I or mine suffer any nonsense, be it protest, resistance or an attempt to escape, three more members of this community will be despatched just as swiftly into the night. I am the Master, so listen.' He raised his arm, fist clenched. 'You must all stay here in the refectory. Food and wine will be supplied from the kitchen which adjoins it. I understand there is a jakes shed nearby. My men will collect paillasses, blankets and braziers to help you rest and keep you warm. If you obey my orders, all will be well. But if necessary,' he pointed to the two corpses, 'you can always keep them company in the death house.'

'What do you want?' Abbot John pleaded. 'Why are you here? Who are you?'

'Very simple,' the Master taunted back. 'Something easy to

achieve.' He paused for effect. 'I am here to take the coffin, the remains of Henry, late King of England, which now lies beneath a slab in the lady chapel of your hallowed church.'

'So they were your spies?' Abbot John retorted. 'The Spanish Benedictine, the married couple, allegedly going on pilgrimage? They were all here to spy out our abbey, the tomb, and so prepare for this?'

'Very perceptive, my Lord Abbot. Yes, we sent envoys, spies. We know more about your abbey than you think. Yes, we have come here to collect a corpse!'

'But that's ridiculous! Why that tomb?'

'Father Abbot, you asked who we were. That is not your business, but at least you know why we are here. We will open the grave, take out the coffin casket and be gone.'

'But why?'

'Again, nothing of your concern.'

'And if I refuse?'

'I will start garrotting more members of your community, then I will take the coffin by force.'

Abbot John rubbed his face. 'So, no more deaths, no more hideous executions?'

'I promised you and I repeat that promise. Cooperate and we shall be gone. No one will die as long as you do what I say. So,' the leader gestured around, 'pick six of your community, six of the brothers, young and vigorous. They will lift the slab and dig. We will also need helpers to serve refreshments and, where possible, they too can help.'

'Most of my community,' the abbot's voice became tremulous, 'are old and weak. The abbey church can, during the winter season, be freezing cold.'

'Then choose six of the strongest.' The Master's voice was hard and betrayed more of an accent. He then lapsed momentarily into Spanish before shaking his head and beckoning Abbot John to draw closer. 'Six!' he rasped. 'Now the sooner we begin, the swifter we leave. Choose six, as well as someone who may cook and serve.'

Abbot John slowly walked up and down each side of the refectory. He caught Katarina's eye, nodded, winked and beckoned her out. He did the same with a young maid and then chose six lay brothers including Jasper.

'Two young women and six strong men.' The Master mockingly clapped his hands. 'Good, good.' He turned back to Abbot John. 'Your prior can remain in charge here. No one leaves. Come, come priest, the dead await.' The Master strode out of the refectory and into the freezing cold morning air. Day had not yet broken.

Katarina, huddled with the rest, felt she was entering another, more sinister world. All around her the abbey lay deathly silent. Few lights glowed and the buildings loomed black and stark above them. A heavy river mist was swirling in to curl across their path to deaden all noise and blur any clear vision. Katarina walked quickly with the others, their escort striding either side of them. Macabre, eerie figures, cloaks billowing out, so they seemed like sinister night wraiths floating through the gloaming. The abbey church was even bleaker, a place of darkness where the shadows did their strange dance. The intruders, however, seemed unaffected by their surroundings. Their leader immediately ordered all the candles in and around the lady chapel, to the left of the high altar, to be lit. He ordered fresh tapers to be brought so the slab covering Henry VI's burial pit could be clearly seen. A barrel full of spades, mattocks, pickaxes and crow bars was brought and, with Abbot John looking on, the self-styled Master demanded that the simple funeral slab, decorated only with Henry VI's name, title and year of death, be prised loose and lifted. Katarina, desperate to speak to Jasper, stood alongside him as the slab was twisted free and laid gently down on the paving beside it. Urged on by the Master, Jasper and the other lay brothers began to hack the hard-packed earth. The coffin casket had apparently been buried deep. Now and again they were allowed to rest and recover. Katarina was escorted to the abbey buttery for jugs of ale and slices of stale bread. During one of these periods of respite, Katarina managed to squat beside Jasper at the base of one of the great pillars which stretched up into the darkness. Katarina and Jasper, talking softly in Welsh, pretended to be studying the host of sculpted faces staring down at them. Babewyns, monkeys, demons and terrifying gargoyles, their snarls and grimaces contrasting so sharply with the serene, beatific faces of seraphs and saints.

'Who are these invaders?' Katarina murmured.

'I don't know, but I think they are Hispanic, mercenaries perhaps.

Only Heaven knows why they are forcing us to dig up the mouldering remains of a dead king.'

'But a saintly one, Jasper! The legitimate, rightful ruler of this kingdom. Anyway, my question still stands. Why violate such hallowed precincts? Who wants the corpse so badly they risk excommunication, not to mention horrid penalties on the scaffold?'

'Could they be the Garduna? You learned about them from the Luciferi?'

'They probably are,' Katarina whispered, staring up at a gargoyle. She clambered to her feet. Jasper followed suit and they moved deeper into the transept, as if eager to examine a wall painting which described Lucifer's fall from paradise, brilliantly executed in a gorgeous array of colours. The artist had depicted the fallen archangel as dressed in costly Milanese armour, his golden-haired head bound by a coronet. He fell from a star-strewn sky, shooting like a blazing comet down towards the hungry flames of Hell.

'The Lord Satan certainly walks here.' Katarina continued to talk swiftly in Welsh. 'The Spanish tribe,' she added, 'the ones we have to defer to, they must be the Garduna, I am sure.'

'So where are the Luciferi? I thought they had set up a close guard on Chertsey.'

'They probably have, but these demons entered in disguise and they now control all the gates, doors and posterns. To any outsider, the abbey is closed but quiet. No fire, no smoke! No one cries, "Harrow harrow"! No clash of weapons or signs along the parapets that the abbey is being fortified. We were roused by the sound of simple hand-bells; their ringing will not be heard beyond the thick, dense walls of the abbey. Oh no, the Garduna are very clever. Moreover, look outside, kinsman, a thick freezing mist curtains off the abbey.' She paused. 'Interesting though, they apparently arrived here on foot.'

'Perhaps their horses are hobbled deep in the woods.'

'Now that would attract attention,' Katarina replied. 'However, if they came on foot, it must mean their lair lies close.'

'Come, come!' the Master shouted. 'The candle burns time and we must finish.'

Katarina and Jasper returned to relieve the others involved in the hard, back-breaking work. The soil beneath the slab was almost rock-like, permeated with hard pebbles and frozen hard by successive frosts. The ground had to be hacked. However, the deeper the diggers went, the looser the soil became. At last they struck wood and feverishly began to scoop out the dirt to reveal a long, oblong wooden casket with a simple cross nailed to its lid. Using ropes brought hurriedly from the stables, the coffin was loosed and raised, the soil and pebbles cascading off in an angry patter, as if the casket itself was protesting at the sacrilege being perpetrated. At last the coffin was free of the pit and placed in a pool of light created by the Master, who'd instructed two of the lay brothers to bring as many candles as they could find. In the dancing light of these tongues of flame, the lid was prised loose to clatter to one side. The Master took his dagger and cut away the rotten linen shroud, pushing it away. For a short while the leader just stared, softly cursing in Spanish before beckoning others to view what he'd seen. Katarina edged forward and hid her gasp at the gruesome tangle of bones and shards of hard flesh.

'More like a butcher's barrow,' she whispered, 'rather than a royal coffin.'

Jasper, standing beside her, nodded in agreement.

The Master, now in a temper, seized the coffin and tipped it over so the bones clattered across the ancient tiled floor. Katarina watched carefully. She was sure the coffin contained human remains; nevertheless, she had enough experience as a butcher on her manor in Pembroke to recognise the leg and head of both a sheep and a pig. The Master himself was now intrigued, sifting the grisly pile with his long dagger. He picked up the remains of a humerus.

'Human!' he grated. 'But this is strange. These,' he shouted, getting to his feet, 'are not just the mortal remains of a prince. These human bones, mixed with those of animals, belong to a man who was decapitated.' He bent down, dropping the shards, and picked up a skull still festooned with scraps of dried flesh and wispy, straggling hair.

'This man,' he declared, 'was decapitated then quartered. My Lord Abbot,' he called into the darkness, 'what is this? Why such pretence?'

Abbot John, who was standing deep in the shadows of one of

the great pillars which ranged either side of the nave, now walked forward.

'I don't know,' he replied, 'who you are or why you are here. And, sir, before you start to rant, I know nothing about the contents of the casket you've just tipped onto the floor.'

'Surely you must? You are lord abbot here. You must know something?'

'No sir.' Abbot John strode purposefully forward. 'No sir, I know nothing of what that casket contained. I was not present when the corpse was dressed for burial or when the coffin lid was sealed. Let me tell you direct. I know nothing. My Lord of Clarence's henchman Mauclerc, together with his familiars, brought this coffin here late last summer and, on the King's orders, buried the casket in the lady chapel. More than that I cannot say.'

'Then take it up,' the Master ordered. 'Reseal it and let's be gone . . .'

The following morning, long before the bells pealed out the first summons to Divine Office, Katarina was shaken awake by Abbot John who then moved across to rouse Jasper.

'Come,' he whispered hoarsely. 'They have left. The demons have flown! The buttery is safe. The fire burns lustily in the hearth and we must meet.'

Once settled in the buttery, Jasper, Katarina and Abbot John shared a bench before a roaring fire; they sipped mulled ale and chewed portions of bread smeared with a herbal cheese.

'So what happened?' Katarina demanded.

'Well, as you know, you and the others were told to stay in the church whilst the rest of the community remained herded in the refectory. I was allowed to return to my own chamber with one guard outside. At first light this riffler must have pounded on my door, yet when I opened it there was no one. No sound, no light; nothing but a thick mist boiling up the stairwell, twisting and turning like a horde of ghosts.' The abbot sipped at his ale. 'I realised many doors must lie open and so they were. I hurried down along the galleries then out across the great cloisters. I could find no one. Nothing to mark what had happened except the four members of our community who had been cruelly slain, their corpses laid out side by side in the cloister garth.' The abbot crossed himself three times in honour of the Trinity. He then got up and walked across to an arrow-slit window. 'As soon as dawn breaks,' he murmured over his shoulder, 'I'll order all the bells of the abbey to be tolled. They have sacred words carved on them. Powerful prayers to drive away the demons, the devils, the lords of the air who hover above the clouds. The sacred bells will disperse them and I shall reconsecrate our buildings with bell, book, candle and holy incense.'

'Father Abbot,' Katarina called out gently, 'what has happened to the demons who invaded here?'

'Oh, they are all gone. I found a postern door open. They must have left as they came, though carrying the casket they'd exhumed. The one they brought still stands in our church.' He turned and came back to his place before the fire. 'Thank God,' he murmured.

'Father Abbot?'

'Thank God they've gone. The Devil's own mist boils outside. I just thank God,' the abbot seemed distracted, 'I did not mention that when our saintly King's remains were brought here, there was one other person, Christopher Urswicke, Countess Margaret's principal henchmen. He was also present. I suspect Master Christopher knows exactly where the true corpse lies.'

Katarina got to her feet. 'Father Abbot, we must return to the church, to the lady altar. The burial pit must be closed . . . and there's one other matter.'

'Which is, Katarina?'

'The demons who invaded here brought a coffin. What did it contain? Why didn't they take it with them?'

Abbot John stood, fingers to his lips, blinking quickly as he fought off the tiredness and exhaustion he must feel.

'Heaven knows,' he murmured, 'what those demons brought in here, but you're right, Katarina.'

They left the buttery, hurrying along the dark cold galleries. Abbot John whispered that the community were truly terrified. They would not even dream of leaving the refectory, not until he assured them all was safe. They reached the abbey church and slipped through the corpse door into the south transept. The candles still flared. The floor of the lady chapel was completely littered with dirt, pieces of stone and hard paving. Katarina ignored this; she simply crossed herself and hurried up the steps through the rood screen into the sanctuary. The coffin stood on its trestles, a simple wooden coffer, more like an arrow chest than a casket. Katarina wrinkled her nose at the foul smell. Abbot John exclaimed in horror, wafting his hand at the stench.

'Something corrupt,' Jasper murmured. 'Something rotten.'

The lid was nailed down so Jasper and Katarina, using crowbars from the tool barrow left in the lady chapel, forced the lid back. A gust of foul air made them retch and cough. They had no choice but to walk away. Abbot John hurried into the sacristy and brought back pouches of fragrant incense, giving one to each of his companions. They then approached the chest again and Katarina stared down at the horrors it contained; the corpses of two men. Both had been decapitated then laid opposite each other, their severed heads wedged between the cadavers' legs. Into the right eye of each of them a blue and gold candle had been thrust, forcing the eyeball to burst. The men's boots and warbelts had been removed, as had any purse or wallet.

'Nothing to identify them,' Katarina declared. 'Except those candles.'

'What do you mean?' the abbot demanded.

'Father, I have been approached by the Luciferi, clerks from the French Secret Chancery. They are the enemies of the demons who swept in here last night. The emblem of the Luciferi is a blue and gold candle, royal colours favoured by their King. I suspect these two were probably spies, searching for the Garduna, the people who invaded us here. They were caught, tortured and killed. The Garduna are sending the Luciferi a message.'

'What shall we do with them?' the abbot asked.

'I would suggest burying them quickly and quietly but, believe me Father, the Luciferi will soon find out. I believe this abbey and the forest around it might well become a battle ground.'

'The Garduna act with impunity,' Jasper declared. 'They truly fear neither God nor man. But come, let's cover the remains, the stink is offensive. God rest their poor souls.'

Once they had washed their hands and faces at a lavarium, they re-entered the buttery. Abbot John built up the fire and went across to the window.

'Dawn is breaking,' he declared. 'Time to rouse the abbey, but—'

'But what, Father Abbot?'

'The invaders, the people you call the Garduna, that's what you called them, yes?'

'Yes, Father Abbot. I only know their name and a little about their reputation.'

'They came here to steal a coffin. I do wonder whether this sacrilegious theft is somehow linked to what I have just learned about happenings at the Abbey of St Vedaste in Arras.'

'In God's name, Father Abbot, what are you talking about?'

'That's the mystery. I truly don't know. I have a letter from one of the brothers there and I need to show it urgently to Countess Margaret. I shall certainly do so today.'

Oswald Hardyng, as he had been baptised when he was held over the font in the church of St Michael and the Angels, was proud to be the steward of Countess Margaret's city mansion, or he had been. He now stood in the jakes cupboard at the rear of that mansion, outside the scullery. Hardyng stared down in total exasperation at the two bloated corpses laid out by the rat catcher only an hour earlier. That busy, garrulous official, who looked like the vermin he hunted, had never stopped talking. He insisted on regaling Hardyng with the story of his life and his constant war against the rats who coursed, legion after legion, through the sewers, ditches and runnels of London. Hardyng, who had already drunk one goblet of wine too many, eventually silenced the rat catcher.

'So you're saying,' Hardyng demanded, 'that both of these rats have been poisoned?'

'Of course. Notice their swollen bellies and the discolouration of their underside.' The rat catcher picked up one of the rodents by its tail and twirled it in front of Hardyng's face. The steward gulped and hoped his stomach didn't betray him.

'Notice,' the rat catcher trumpeted, 'the swollen belly, but also the mouth and snout. See how they are stained with a thick, dirty froth. Oh, they've definitely been poisoned. Some deadly noxious potion such as henbane or foxglove.'

'Are you sure?' Hardyng insisted. 'I mean, these rats devour all kinds of filth.'

'Aye, and they have the world's strongest bellies. Rats can only be killed by powerful poisons, and do you know what? Sometimes even that fails. But why do you ask? What is the problem? Why worry, the rats are dead, the enemy depleted.'

'I found three other rats.' Hardyng gestured across the small scullery yard. 'Just lying there. They were like these two, a creamy filth around the mouth and muzzle, bellies all swollen.'

'Then that's further cause for rejoicing. Five more of these filthy buggers have met their end. Anyway, Master Hardyng, that's all I can say. You can thank God that the rats are brown and not black. Some people, men skilled in hunting these vermin, believe the black rat brings the pestilence, but listen to my view . . .'

Hardyng had cut the man short, paid him good coin and despatched the rat catcher as fast as he could through the garden gate. Once he'd gone, Hardyng just slumped on the bench in the jakes cupboard. He pulled across the slat to seal the shithole through which the rats must have emerged from the cesspit below. Hardyng, all confused, sat head in hands. He took his responsibilities very seriously. He was steward to the countess, an important member of her household. But all that had changed and now due to this. I mean, Hardyng reflected to himself, five rats poisoned, five at least, but the laying of poison lies strictly in my hands. It has to. Hardyng beat his fists against his thighs. Poison was a serious matter. The potions were always kept in a locked cupboard, and every time one was taken out an entry was written in the ledger. No such entries had been made, yet poison had definitely been laid in the mansion. But by whom? And above all, on whose authority?

Hardyng had questioned those servants who still worked for the countess, but all he had elicited were stout denials and strange looks. Of course he realised the servants were laughing at him behind their hands: his speech was slurred, his walk awry and his poise unstable. Nevertheless, none could help him in his enquiries, and this intrigued Hardyng. He had laid no poison nor authorised it to be done. Whoever had decided to pour it down this jakes hole must have bought it from an apothecary. But again, who and why? The only other mention of poison was the abrupt and mysterious death of that Frenchman. Hardyng could not understand that. He had locked the French visitor in the waiting room, served him a goblet of wine and returned to his usual duties. Indeed, he'd never given the Frenchman a second thought and had almost forgotten about him. So how had he been poisoned, why and by whom? True, Hardyng had served him a goblet, but it was from the common store and he himself had sipped from it to ensure its flavour. He had tasted nothing amiss. Later Guido the physician had sent him down to the cellar, where Guido had left morsels soaked in the wine taken from the goblet the Frenchman had used. This wine had been fed to the rats which swarmed there, but all the rodents had remained unscathed. No corpses were ever found in that cellar, only here – in or near – this jakes cupboard. Physician Guido had pronounced the wine sound, so how had Bernard been poisoned? Had someone else gone into that waiting chamber and murdered the Frenchman? And who could have done that? Hardyng scratched his head; that was a matter for Urswicke and Bray. He was steward here and he needed to find out where this poison came from.

Hardyng lurched to his feet, left the latrine and staggered back through the scullery into the house. The galleries and rooms lay silent. Hardyng returned to his own chamber. He tried to pray but became distracted. He went over to his chancery desk and sat down before it. He thought of Andre Bernard. Hardyng blinked. 'Andre?' he whispered. 'How did I get to know his first name; he never gave it to me.' Hardyng tried to recall every single moment in that brief encounter with the Frenchman. No, he was certain Bernard had never given him his full name. Very recently Master Urswicke had asked him the same and he couldn't answer the clerk's question. Bernard was simply anxious to speak to the countess as soon as possible, nothing more than that.

Hardyng sat listening to the sounds from the street. He closed his eyes for a moment then opened them. The noise from outside reminded him that there was also the mystery of those two clerks. They'd seemed personable enough. Hardyng had said as much to Sir John Stafford and Guido the physician. They'd asked him and the other servants some questions, then the disaster had occurred: those severed fingers, all bloodied beneath the door. For the rest the chamber was completely empty. Eglantine and Clairvaux appeared to have vanished into thin air. Both clerks had disappeared during the afternoon when that mummers' troupe The Clerks of Oxford, had performed in the street outside. All the remaining servants, himself included, had flocked to watch it. So who had not been there? Was it a coincidence that this troupe should appear on the very afternoon two royal clerks were abducted? Were people in the house involved? Or, and Hardyng felt a pang of guilt, had someone crept in? Yet he was steward responsible for the security of the countess's house. Hardyng felt his panic deepen. On that particular afternoon, despite all the strange occurrences happening in and around the mansion, had he secured all the doors and entrances? Had he been remiss in his duties? Had some villain, or a gang of them, stealthily entered through an unlocked door to perpetrate bloody mischief?

Hardyng tried to control the spasm of fear which gripped his belly. So many questions could be asked of him. Yet how was it his fault? He was a household steward who had to confront sudden death, mysterious murder, not to mention fire arrow attacks on the mansion. Hardyng realised the challenges his mistress had to confront, but Hardyng never wanted to be drawn into the affairs of the great Lords of the Soil. Hardyng's world was quite simple and straightforward: the sealing of indentures; the hiring of servants; arranging purveyance from the markets. He had to ensure the pantry, buttery, kitchen and scullery were kept scrupulously clean and ready for use. 'Matters politic', as he assured his colleagues, were not his concern and shouldn't be theirs. Such matters were best left to Master Urswicke and Master Bray.

Hardyng rubbed his chin. Both of the countess's henchmen had also been swept up in the turbulence which had engulfed Lady Margaret's household. Only recently, both Urswicke and Bray had warned Hardyng and the servants not to go down to the cellar where the countess had lodged two important prisoners she wished to question. 'All this confusion,' Hardyng breathed. 'I need some wine, a generous goblet of Bordeaux.' He would not have it here in the house, the servants would see him then gossip about it.

Hardyng pulled himself up, grabbed his cloak and left the house. The light was fading as he hurried across the silent garden and into the small but dense copse of trees. He reached the clearing, his favourite place, with the stool he always sat on, his goblet and, beside it, a bulging wineskin.

Hardyng sat down on the stool and, hands shaking, unstoppered the wineskin and slopped the Bordeaux into the goblet. He gulped greedily at the brim then refilled it again. Hardyng smacked his lips, lost in his own thoughts. 'It is time I sobered up,' he murmured.

Yes, he would sleep well tonight, then he would marshal his thoughts. He would draw up a memorandum as if he was drafting an indenture. He would list all his concerns for the countess and her two henchmen. He would describe in great detail what happened on the morning the Frenchman was poisoned and the afternoon when the mummers performed outside. He would list certain questions and pray that Urswicke and Bray would find the answers. He was sure this would help.

Hardyng looked down at the wine. Now he remembered other matters which, at the time, he dismissed as of no consequence. Hardyng, like all servants, tried to eavesdrop on those he worked for. The steward now appreciated that some coven had emerged from the dark to loose those arrow storms. They seemed to know a great deal about the house, be it the front or the back, and its jetty.

'I wonder!' Hardyng exclaimed to himself. Some time ago, during autumn, two visitors had knocked on the door. Both were Spanish. Both said they were visiting England on pilgrimage to Chertsey then on to Walsingham. Anyway, they simply wanted to see a refined London house. Hardyng, of course, had been flattered and escorted them around, deeply appreciating their constant murmur of approval. About the same time a young man, also Spanish, who claimed to be pursuing a vocation to enter the Benedictine order, knocked on the door asking for alms. The countess was always generous, and the young man had spent hours in the buttery. He too claimed to be on pilgrimage. On reflection, was all this a coincidence? Or were these visitors simply trying to discover as much as they could about the countess's mansion and her household? Hardyng took another gulp, unaware of the dark, sinister presence in the trees behind him.

Christopher Urswicke sat deep in the pavilion, at the far end of the countess's winter-bound garden. He was wrapped in a heavy military cloak. Two warming pots flanked either side whilst the brazier before him was crammed with glowing charcoal. Urswicke was comfortable enough. The early morning was not too cold and he just wished to escape from the hustle and bustle as the countess's household prepared for its imminent departure to Woking. Urswicke had risen early. He had visited the countess but she, worried deeply about her son, was lost in her devotions, kneeling, hands crossed, before a triptych of the crucified Christ and Our Lady of Walsingham. Urswicke realised she was not to be disturbed, so he'd collected his own psalter and retreated to this garden bower. In truth, he found it difficult to pray. He was too deeply distracted by his return visit to Westminster. He had arrived back long after vespers. He and Bray had checked on the two prisoners still incarcerated in the cellar beneath the house. Urswicke had wasted little time on them before going to visit the Luciferi's messenger, Malachi, who seemed happy enough on his bed of straw in one of the warmest haylofts in the countess's stable room.

Urswicke had been tempted to share his suspicions with both his mistress and Bray, only to decide that he would let matters rest as he reflected further.

'A square of parchment,' he murmured to himself, 'an inkpot and a genealogy of kings. I ask myself, are these all keys to the mysteries confronting us?' Urswicke sighed and opened his psalter on the chapter of devotions to St Julian the Hospitaller. The saint's life was told in a series of miniature paintings, a veritable parade of exotic costumes, golden harness, a whirl of deep colour and bejewelled clasps. In contrast to this, on the opposite page, the incarnation of hellish terror: a leering crone floating high against a dark, menacing sky, lit by fires burning below. All these pictures told the story of Julian, who returned home to find two sleepers in his bed. Believing his wife was betraying him, he slaughtered both, only to discover he had murdered his own parents, who had decided to pay their beloved son a surprise visit. So, overcome by guilt, Julian had spent the rest of his life in reparation and penance, caring for sick lepers in particular.

Urswicke always felt drawn to this particular devotion. He truly despised his own father, who had driven Christopher's beloved mother to an early grave. A born intriguer and a most dangerous soul, Urswicke sometimes felt tempted to challenge his father to a duel and kill him. He had confessed the same at the shriving pew, and the priest who was to absolve him, an ancient Franciscan, would simply murmur words of consolation. Countess Margaret had been more pragmatic, saying that Christopher's desire to kill his arrogant father was simply a reflection of the deep animosity he felt towards Sir Thomas. 'You would not kill him, Christopher,' she once declared. 'Temptations are like birds; they fly through the trees but rarely nest. You have a good soul, Christopher, and the temptation is understandable. Your mother was beautiful, loving, faithful and devout. I never heard her utter a word against your father or, indeed, anyone else. Nevertheless, we know what Sir Thomas is like, what he's truly capable of. What you must do, Christopher, is become and remain a better man than he.'

'True, true.' Christopher crossed himself. 'St Julian, help me, and above all help me discover what my esteemed father wishes to gain from this present mischief.' Urswicke leaned back against the seat. A true shadow-player, Urswicke's father hated the countess and would do all in his power to inflict damage on both her and her household. He would do it cleverly, subtly, treacherously. Urswicke had no doubt that his father was the moving spirit in these present troubles. But why?

Urswicke broke off from his reflection. The crows in the small copse of trees to his left were particularly noisy. The clamour of the birds even drowned the cries of the hot water man in the street beyond, yelling how tubs of hot, perfumed water were now ready in a nearby bathhouse. Urswicke watched the crows burst out of the copse in a flurry of black feathers. 'Something's disturbed them,' Urswicke murmured to himself. 'Perhaps one of the cats.' The cries of the crows stilled somewhat. Urswicke reopened his psalter. He stared at the different miniature paintings and wondered yet again about the mischief that his father and others were plotting. A door abruptly opened and a servant came out, enquiring about Hardyng. Urswicke shook his head, muttered he could not help, and the servant hurried back inside.

Urswicke decided it was time for him to join the preparations within. He rose to his feet then paused as a huge, sleek, black-feathered crow glided down, some morsel in its sharp beak. Urswicke, startled, stepped forward, and the crow dropped the blood-encrusted fragment and flapped away, cawing its annoyance at being disturbed. Urswicke drew his dagger and went to crouch near to what the bird had dropped. Urswicke turned it over with the point of his knife. 'In God's name,' he whispered, 'what is this?' He breathlessly got to his feet, staring across at the copse of trees. 'A human eye!' he murmured. 'So what's in those trees? What's causing the furore amongst the carrion?'

Urswicke strode across the grass into the deep green darkness of the copse. He stared around and glimpsed a flash of colour amongst the trees. He walked towards this. A thin mist seeped backwards and forwards. Urswicke truly felt as if he was entering the kingdom of ghosts. The cawing crows had fallen silent, no surging echoed from the undergrowth either side. Nothing but a baleful silence, a dreadful stillness, as if all that lived cowed at the presence of death. Urswicke walked slowly towards the grue-some scene. The mist shifted like a curtain being pulled aside and Urswicke immediately recognised Hardyng: the steward hung like a doll, the noose around his throat tied tight, its knot fastened cruelly just beneath the steward's left ear. Hardyng was fully dressed. On the ground beside him lay his cloak and a flattened wineskin, next to a stool which he must have brought out to squat on before deciding to hang himself. Hardyng's corpse swung slightly in the morning breeze, an ominous sound, the creak of both rope and branch playing out like some mournful music. Urswicke noticed how the unfortunate man's bladder had emptied, the front of his blue hose was soaking wet.

'You drank and you drank,' Urswicke declared. 'Then you killed yourself. You brought a rope and fastened it over that branch, you tied a knot and stepped off the stool. Is that the truth?' Urswicke drew nearer and clasped the dead man's hand. It was freezing cold. Christopher crossed himself, murmuring the requiem, when he heard Bray calling his name. Urswicke turned to leave but remem-bered Hardyng's great bunch of keys, his 'badge of office', as the dead steward often jokingly referred to them. Urswicke returned to the corpse, lifted the dead man's jerkin and took the ring of keys hanging from a hook on the steward's broad household belt. Clutching these, and hurriedly whispering a prayer, Urswicke left the copse. Bray was waiting, pacing up and down snapping his fingers, lips soundlessly moving, as if deeply immersed in some problem. He stopped and stared at Christopher.

'Come,' Bray beckoned. 'Come, Christopher, you must see this.' Not waiting to answer any questions, Bray led Urswicke back into the house and down to the cellar where they had lodged the two prisoners. Bray took a key from his pocket and opened the door. The chamber now reeked of foul smells. The light was dim.

'Sweet angels,' Urswicke whispered, peering through the murk.

Their two prisoners now sprawled against the wall bench. Both men had been killed by bolts from a powerful crossbow. Loosed close, the barbs were deeply embedded, shattering the forehead of each victim, reducing their faces to nothing more than a gruesome mess of ripped flesh and black-red blood. Urswicke knelt between them, swiftly scrutinised the two corpses, before glancing back over his shoulder at Bray.

'No other mark,' he declared.

'I agree. I found the same. A bolt to each of their heads, nothing more.'

'But how?' Urswicke got to his feet and walked back to push the door shut, wrinkling his nose at the foul smell. 'How?' he repeated. 'Reginald, that door was locked. You had the key.' He paused and drew from his deep pocket the ring of keys he had taken from the dead steward. He fumbled amongst these until he found one identical to the key held by Bray.

'Did Hardyng give you that?'

'He had no choice.' Urswicke went and fitted the key, turning the lock.

'Well, did Hardyng give you that?' Bray insisted.

'As I said, he had no choice. He's dead.'

'What?'

'Hanged himself in that copse of trees. I found him dangling there just before you arrived.'

'Murder?'

'It looks like suicide. But leave that for the moment. Let's concentrate on our two prisoners. Reginald, both men were murdered. For a short while, we will leave their corpses. The mystery is clear enough and the solution probably lies deeply hidden.' Urswicke gestured around that forlorn chamber. 'Reginald, for the love of God, what do we have here? Both victims were young, strong men, quite capable of defending themselves, even if they were manacled. But look, there is no real sign of any struggle, any attempt to defend themselves. Just as importantly,' Urswicke crouched by one of the corpses, carefully scrutinising the crossbow barb, 'this bolt,' he declared, 'was loosed from a heavy battle arbalest, the type used by Genoese mercenaries. Those crossbows are heavy, clumsy, yet very powerful; their bolts can even shatter stone.'

'So only one can be carried?'

'Precisely, which means, my good Reginald,' Urswicke got to his feet, 'that there were two assassins, each carrying a war bow. Somehow they got through that door, killed our guests and left. Again, another mystery. You found the door locked?'

Bray nodded in agreement, ushering Urswicke out and turning the key behind them.

They left the house, going out into the copse. Drawing his dagger, Bray helped Urswicke cut the hanging rope, then lowered Hardyng's corpse to the ground. Bray murmured a prayer as he cut the noose free, the corpse shaking, allowing the last breath out.

'Good Lord.' Bray studied the hanged man's purple, twisted face, all bloodied and torn where the crows had feasted on the soft parts, the nose, ears, cheeks, and the blood-filled sockets from which the eyes had been plucked.

'So,' Bray sat on the stool Hardyng had used to hang himself, 'our good steward, whose wits had been disturbed by all the strange happenings here, takes a stool and a wineskin out to this copse. He drinks himself stupid and his mood darkens even further. He cannot go on. Hardyng gets a rope, fastens one end around the branch of that oak, fashions a noose and slips this over his head. He stands on the stool, tightens the knot and steps into eternity.'

'So it would appear,' Urswicke replied. 'There's no sign of ligature or binding. Nothing to demonstrate he was murdered.' Urswicke lifted the dead man's left hand and stared at the ink-stained fingers.

'Oh my lord,' he murmured.

'Christopher?'

'Reginald, look at Hardyng's fingers. He was left-handed. Now, when he allegedly fixed the noose around his neck, he would tighten the knot, yes?'

'Yes.'

'On what side?'

'Well, if he was left-handed the noose would be tightened on his right side. He would do this, especially at a time when he was fey-witted and deep in his cup. But the knot wasn't on his right side, was it? Oh no, the noose was expertly fastened on his left.' Bray got up and moved the stool back to the branch from which Hardyng hanged himself. He positioned himself carefully then stood on it, reaching out to grasp the branch. 'Hardyng,' Bray declared, 'was left-handed. The knot should have been tightened on his right side and it wasn't. Christopher, look at me. I'm taller than Hardyng and yet I find it difficult to reach out and grasp this branch. Straws in the wind,' he murmured. 'But I don't think Hardyng killed himself.'

'Straws in the wind indeed,' Urswicke retorted. 'But I think you're right.'

Three days after the Garduna had left Chertsey, Katarina, Jasper and Henry were summoned in the dead of night to the abbot's private chamber. The Benedictine looked worried as he bolted and locked the heavy door before gesturing at them to sit on the chairs before the roaring fire. Abbot John served mulled wine, richly laced with herbs, and urged them to eat the croutons basted with a savoury spice. Once he had made his guests comfortable, he sat down, crossed himself and administered a blessing.

'Are we going to need that, Father Abbot?'

'We certainly are, Katarina.' The abbot drew a deep breath. 'Cornelius the anchorite has disappeared. He has been gone some days, God knows where. He just disappeared, vanished like dew beneath the sun. I have carried out careful search but there is no trace of him. No one knows anything. Nevertheless, he has vanished, leaving his few possessions in the anker-hold.'

'Father Abbot?' Katarina kept her face schooled. 'Why should such a disappearance concern you? I mean, Cornelius may have been a Yorkist spy . . .'

'He certainly was, and a much valued one. I was under strict instruction from the Royal Council to report anything wrong or worrying about our anchorite, whether he fell ill or, as is the case, simply disappeared. Now before the arrival of those demons who pillaged the tomb, I despatched a courier to Westminster bearing messages about Cornelius's disappearance. I have also despatched another about the desecration of the royal grave. Ah well, to cut to the quick, a messenger from Westminster has visited us with the news that Mauclerc, George of Clarence's henchman, along with the comitatus of mounted archers, is already on his way here.'

'Mauclerc,' Jasper breathed, 'a true blood gulper. Clarence's creature. A killer who has shown the likes of us no mercy.'

'I have heard of him.' Katarina sipped at her mulled wine then sat holding her goblet, staring into the flames, half listening to the winter wind clattering the shutters. Cold draughts seeped in through the gaps and cracks to send the tapered candle flames dancing. Katarina watched the circle of golden glow and shivered. She knew enough about the Yorkist court to be wary of its dangers. Clarence and Mauclerc were truly threatening, murderous souls who'd revelled in the bloodletting after Tewkesbury.

'What's Mauclerc's purpose in coming here?'

'It's obvious, Katarina, the pillaging of a royal tomb is cause enough.'

'Father Abbot, I disagree. The House of York couldn't give a fig about Henry's tomb. Indeed, they may be only too pleased to be rid of any remains and so destroy the shrine to our martyred King.'

'True true,' Abbot John agreed. 'It's ironic that Mauclerc has been despatched to view the damage. We all know the true contents of that coffin. Certainly not the remains of our departed King. We know, as does Master Urswicke, that the coffin was exhumed and opened. What can be found there is nothing more than the work of Mauclerc and his henchmen.' Abbot John chewed the corner of his lip. 'I do wonder if Mauclerc knows the where-abouts of the true corpse.' Abbot John paused. 'Katarina, you are correct. I don't think Mauclerc gives a fig about the remains of King Henry, but he would certainly be keen enough to know the whereabouts of the Yorkist spy, Cornelius, our self-proclaimed hermit.' The abbot turned in his chair and gently tapped Katarina under the chin. 'Katarina, do you know where he is? You see, Brother Sylvester, our refectorian, or one of them, came to see me recently. He claimed that Cornelius was deeply interested in you.'

'Was he now? I certainly never returned the compliment. Father Abbot, I can honestly say that I do not know where Cornelius might be.'

Abbot John smiled and turned back to the fire.

'Cornelius will not be missed,' Abbot John rasped. 'Our self-serving anchorite was not what he proclaimed to be. He was not a man of prayer, but a soul steeped in great deceit and lechery.' Abbot John glanced quickly at Katarina. 'Oh yes I have heard stories about him bullying washerwomen. In truth, we became poorer because of his presence, so we are certainly richer for his going. However, Cornelius was only part of the disease.'

'Father Abbot?'

'There are two cheeks to every arse.' Abbot John shrugged at his bluntness. 'Cornelius was one, Brother Sylvester is another. I believe, and I always have, that Sylvester is a spy in the pay of York. No no, let me explain. Cornelius watched the tomb, the shrine, visitors to it, and so on and so on. Now the Crown, whoever wears it, is always interested in Holy Mother Church and what goes on in its great abbeys up and down the kingdom.'

'In a word, they have a spy in such religious houses?'

'Oh Katarina, often more than one. I suspect that was the same here. Cornelius would watch the shrine whilst Brother Sylvester, as a refectorian, would get to know about all the visitors to Chertsey. More importantly, our abbey lies directly on the approaches to London, both along the highway as well as the river. Couriers, messengers and others of that ilk rest here before the final ride into London, some seventeen miles away. Sylvester, of course, would entertain them. He would serve refreshments. He would also give them messages, secret messages, assuring the couriers of being well paid when these were delivered in the Halls of Westminster.' The abbot rolled his goblet between his vein-streaked hands.

Katarina's apprehension deepened as she recalled how often she'd seen Sylvester in the refectory, chatting in such a friendly manner with Henry as he did with other scullions. Katarina had viewed the refectorian's curiosity as harmless enough. Now she certainly didn't.

'Everything that has happened here,' Abbot John declared, 'must have whetted the curiosity of both Cornelius and Sylvester. Now that Cornelius has disappeared, Sylvester will be snuffling for secrets with all the skill of a hungry pig.'

'And any information he has garnered despatched to the Secret Chancery at Westminster.'

'Undoubtedly, Katarina.'

'What can we do?' Jasper groaned. 'We should flee Chertsey.'

'Nonsense, kinsman.' Katarina repressed her own deep chill of fear. She breathed. 'If we fled, that would only provoke suspicion. Mauclerc would summon his huntsmen, whip up his dogs and pursue us the length and breadth of the shire. And where could we hide? How could we secure passage abroad? More importantly, we have no choice but to stay here. The Countess,' she smiled at Henry who, as usual, sat still as a statue, his face all watchful and wary, 'the Countess,' Katarina repeated, 'your mother wishes to take urgent counsel with you.'

'Do you think that is another reason Mauclerc is coming here?'

'No, Jasper, they know nothing about our arrival in Chertsey. Moreover, the Brothers York are keen not to depict themselves, when it comes to the countess, as overbearing intruders. Well, at least when it comes to appearances. They do not want to be seen as hounding the Lady Margaret. So we stay here until she comes. We shall shelter deep in the shadows of this abbey and, what is crucially important, we must not provoke any suspicion.'

'Easy enough,' the abbot declared, 'if it wasn't for the disappearance of Cornelius and the constant spying and snooping of Sylvester. I hate him,' the abbot added heatedly. 'I truly hate him,' the abbot repeated. 'And perhaps it's time—'

'For what?' Jasper demanded.

'Close your ears, young man.' The abbot leaned across and tapped Henry on the arm. 'Though you may know this already.' The abbot murmured a paternoster. He kept repeating the phrase 'and deliver us from all evil' before opening his eyes. 'Amen,' he declared. 'Amen! I have seen and I have seen but I have done nothing. Perhaps now is the time. Our anchorite,' he continued hurriedly, 'our so-called hermit, was a lecher for the ladies.' Abbot John drew a deep breath. 'Brother Sylvester has a predilection for young boys, young men. He lusts after them.' Abbot John let his words hang like a noose in the air. 'I agree, I concede,' he murmured haltingly, 'that I have failed in my duty. Many of the boys who work in the abbey, be it in the kitchen or the gardens, are orphans we have taken in. They are innocents and vulnerable. They have no kin to protect them, nothing but me and my abbey. They are happy enough, contented with their lot. Some will join our order, others will learn a craft then leave. As I said, they are happy enough, but I have heard rumours, gossip about Sylvester. At first I thought it was nothing more than salacious chatter, but I have glimpsed things I wish I had not.'

'Sylvester is sweet on Alcuin,' Henry abruptly blurted out. 'Lady

Katarina, you must have seen him. Alcuin is a young man, tall, slender as a willow, with corn-coloured hair.'

Katarina nodded. She'd seen Alcuin who, despite the grime and dirt of the scullery, was a truly beautiful young man of about sixteen summers. Katarina then recalled the skeletal-faced, bald-headed refectorian talking to Alcuin. Now she understood the real reason. The abbot was correct. For a monastery to house such a vile creature was truly heinous. Here at Chertsey it was sacrilegious. Outside the abbey, such abuse would be punishable by death.

'Yes yes,' the abbot declared. 'Sylvester, as you say, is sweet on Alcuin. He is also a spy, probably deeply interested in Henry and yourself, Katarina.'

'Then he must be silenced,' Katarina replied. 'Father Abbot, we are not responsible for the deep danger now forming around us.' Katarina stretched out and clutched Henry's shoulder, squeezing it tight as she fought back her tears. 'This young man is more precious than life itself. He is our true King. The Crown of England is his inheritance. I will do whatever it takes to defend both him and his rights.'

'Very well, very well,' the abbot sighed noisily. 'This evening, when the vespers bell tolls, come here. I will take you into the caverns beneath the abbey. You and Jasper wait there. You will be armed. You will find a crossbow, a quiver of bolts, as well as sword and dagger. Take these. I will then leave. Go into one of the rocky enclaves which stretch off the passageway. Hide deep in the dark and wait.'

'For what?'

'Why, Brother Sylvester. I know, God forgive me, all about his filthy lusts. Catch him in the act at the very heart of his sin, then do what you have to . . .'

Katarina settled herself in the recess halfway down the shadow-filled tunnel, in the cloying darkness, with only a few sconce torches flaming vigorously against the murk. Abbot John had met her secretly at the entrance to this cavernous crypt, which lay beneath a disused outhouse. The abbot had explained how, centuries earlier, during the savage attacks by the Northmen, the Benedictines had found this crypt hollowed out by nature. The monks had developed this further, deepening the enclaves, laying down a pavement and creating gulleys to take away the water constantly seeping in. During the Season of the Wolf, when God and his angels had slept and the kingdom had been ravaged, the Benedictines had sheltered below ground, taking all their precious, sacred items with them. They had made themselves as comfortable as possible, hiding here until the danger passed.

'Danger now threatens again,' Abbot John whispered. 'But of a different kind.' He pointed to a ledge where he had placed the weapons, including a ready-primed arbalest. 'If you have to use them, do so.' The abbot stepped closer, staring into Katarina's eyes. 'God forgive me, daughter. I was going to make my excuses, saying I had to leave before Sylvester arrives.' He beat his breast. 'Please forgive me for being such a coward. I detest Sylvester. He is the most sinister of souls. I cannot leave you here by yourself to confront him.'

'I am not afraid, Father Abbot. Jasper would have come but he must protect Henry.' The abbot murmured his agreement.

To distract herself, Katarina moved to examine the crude but vivid wall paintings which long-dead artists had etched in a range of brilliant colours along the occasional smooth slab of wall rock. One in particular caught her attention: a searing portrayal of the torments of the inferno. A journey into Hell and the horrors it housed. The artist had depicted a white demon on the left and a yellow devil on the right. These were holding up a bridge of spikes, across which five little naked souls were trying to cross, only to be caught and gashed on the sharp spikes. One of these souls was a man carrying a bowl of milk, another was a woman with a huge bundle of unspun wool, a third was a smith with a mallet and an iron bar. Because of what they held, all three souls could not pass on. Katarina was about to move to a second painting when a sound echoed along the passageway.

'Come, come!' the abbot hissed.

Katarina joined him in the shadows. The noise grew. Sylvester's grating voice almost drowned the whimpering protests of Alcuin, their steps drawing nearer. Katarina watched as both passed the recess, Alcuin's bare feet slapping the slabs. He looked frightened and cold in the thin white gown that scullions wore. He paused almost opposite where Katarina and Abbot John were hiding and pleaded with Sylvester to allow him to go back to the kitchen.

'Nonsense, you know why you are here.' The refectorian pushed Alcuin on, their voices echoing ominously back.

'They have entered an enclave,' Abbot John whispered. 'Sylvester has a makeshift bed there.' Katarina stood listening to the cries of both the assailant and his victim.

'Enough,' she whispered, picking up the arbalest. 'I can only stomach so much.' She swept out of the gallery and down to where the entrance to Sylvester's enclave glowed with light. She entered. Alcuin was lying face down, a sweaty, naked Sylvester bestriding him.

'*Pax et bonum*, Brother,' Katarina greeted.

Sylvester rolled away from his victim, who just lay crouched on the floor. The refectorian grabbed his cloak, holding it close to cover his nakedness, his bony face and head sheened in a thin sweat. For a while he just gaped at Katarina and his abbot. He then licked his lips as he stepped deeper into the darkness, away from the light of the lanternhorn. Katarina edged closer, raising the arbalest. Sylvester simply stared back, then his surprise was replaced by a look of deep cunning.

'So,' he gasped, 'Father Abbot and his bitch.' He pointed at Katarina. 'I've been watching you and that kitchen brat. Lord Mauclerc will be arriving soon. I think he is going to be interested in what I say about you, your brat, and the disappearance of poor Cornelius. Oh yes.' Sylvester stretched out his hand. Katarina thought he was trying to steady himself against the wall, but then his arm swept back, his hand holding an arbalest similar to the one Katarina carried.

'Like you my dear,' he taunted, 'all primed and ready, as I was for this soft creature.' Sylvester callously kicked the still prostrate Alcuin.

'Brother Sylvester!' the abbot growled.

'Oh shut up.'

The refectorian edged closer. Katarina steeled herself. She should have known the likes of Sylvester would be armed. A dangerous soul, who would never leave anything to chance.

'What are you going to do, Father Abbot?' Sylvester taunted. 'Report me? To whom? To the King? His royal brothers? Oh, of course.' The refectorian lifted his fingers to his lips, as if startled by some new thought. 'Oh no! Why go to London? Lord Mauclerc will be here soon. He will be very, very interested in what I have to tell him. We'll find out, woman, who you really are. And that kitchen boy. Oh yes. I will . . .' He broke off, turning as Alcuin abruptly leapt to his feet and brought his arm back to smash the thick broken tile he'd grabbed from the floor against the side of his tormentor's head. Sylvester groaned, dropping the arbalest which crashed to the floor. Alcuin struck again. A ferocious blow, which smashed the back of Sylvester's head so violently that blood spurted out of the refectorian's nose and mouth before he collapsed to the floor. Alcuin would have delivered another blow, but the abbot intervened, pushing him away, prising the slab from Alcuin's grasp. The young man just leaned against the wall, chest heaving, face all sweat-soaked.

'I hated him, Father Abbot.' He kicked the refectorian's corpse. 'I am glad I killed him. He treated me like a whore, a piece of flesh meant for his pleasure. Believe me, Father Abbot, Sylvester was no man of God but a demon incarnate. He should have been executed years ago. He should never have been allowed into this abbey.'

'Now now.' The Abbot soothed Alcuin, telling him to crouch down and compose himself. Once he had, the abbot and Katarina squatted opposite him. Alcuin grew calmer, allowing Katarina to stroke his hair. She then grasped his hand and squeezed it.

'Sylvester's gone to God,' she declared. 'He will answer to a higher justice. But time is passing, what can be done? Mauclerc will soon be here, mouthing curses and threats. He'll be furious that two Yorkist spies have disappeared from this abbey. Father Abbot, I have heard of Mauclerc. He will organise the most thorough and cruel search. God knows what would happen if he got his hands on Alcuin.' Katarina swallowed hard. 'Mauclerc hates the countess: if he discovered the truth about our visit to Chertsey, he would seize the Lady Margaret, her household and all of us here.'

'Listen.' The abbot pointed at the corpse. 'Alcuin, what you did was in self-defence. Mauclerc wouldn't give a penny for that. He'll hang you from the gatehouse and that would be the end of you. God knows what he'll do to us. Alcuin, you must go. Now look, I have been thinking. You are the same height as Sylvester, so strip his corpse. Take his robe and his stout sandals. Stay here. I will leave and return with a small purse of money and a satchel of food. I do not want to attract attention by collecting a fresh robe and sandals from the abbey stores. Crispin, our wardrobe master, is very scrupulous. He would ask a hundred and one questions and it is best if I say as little as possible. Yes.' The abbot got to his feet. 'Alcuin,' he declared, 'you must leave this abbey dressed as a Benedictine monk, and journey as fast as you can, perhaps to our brothers at Westminster.'

'No no,' Alcuin shook his head. 'No more abbeys, no more churches, no more so-called houses of prayer. No, Father Abbot, forgive me, but I want nothing of that. I will leave here and go back to kin at Thorpe Le Soken in the wilds of Essex. I will settle down there and try to forget this nightmare.' He forced a smile. 'And yes, I will miss Chertsey, especially you, Father Abbot.'

'Very well.' The abbot sketched a quick blessing over the corpse. 'Take Sylvester's remains down to the end of the passageway. There is an iron gate, rusted and old but still in use. Pull it back, but be very careful. A causeway leads out, it cuts across a very deep, treacherous morass before it reaches firmer ground. Bury Sylvester's corpse in the morass. It will sink without trace. I doubt,' he added grimly, 'if this will be the first corpse buried there but, once in, it will sink into the earth and be gone.' The abbot crossed himself. 'Do what you have to,' he rasped. 'I shall return.'

By the time he did, Katarina and Alcuin had dragged Sylvester's corpse down the damp, dank passageway. They slopped through pools and puddles, gasping at how heavy and slippery the corpse proved. At last they reached the heavy iron grated door. Once opened, they braced themselves against the freezing darkness which threatened to engulf them.

'We must be careful,' Katarina whispered. 'I've seen marshes like this in Wales. As long as we stay on the path, or in this case the causeway, we are safe. Take the wrong step,' she smiled thinly, 'and we'll be joining Sylvester deep down in the wet darkness.'

Edging carefully forward, lifting the lantern, Katarina could make out the red brick causeway cutting across the quagmire. She and Alcuin grasped the corpse, shuffling along the narrow path. Once they had reached what Katarina reckoned to be halfway, they dropped the cadaver into the marsh where it sank immediately. They slowly made their way back to the recess. Alcuin quickly dressed in the dead man's robe and sandals. Abbot John returned with a food parcel and a purse of coins, as well as a dagger carefully hidden in a shoulder satchel. Alcuin made the bleakest of farewells, allowing Abbot John and Katarina to lead him back to the causeway. Katarina and the abbot watched him go, the small lantern Alcuin carried glowing against the dark before it disappeared into the night.

'Thank God,' Abbot John breathed. 'I am sure that Mauclerc will arrive soon.'

The abbot's words proved prophetic. The following morning, just after the Jesus Mass, with the abbey bells booming into the mist and the windows all aglow with candlelight, Mauclerc arrived like God's own anger on horseback. He and his comitatus of mounted archers clattered into the great forecourt. As the horsemen dismounted, Katarina, watching keenly from the shadow of the kitchen door, abruptly felt a cold spasm of fear as a huge, caged cart trundled through the abbey gate. Four verderers, professional hunters, manned the cart and its inmates, two massive war dogs; mastiffs, these yipped and barked as they caught the different smells drifting across the courtyard. Abbey ostlers tended the horses but stayed as far as they could from the mastiffs. Katarina knew why. She had seen the likes in Wales. The hounds were ferocious hunters, with the added skill of raising a scent, then following it ruthlessly until they came across their quarry or the scent simply ran out. Katarina closed her eyes and clutched her ave beads. She fervently prayed that the hounds would never pick up the scent of the two men – dead though they be – whom Mauclerc wanted to meet.

York's principal henchman certainly did not waste time on niceties. He loudly demanded an immediate audience with the abbot. This proved to be brief and fruitless. So Mauclerc, like the Garduna, ordered the entire abbey community to assemble in the great refectory. Mauclerc, his lean, wolfish face twisted in anger, demanded the whereabouts of his good servants, Cornelius the anchorite and Brother Sylvester the refectorian. He stamped his booted feet, clapping his hands as he repeated the names. But a wall of silence greeted his strident questions, which he repeated time and again. Katarina sensed that, unlike the first confrontation with the Garduna, many in the refectory realised that, for all his bluster, Mauclerc could do little here in a royal abbey, defended by Holy Mother Church with all the power of bell, book and candle.

As she watched Mauclerc rant and threaten, Katarina wondered why Mauclerc had really come to Chertsey. The desecration of the mysterious grave? The visit by the Garduna? The disappearance of two Yorkist spies? Or was it something else? Had Mauclerc and his masters learned about the impending visit of the countess to Chertsey? After all, it was logical. The countess's manor at Woking was only a few miles away and, whenever she adjourned there, she must visit this abbey with whose abbot she was on very close terms. Did the Brothers York suspect there was more to the countess's planned visit than just the usual pilgrimage to what she considered a Lancastrian shrine?

Katarina watched intently. Mauclerc was certainly seizing the opportunity to study those he'd summoned here. He stood at the great lectern and constantly moved, as if trying to discover something amiss. Katarina drew comfort from her own tawdry appearance. Jasper looked every inch the simple lay brother, whilst Henry was a greasy-haired, dirty-faced spit-boy, nothing to provoke Mauclerc's suspicions.

At last Mauclerc ceased his ranting and climbed down from the lectern. He then swept out into the great yard where the verderers and their huge dogs were waiting. Katarina watched as both hounds were given the scent of the missing men from items taken from their cells. She pretended to busy herself about a whole range of tasks, fearful that the hounds racing backwards and forwards might discover something amiss. They did not and, just after midday, Mauclerc made his brusque farewells with the abbot, then he and his escorts cantered out towards the London road.

After vespers, Katarina, Jasper and Henry met the abbot in his lodgings. They'd crept through the dark into the precincts, then up the spiral stone staircase to Abbot John's private chamber. Once they'd satisfied their hunger with strips of bread and morsels of spiced ham, Abbot John gave an account of Mauclerc's visit, posing the same question Katarina had. Why had Mauclerc visited Chertsey?

'Undoubtedly,' Abbot John whispered, 'the mysterious disappearance of two Yorkist spies.' He laughed sharply. 'All their hounds managed was to trace a scent to the edges of the abbey, but after that nothing.'

'And the desecrated tomb?'

'Katarina, he acted as if he couldn't care less. However, Mauclerc did murmur that Urswicke, Countess Margaret's henchman, probably had the truth about the tomb, which I would I agree with.'

'Father Abbot?'

'When Urswicke comes he will enlighten us. Two matters did intrigue me,' the abbot continued. 'First, I concede, the Yorkists care about King Henry's tomb as much as they would a midden heap. Indeed, Mauclerc didn't seem in the least bit interested in our previous visitors, those you call the Garduna. Secondly, I talked to Mauclerc's captain of archers. The man was pleasant enough. He said he had a brother in the order. Anyway, he informed me that Mauclerc did not journey from London with them, but they were under instruction to meet him close to the forest crossroads at first light. My question is this, where had Mauclerc been? What had he been doing in this desolate part of the kingdom?'

The abbot paused. 'Something stirs; a malignancy forms deep in the shadows of the kingdom of Darkness, but I don't know what. People argue that we are body and soul, we often forget the soul. We are spiritual beings so we can sense the flavour of things unseen, of the invisible which still exists beyond the curtain, beyond the pale. I believe great danger threatens the countess and all those she loves. I must see her. I have received a letter from a brother, a good friend of mine, sacristan in the Abbey of Saint Vedaste in Arras. A great listening post for what happens in the Duke of Burgundy's kingdom, but also beyond. France to the west, Italy to the south and the kingdoms of the Rhineland to the east. The great victory at Tewkesbury, the abrupt murder of Henry and the seizure of the throne by the Yorkists has stirred up a storm across the Narrow Seas which is still not spent.'

'Father Abbot, why do you say this?'

'As I said, I received a letter from a friend. I have deciphered it and despatched it to the countess. She may well see it as another strand in the dangers massing against her. Oh lord, it will be so good to meet her.'

PART FIVE

'The Garduna maintained that everything they did was an expression of God's will'

Margaret, Countess of Richmond, sank deep in the thick woollen shawl she'd thrown about her shoulders as she sat before the hearth in the great solar of her manor of Woking. She stared across the room. Christopher Urswicke was busy with pen and parchment. Bray was absent, checking what damage had been inflicted by those mysterious arrow storms, as well as preparing against any future attack. Margaret was pleased to be in Woking. She loved her manor in its exquisite setting close to the River Wey, all screened by thick copses and lush parkland. Woking was a well-furnished, moated residence, with its grand entrance leading into stable yards, cattle byres, a forge master's smithy, barns, granges and other outhouses. Beyond this, a lavishly tended deer park, stew ponds, poultry pens, piggeries and fertile orchards.

On her arrival at Woking, Margaret had mounted her favourite palfrey and made a progress around her estates. She had been pleased by the work of her stewards, bailiffs and household retainers, though the damage inflicted by the mysterious assailants and their fire arrows was clear to see. Margaret was determined to wait a further day before journeying on to Chertsey to see her beloved son, a secret shared only with Urswicke and Bray. Indeed, Christopher had begged her to be most prudent, to watch and say nothing. To betray no emotion or provoke suspicion. He had informed his mistress about Hardyng's mysterious suicide and the brutal yet equally mysterious murder of the two mummers. The countess had mourned and prayed for Hardyng before asking Urswicke to remove the three corpses to the Paradisium, London's greatest death house. Once there the remains would be dressed for burial and a requiem sung for their souls.

Margaret closed her eyes and murmured a prayer for the

departed, threading her ave beads through her fingers as her mind drifted back to the business at hand. Urswicke had undoubtedly uncovered a subtle plot against her, and one in which Christopher's most sinister father played a prominent, if not leading, part. Yet what was the purpose? What are my enemies trying to make me do? she wondered. She felt as if she was being driven out of the kingdom. Margaret recalled her recent meeting with the Brothers York. They wanted her gone. Surely? They would give her every assistance to achieve this. Urswicke and Bray believed the same. Yet, like herself, they wondered for what purpose. Did York hope that if she went into exile, she and her cause would wither like fruit on the branch? Would she and her household become nothing more than a group of hapless English exiles, desperate for the protection and sustenance of a foreign prince? Yet the reverse might also be true. What would happen if she went abroad and set up a court in exile? Once joined by her son, Margaret and Henry could become the rallying point for all opposed to the rule of York.

'Yes yes,' she whispered, 'that is possible, but that's their thinking not mine!'

Margaret put her ave beads away. Prayer was out of the question, but plotting certainly wasn't. The game now being played was not just the usual tensions between her and the Brothers York. Other great princes were becoming involved. Urswicke had informed her about the Luciferi and their doings in London. In fact, their courier Malachi, that handsome young man, was now disguised as a member of the countess's household, an ostler, apparently skilled in all matters of horseflesh. The Luciferi were one thing, the Garduna were another. Urswicke had learned all about these in the bleak chancery offices at Westminster and told her what he'd found. Undoubtedly the Garduna were a blood-thirsty, war-like tribe, a murderous battle group – yet they had no grievance against her, surely? Nevertheless, they had been hired to inflict great damage on her. Who was responsible for that and why? Had York decided to use the Garduna to drive her away? But that took her back to the heart of the mystery and that unan-swered question, why? And why now?

True, her husband Sir Henry Stafford had recently died. She could no longer be totally reliant on the Duke of Buckingham and the powerful influence of the Stafford brood. True, she had her good half-brother Sir John; however, he too would soon leave. Both Sir John and Physician Guido had begged her to join them. They had urged her to avoid France and Spain but seek refuge with Charles, Duke of Burgundy. He would be delighted to welcome her and would accord the countess every dignity. Of course she had broached the matter with Bray and Urswicke. The former was non-committal. Christopher just stared hard at her, shaking his head. And now there was the business at Chertsey. Abbot John May had sent her cryptic messages that he had safely taken in three pilgrims, though the abbey peace had been shattered by the interference of York, the invasion of the Garduna and the threatening arrival of Mauclerc. Quite recently, Abbot John had also sent her a letter from Arras, written in a cipher. Abbot John May had translated this before sending it by careful messenger to Woking, who'd waited until the countess had arrived to deliver it. Margaret was intrigued by the contents. She had given it to Urswicke, who was now studying the letter on the other side of the chamber.

'Christopher,' she called out. 'Come and join me. Bring that letter with you.'

Urswicke, scratching his head, left the chancery desk and sat across from his mistress.

'You've read it, Christopher?'

'Of course, mistress. The contents intrigue me. There is no doubt that Duke Charles is preparing a memorial to an English King and there's every indication this will be to our late lamented Henry VI. But why should he do that? I don't recall Burgundy being a fervent supporter of our cause. Indeed, the opposite. Thanks to him, Edward of York successfully invaded this kingdom, what, a matter of months ago. So why the change? Why in God's earth is a mausoleum, a shrine to an English King, being erected in Arras? I doubt if it would be popular; Henry VI certainly wasn't. Indeed, despite Sir John and Physician Guido's pleas to join them, I am not too sure that our reception in Burgundy would be as friendly as they propose.'

'Never mind them, Christopher, let's keep to the matter in hand. Abbot John's writing is extremely small and tight. You have the eyes of a hawk. Christopher read it. Read it aloud so I can catch the nuances. Do so now, slowly. Try and put yourself in the mind of Ricard, the Benedictine monk who wrote it.'

Urswicke made to reply but the countess lifted her hand.

'Please, Christopher, read it. Indulge your mistress.'

Urswicke smiled, shrugged, cleared his throat and began.

'Ricard, sacristan in the abbey church of Saint Vedaste in Arras, sends to his beloved father in Christ, John May, abbot of Chertsey, greetings in the name of the Lord Jesus, Mary his Mother and our founder St Benedict of Nursia. Father Abbot, I wish you peace as we travel through the valley of deep shadow to the kingdom awaiting us. I promised that when I left Chertsey I would keep you informed about what is happening in Arras, which truly is the crossroads of the world. What chatter and gossip I glean, I pass on to you. For that is the purpose of our Order, to keep the affairs of the world under our constant scrutiny. I write in the clear cipher you taught me, whilst the courier who carries this is a true Benedictine and a good brother to both you and me. Now to the chatter and gossip I mention above. First the city of Arras is in great turmoil, not due to any tumult – be it within or without – but to the arrival of our Lord Duke Charles and all his court. At first sight nothing strange, except that our Bon Seigneur has paid frequent visits to our abbey. The true reason remained hidden. Rumour has it that our Father Abbot was sworn to silence over some great secret: that is all I learned until sometime later, when I stumbled on what might be planned. As I wrote above, the duke became a constant visitor to our abbey, invariably accompanied by Marcel Lancthom, his architect and master mason. On these occasions both men would be closeted in our abbey church, the doors locked, bolted and closely guarded by the duke's mercenaries. Apparently, or so rumour had it, they would walk the church from the high altar, down the nave and along the transepts, closely inspecting the chantry chapels either side of our church.

'Three weeks ago, two of these chantry chapels, dedicated respectively to Saint Remigius and Isadore, were closed down, hidden behind a lofty, very sturdy wooden palisade. Workmen, masons and carpenters, were assembled and given their instructions. The wooden trellis screens which marked off the chantries were removed and the window in each chapel enlarged.' Urswicke glanced up. The countess was now deeply immersed in what she was hearing, lips moving as if repeating the words, concentrating on what they implied.

'Read on,' she murmured. 'Please!'

'The paving stones from each chantry chapel were removed from the church,' Urswicke continued, 'and the coffins they once covered were carted away for burial in God's Acre. Naturally I was both surprised and intrigued. No, I beat my breast, I had a right to know. After all, I am the sacristan of Saint Vedaste: the care and upkeep of these chantries are my responsibility. I plucked up courage and approached Father Abbot but he was adamant. He refused to discuss what was happening and forbade me ever to raise the matter with him again, adding that in the fullness of time, all would be made manifest. I must be honest, I was not happy with Father Abbot's attitude. Our master is the Rule of St Benedict, not the will and the whim, the selfish decrees of some temporal prince. I was determined to discover what was happening.

'Now, as you well know, the sacristan in our order is responsible for the security and safety of God's house, as well as the sacred precincts around the abbey such as the cloisters and crypts. By now the duke's guards had been withdrawn. Father Abbot did object to armed men patrolling the abbey. Accordingly, Master Marcel was given his own ring of keys. He would secure the palisade around the building work then leave the church through the Devil's door, locking it behind him.

'Eventually my determination got the better of me. One night I entered the church. Earlier in the day I had secreted a narrow scaling ladder behind the baptistery. I used this to climb the palisade then lower myself down the other side. The devastation which greeted me was surprising. Both chapels had been truly levelled, not one stone left upon another. Altars, aumbries, stoups, statue ledges and plinths had been removed. I had brought a small lantern with me. I used this to search around. I noticed a thick, soft paillasse rolled up in a corner, as well as a silver tray with a flagon of wine and two goblets. At the time I thought Monsieur Marcel was partial to a little ease and comfort. I also glimpsed a chancery wallet lying nearby. I undid the clasps and found sheets of parchment, the type used by masons and artists to conjure up some projected carving or painting. One sheet depicted an antelope, a five-petalled rose, a king's head and a coat of arms, a shield quartered with golden lions rampant on a scarlet background and silver lilies against a deep blue field. I studied this and other sketches and wondered what was being planned.

'Any further search was fruitless, for I heard sounds from outside the church. I hurriedly put the parchments back in their pouch. I grabbed my lantern and climbed up out of the enclosure, making sure I took the scaling ladder back into the deep shadows around the baptistery. I waited there, straining my ears, whilst reflecting on what I had discovered. I was about to move out of the darkness when the sound of voices carried along the nave. People whispering, yet in such a cavernous place any speech, however hushed, will carry. Two voices, I was sure, a man's gruff tones and the lilting giggle of a woman. I crept forward and glimpsed the faint glow of candlelight. I heard the door in the palisade open and shut. I crouched down. Our midnight visitor, I reasoned, must be Marcel, and he'd apparently brought a woman with him. I waited; there was chatter, whispers, and muffled cries of pleasure. Undoubtedly Marcel was holding a love tryst. I recalled the phrase "*Carpe diem* – Seize the day". Marcel had prepared all this, which explained the flagon of wine and the goblets. I felt angry. This was our abbey church, not a brothel, so I decided to exploit this blasphemous fornication. The low moans of pleasure continued to echo faintly as I crept forward. The door to the palisade hung slightly open; a mistake by Marcel in his hasty lust. I approached the sliver of light and peered through. Marcel was playing the two-backed beast; his paramour had beautiful long blonde hair. In the throes of her excitement, she tossed back her head, revealing a face I knew only too well: Isolda Gruthys, wife of Arras's leading lawyer. Every Sunday both she and her husband proudly processed into the abbey church, garbed in all their finery, to receive the plaudits of their peers. Isolda must have been besotted by Marcel for, if her sin was discovered, it would mean humiliation and disgrace for the rest of her life. I took a deep breath, pushed open the door and leaned against the lintel, loudly clapping my hands. The two lovers, startled and confused, immediately grabbed discarded pieces of clothing to cover, as did Adam and Eve, their shameful nakedness.

'"Well, well, Monsieur Marcel." I strode towards him as he made to pluck his dagger from its sheath. I kicked this aside. "Do not add murder to your sins. You could not explain that away. Instead, think about what will happen if I sound the tocsin? What will people say? What punishment would Holy Mother Church impose on you, Marcel? To walk the city and this abbey garbed only in your shift, carrying a candle with placards around both your necks proclaiming your lust, your lechery and your sin? To be ordered to fast on bread and water for forty days and to spend a day in the stocks of the market place?"

'Isolda, face terror-struck, pushed a piece of clothing into her mouth to stifle her cries and moans. Marcel however, his lean face all tense, stretched out a hand in supplication.

'"What is it?" he grated. "What do you want? You want something, otherwise you wouldn't be talking to me. You would have sounded the tocsin."

'"This." I gestured around. "Two chantry chapels have been destroyed. Why?"

'Marcel glanced across at his paramour who nodded.

'"If I tell you," Marcel retorted, "this will remain secret?"

'"I have something else to ask you," I replied. "But yes, tell me what you know and this will all remain secret." Once again Marcel glanced despairingly at his lover before turning back to me.

'"Duke Charles, and I do not know or even suspect the true reason, fully intends to erect a splendid shrine to an English King."

'"Which one?"

'"I am not too sure, but I suspect it is Henry VI, the saintly monarch, allegedly murdered in the Tower of London by Yorkist captains."

'"Why?"

'"I asked the same and was told in no uncertain terms that it was none of my business. I was to design and build a majestic shrine in strict accordance with Duke Charles's instructions." Marcel then crossed himself. "I can tell you nothing more."

'"Oh, I am sure you can," I declared. "You are designing a tomb, a shrine to a fallen King, to the late, lamented King Henry VI. Now why should Duke Charles do that? What link does he have with that poor soul? Indeed, Duke Charles fervently supported Edward of York. So what is this?"

'Father Abbot, I needed to know. On your behalf I pressed

myself to ask. You remain a most zealous supporter of the Lancastrian cause and of the countess in particular. Your abbey, a Benedictine house, holds the mortal remains of a martyred King. You deserve to know what is happening. I was determined not to let Marcel wriggle off the hook.

"'Look,' I edged a little closer, "I promise, I swear here in this holy place that if you divulge the reason for all of this, I will never mention it to anyone here in the kingdom of Burgundy." Marcel looked askance at me.

"'You are telling me the truth?' he demanded.

"'If you do the same."

Marcel drew a deep breath and stretched out to stroke Isolda's hair.

"'My lady's husband is, as you know, a leading lawyer in this city, a royal notary. He has been summoned to a secret meeting in the duke's palace tomorrow."

"'My husband has gossiped,' the woman broke in, "he always wants to impress me. He informed me about the meeting, adding that it had something to do with the secret work being carried out here in Saint Vedaste, that's all I can say."

"'I promise,' Marcel murmured, "once I know, Brother Ricard, so will you."

'I replied that I would be waiting and that I must know immediately. I added how they must never repeat their lechery in such hallowed precincts, and left them to reflect, and I hope repent, of their sins. So, Father Abbot, you know what I have discovered, no more, no less, nothing else. However, I assure you, once I discover the true reason for the desecration of our abbey church, I shall return to you. God save you. Brother Ricard.'

Urswicke rolled the scroll up and handed it back to the countess, who promptly dropped it into a nearby brazier and watched it turn to fiery ash.

'The letter is some days old now,' she murmured. 'Given time here, given time there, I suspect Brother Ricard now knows what the purpose of that building work is. Let's hope we receive it soon.' She tapped the brazier. 'The translation,' she declared, 'is gone but not the original cipher.' She leaned across and gently shook Urswicke on the shoulder. 'What is it, Christopher?'

'Well, the mystery curdles deeper. Why does Duke Charles want the corpse of our saintly King? I mean, that's what's happening, isn't it? The Garduna have stolen what are supposed to be the remains of a holy King. They have been hired to do that by Burgundy. But why?'

'To spite his opponents, the Brothers York? It could well be that. The removal of Henry's remains to coincide with our possible flight to Burgundy?'

'Yet that is only matter of conjecture, mistress. We may well decide not to go. No no,' Urswicke continued. 'There must be other reasons.'

'True true, Christopher, we may journey to Burgundy or we may not. We might go now or sometime in the future. However, this shrine that Duke Charles is preparing could be promulgated as the rallying point for all of York's enemies, a list which should grow longer every year.'

'I would agree, mistress, but there is a lack of clarity. The involvement of the Garduna is highly bizarre. They attack us, the House of Lancaster, yet they are intent on seizing the mortal remains of our sainted King, the leader of our House. There's the riddle.' He continued. 'Think of it as a triangle, mistress. On the apex, Duke Charles building his shrine. On the right corner, the Garduna seizing Henry's corpse. On the left, the Garduna attacking us.'

'I agree, I agree,' the countess retorted. 'The Garduna are most hostile towards us – yet, on the other hand, they are most active in assisting Duke Charles to create a great Lancastrian shrine.'

'Unless . . .?'

'Unless what?'

'The Garduna are truly treacherous. Perhaps they are working for someone else who also wants to see that coffin removed from Chertsey Abbey. But there again, I cannot understand that. Who could it be? Why?'

The countess was about to reply when Bray, cloaked, booted and spurred, swept into the solar.

'My lady,' he declared. 'Your manor is now fortified and defended as best we can. Sir John and Physician Guido also wish to meet. They have certain matters to discuss.' Bray glanced quizzically at Urswicke. 'What is going on here, my friend? I sense something important.'

'Not now, not now.' The countess winked at Urswicke and rose swiftly to her feet. Grasping her walking cane, she walked to the elmwood, oval-shaped table.

'Let us meet our friends. Christopher, sit here on my right.'

A short while later, Bray brought Guido and Sir John into the solar; as usual the latter was accompanied by his silent shadow, Squire Lambert. Urswicke studied the young man, who looked withdrawn, worried and tense. The two older men, however, seemed all busy and distracted: each clutched a sheet of parchment, which Guido smilingly declared were some of the fruits of their studies into the history of the Stafford family.

'My Lady,' Sir John pompously tapped the table, 'we must be gone soon. We beg you to collect your most precious possessions so you and,' he gestured at Bray and Urswicke, 'your henchmen can join you in exile in Burgundy.'

'Better still,' Guido intervened, 'your two loyal stalwarts could remain here to look after your interests.'

'I don't know. I don't know.' Countess Margaret acted all flustered. An attitude Urswicke had begged her to show as he secretly searched for the best path forwards out of the tangle of murderous mystery which confronted them.

'I don't know,' the countess repeated. 'But tomorrow, just after first light, I intend to visit the Abbey of Chertsey, where I shall pray and reflect.'

'Good sister, we must accompany you,' Sir John insisted.

'No!' Margaret's voice turned hard and sharp. 'No, sweet brother, I want you, Guido and Master Lambert to stay here and guard the manor.'

'But good sister,' Sir John, all flustered, waved his hands, 'I need to consult a book the abbey library holds.'

'What book?' Urswicke demanded. Both he and Bray were as determined as their mistress that no one would ever discover the true purpose of their visit to Woking or the nearby abbey.

'I need to read what's called the *Liber Lancastriae – The Book of Lancaster*. The chancery at Westminster says the only copy is kept at Chertsey Abbey.'

'Then worry no more,' Margaret smiled. 'We shall bring it back with us.'

Both Sir John and Physician Guido looked quite upset at this. But Margaret kept smiling at them reassuringly.

'Good sweet brother,' she declared, 'as I said, this manor could come under attack. I need you here. Don't worry, we shall return shortly.'

Urswicke watched his mistress's guests. Did they suspect, he wondered, who might be sheltering at the abbey? He was never too sure about Sir John's allegiances. But there again, he mused ruefully, the same could be said for many in the kingdom.

Lady Margaret rose. 'We shall leave at first light. Christopher, Reginald, make sure my entourage is ready.' She clapped her hands softly. 'I do look forward so much to meeting Abbot John May, an old friend and a constant ally.'

Late the following evening, Countess Margaret held secret council in the abbot's private chamber. After an uneventful evening, they had left for Chertsey just after first light and arrived safely late in the afternoon. Margaret and her entourage acted as if they were pilgrims visiting the royal grave and, of course, discovering what happened during the recent desecration. Only after compline had been sung, the bells silenced and the candlelight doused, did Abbot John arrange for Katarina, Jasper and Henry to secretly join the visitors in his private chambers. Katarina and her companions had sloped like shifting shadows along the cavernous stone galleries and up the different stairwells, flitting like midnight wraiths across cloisters and gardens. The abbey lay silent. Abbot John had arranged it so and now they were all safely ensconced in his chamber. For a while they broke their fast as the countess took her beloved son into the abbot's narrow bedchamber so she could greet him tenderly and hold him close. She and Henry had then joined the others to drink and eat before the countess called them to order. For a while she just sat, listening to the night sounds echoing across the abbey grounds, the sharp rustle of trees, the blustery wind and the ever-constant hoot of the owls.

'A bird of ill-omen,' Countess Margaret murmured. 'Look my friends, my allies.' She looked at Henry and her smile widened. 'And my dearest son. I admit,' she beat her breast, 'I have drifted like a leaf on the water during this present business. I'm like a chess player where all my pieces, or so our enemies think, are blocked.' Margaret paused, drawing herself up. 'We have to dig deep into our souls for both courage and cunning. Our adversaries believe they hold the whip hand. They think that we have fallen and may well never get up. They are mistaken. So, let us concentrate on these mysterious attacks. No personal danger to me but to my henchmen, yes. Constant assaults and ambuscades as well as those horrid proclamations posted about me at St Paul's and in Cheapside.'

'Christopher has told us all about these,' Katarina declared. 'Who could write such filth?'

'Mistress,' Urswicke intervened, 'let us grasp the nettle, let us be blunt. I strongly believe that all this mischief is the work of my father and the Secret Chancery. Sir Thomas, acting for the Brothers York, simply wants to drive you away, to create a total constant nuisance, so you'll break and flee.'

'And you think there is an alliance between your father,' Margaret asked, 'and the Garduna?'

'I suggest there is.'

'Yet the Garduna came here,' Margaret declared, 'They plucked what they thought was the saintly Henry's corpse from his tomb. Why should they do that? What's the purpose?'

'I agree,' Urswicke replied. 'That does puzzle me greatly. You see, I was here when that coffin was first buried. I know what happened. Henry's corpse was brought by barge down to Chertsey. Mauclerc and his gang of ruffians were intent on desecrating the corpse and mocking the saintly King's grave. In the end they did not coffin Henry's corpse but the tangled remains of Edmund Quintain, a gentleman out of Kent who fought for Faucomburg during the recent tumult in London. Quintain was proclaimed a rebel and a traitor. He was eventually captured and sentenced to be hanged, drawn and quartered and was duly punished. Quintain's butchered remains were pickled in a barrel and also brought here. Clarence was determined that the royal grave would receive this sordid mess. Consequently, any attempt to claim miracles being worked at the King's tomb would be regarded as highly spurious. A sacrilegious attempt to exploit the dead King's bones for partisan polemics. After all, how can the tangled, bloody remains of a killer, a traitor, such as Quintain, do anybody any good?'

'And the true corpse?' Jasper asked.

'Oh, Clarence wanted that and its casket tossed into the river or buried deep in some forest marsh. I pleaded with him, arguing that one day the remains might become useful. Thank God he agreed.'

'And?'

'And, Sir Jasper, only I know the true burial site of King Henry of England. It will remain a secret until young Henry,' Urswicke bowed to Margaret's son, 'the rightful heir to the throne, seizes the crown and orb of this kingdom.' Urswicke smiled. 'I've done more. I have also hidden away precious relics of our saintly King; his hat, his jerkin and gloves.' Urswicke fell silent as the abbot murmured his agreement.

Bray rose and went to make sure the stairwell outside was still quiet and deserted. He returned to his seat, shaking his head.

'I hear what you say, Christopher,' he declared. 'But one matter does concern me, I am sure you have thought of it already. If Mauclerc and his masters know the truth about the tomb. If the Garduna are in some kind of unholy alliance with the Yorkist lords, then why did the Garduna come here to seize what is nothing more than a bundle of old bones?'

'I agree.' Urswicke drew himself up, rubbing his hands. 'That's a real mystery which, for the moment, I cannot resolve. My Lady, to other business. You have spoken to your son about the challenges which confront us?'

'I have, and I have also discovered that Henry's refuge in Brittany may not be as safe as we thought, that is why I needed to meet him. Jasper and Katarina will carry out our decision but what is it? Are you saying we should seek refuge in Burgundy?'

'Nonsense.' Urswicke's voice was almost a shout, startling those in the chamber. 'Nonsense,' he repeated softly. 'I believe it's time we carried the war into the enemies' camp. But first, Father Abbot, does your library here hold a book called the *Liber Lancastriae*?'

'It certainly does.'

'And can I borrow it?'

'Of course.'

'But taking the war into the enemies' camp,' Katarina heatedly demanded, 'how in God's name do we do that? Christopher, look around you. We are few and relatively weak. The Garduna could annihilate us in a matter of heartbeats. So how can we enter their camp, we don't even know where it is?' Katarina stared at the

countess's highly trusted clerk. Ever since she and Urswicke had
first met, Katarina was fascinated by this fair-haired young man,
with a face and voice of an innocent. Yet, Katarina now reflected,
Christopher Urswicke was as cunning as any man she'd ever dealt
with. Bray she knew of old: dark, taciturn, even a little sinister.
Urswicke however, was the countess's true man, the embodiment
of her will. If he talked of taking the war into the enemy camp,
then Katarina knew he meant every word of what he'd said.

'Listen.' Urswicke took his hands away from his face. 'Listen,'
he repeated, 'and listen well. We know that a Garduna battle group
entered England and now lurk deep in the darkness. We do not
know where they hide or the whereabouts of their lair. Undoubtedly
a cohort of these sinners ran free in London. However, I suggest
that is not the main battle group. So where are they?'

Margaret caught the rising excitement amongst those gathered
around her. Urswicke had certainly been reflecting and plotting.

'Remember,' Christopher continued, 'when the Garduna entered
Chertsey, they carried a coffin and they left in the same manner.
I have made enquiries amongst your stable boys, my Lord Abbot.
In the main, the Garduna came here on foot and left in a similar
fashion. Mauclerc travelled into Surrey, only meeting his retinue
just before they arrived here. Finally there are the recent attacks
on Woking Manor, undoubtedly the work of the Garduna. So we
have a group on foot, dressed like Friars of the Sack. We have
Mauclerc appearing abruptly out of the forest and we have a war
band not far away who attacked the countess's manor.'

'So the Garduna must lurk close?' Bray declared.

'Precisely,' Urswicke retorted. 'But where? Abbot John?'

'There's chatter amongst the forest people,' the Benedictine
murmured, 'of something quite unpleasant. Nothing distinct, just
shadows flitting between the trees, strange sounds and cries.'

'Do you have a chart of the forest?'

'Yes, Christopher. But the forest is one dense copse; there is
very little there. But see for yourself.'

The abbot rose, crossed to a chest, opened it, fished amongst
the contents and brought back a yellow scroll which he opened,
stretching it out across the table and holding it down with parchment weights.

'So what do we have here?' Urswicke asked, stretching across the yellow map, tracing different entries with his finger. 'There are trees,' he lifted his head and smiled, 'of course! Woodsmen's cottages, the abbey and its outhouses and this.' Urswicke jabbed a finger at a crudely drawn manor house.

'The Chasuble,' Abbot John replied. 'Once a hunting lodge, then a tavern, now a building much decayed. But we have journeymen who say they have stayed there and they report nothing untoward.'

'Do they now?' Urswicke retorted. 'But let's see for ourselves.'

'Why?'

'That,' Urswicke tapped the chart, 'is the only place which could safely house a war band.'

'But as I have said, journeymen, tinkers who have stayed there, report nothing amiss.'

'Father Abbot, what if they were sent to peddle such lies and sustain the illusion of nothing untoward? Think,' he added heatedly. 'The Garduna must be close by, that's a matter of logic. They could well lurk in a place like The Chasuble, feeding into the local community whatever they wish. Father Abbot, you talked of having visitors to Chertsey some time ago. Pilgrims from Spain. Of course they were no more pilgrims than I am. They were spies, despatched to collect as much information as possible, be it here in the abbey, my Lady's manor house, or a majestic but dilapidated tavern which no one really frequents. No.' Urswicke pushed back his stool. 'Mistress, my friends, I think it's time my good comrade Reginald and I visited The Chasuble.'

'And I will come.'

'No Katarina,' the countess declared. 'I need you and Jasper here, for only God knows what the darkness outside truly holds . . .'

The countess was about to move to other business but paused at a furious knocking at the door. Bray, drawing his dagger, answered it; Urswicke stood behind him with a primed arbalest at the ready. The figure was cowled and visored, head and face almost hidden by the thick folds of a military cloak.

'Fleetfoot!' the countess exclaimed, rising to join her henchmen. 'Fleetfoot, only you could present yourself with such drama.' The countess's messenger was ushered into the chamber, where he doffed his cowled cloak, warming his mittened fingers over the brazier. He gratefully accepted something to eat and drink.

'Well?' Urswicke demanded.

'Mistress.' The lanky, narrow-faced courier glanced earnestly at Lady Margaret. 'I have sworn a great oath. I can only deliver my messages to you and Master Christopher, no one else must be present.' Lady Margaret glanced at the abbot, who gestured towards his bedchamber. The countess and Urswicke led Fleetfoot into the room, closing the door behind them.

'The message is not written?'

'No, mistress.' Fleetfoot tapped the side of his head. 'I learned both messages by rote, especially the second.'

'Of course,' Urswicke breathed. 'You, like all your tribe, have a great gift, a singular talent. What you commit to memory is even more accurate than the written record.'

'Be that as it may,' Fleetfoot replied in a flat tone of voice. 'My first message is from Lord Thomas Stanley. I found him at his fortress of Latham. Mistress, Lord Thomas is deeply interested in your proposal. He believes there is no obstacle in proceeding forward. He passionately hopes this enterprise will be swiftly carried through. That,' Fleetfoot declared sonorously, 'is the end of the first message. Except that the Lord Thomas believes it is prudent not to commit anything to paper.'

'I agree. And the second message?'

'This is for you, my Lady, and Master Christopher. I was returning to your house in London. By the way, all is well there. Anyway, a Benedictine monk was waiting for me, standing deep in the shadows. He hoped someone of note from your household would come and of course that was me.' Fleetfoot paused, almost quivering with pride at his own importance. 'Anyway, the good brother was waiting in the shadows of the main door.'

'And his message?' Urswicke felt a tingle of excitement, a premonition of startling news about to break.

'Brother Anselm, as he styled himself, asked me to give you the following message from Sacristan Ricard at Saint Vedaste. The message is based on the testimony of a leading lawyer who drew the instrument up, a formal memorandum signed, sealed and blessed in the Duke of Burgundy's Palace in Arras on 10 November last. The message is as follows.' Fleetfoot spoke measuredly. He did not, of course, know the full significance of what he said. The message was greeted with a stunned silence. Fleetfoot was asked to repeat it until Urswicke, trying to curb his own excitement, listened carefully to what was said . . .

The following morning, two weary journeymen, travelling peddlers, entered the courtyard of The Chasuble. Both looked travel-stained and desperate as they whined for food and warmth. A close-faced ostler ushered them into the tavern's spacious taproom, past the great buttery table where Minehost, a tall, swarthy-faced individual, held court over those breaking their fast at tables around the eating hall. The air was sweet with cooking smells. A busy place, Urswicke thought staring around, and yet it was almost too orderly. Servants hurried about, dogs barked, horses neighed shrilly from the stables. Urswicke, the journeyman, glanced up at the flitches of ham and chunks of cheese, wrapped in nets and hanging from the beams, to be smoked by the tendrils curling out of the mantled hearth where a fierce fire roared. Urswicke was still deeply distracted: he found it difficult to accept what Fleetfoot had announced the previous evening. And yet the message made sense and was a logical piece in the solution to the mysteries confronting them.

'So clever,' he whispered to himself. 'So very, very clever! Subtle and cunning.' He was now convinced that his father was the root of all this mischief, yet the Garduna seemed to be playing a game of double hazard and Urswicke wondered how the game would end. How would the dice roll? How would the different players react? Any yet it seemed so astonishing that what was being plotted in a luxurious palace in Arras would have such importance for a lonely, shabby tavern deep in an English forest.

Once he had digested the message, Urswicke had exchanged urgent words with the countess before preparing for his early departure. He had not been given the time or the opportunity to discuss matters with Bray. Instead they were here in The Chasuble and Urswicke was beginning to wish they were not. Nothing extraordinary, no emerging danger, just a feeling of deep unease. Urswicke relied on this. He truly believed the soul could see, hear and understand things the ordinary five senses could not. He had listened to such a theory being expounded in the halls at Oxford, and, at the time, he found it difficult to accept. Now he did not. In his view The Chasuble was a truly evil place. There was a malevolence about it, a malignancy which might prove threatening. To distract himself he studied the other customers, which included a group of mounted archers. Urswicke couldn't decide whether they were Tower bowmen, the retainers of some lord, or just mercenaries looking for fresh employment. Nevertheless, the more he stared at them, the more convinced Urswicke became that he had seen their red-haired captain before. He glanced around; the taproom was filling up. Bray, slouched beside him, pretended to sleep, turning slightly so he could watch both the door and his wooden carrying frame for his satchel and pack. Urswicke's unease deepened. They had made a mistake.

'I'm going to the jakes,' he whispered hoarsely, rose and slouched down the narrow corridor leading to a shed just outside the taproom. He abruptly turned and glimpsed a shadow dart back to join the rest.

'That's it,' Urswicke breathed. He went to the jakes then hurried back to the taproom where he shook Bray.

'Come,' Urswicke urged. 'It's time we left. I now know what lurks here.'

They fastened on their wooden frames, grasped their staffs and made to leave. However, as they approached the door leading out into the courtyard, Minehost moved to block their path. He carried a heavy war arbalest and was flanked on either side by two of his household, similarly armed.

'Good sirs,' Urswicke pleaded, 'we are finished here. We wish to go.'

'Master Urswicke, Master Bray,' Minehost retorted in a strong accent. 'You are to stay, you cannot leave. Did you think we would not recognise you? We have your descriptions.' He smiled thinly. 'Oh yes, we have your descriptions etched on our memories. Did you not realise we watch the approaches to this tavern? You claimed to be travelling north from Dover, yet my scouts said you travelled south from Chertsey or beyond.'

Urswicke kept his face impassive but he silently cursed. He'd made a terrible error. The Garduna were much more highly skilled and organised than he thought. They were professional killers, mercenaries. They had probably thrown at least two to three rings around this tavern, silently watching all those who approached or passed through their territory. He and Bray had dirtied their faces, pulled up hoods and mufflers, but the Garduna had seen through this.

'We are the henchmen of Margaret, Countess of Richmond,' Bray declared. 'Stand aside.' Reginald's hand fell to the handle of his dagger.

'I couldn't care if you were the offspring of the idiot who calls himself the Pope. You, sirs,' Minehost jabbed the arbalest at them, 'are to remain here. Master Bray, keep your hand away from your knife and come with me.'

Urswicke and Bray had no choice but to follow Minehost up into a dirty, derelict room. The taverner sarcastically informed them it was the bridal chamber and they should make themselves as comfortable as possible. He left, slamming the door behind him and turning the key. Urswicke immediately crossed to the shuttered window but the bars were fastened securely, and when he peered through the slats he glimpsed the armed men milling below. He went across to the stool pushed up close to a brazier whilst Bray, mouthing curses, stretched out on the bed.

'My apologies, my friend,' Urswicke declared. 'I made a grievous mistake.'

'True true, but yet not true,' Bray retorted. 'We now know where the bastards lurk and I suspect they are arming themselves for fresh mischief.'

'They could be leaving,' Urswicke declared, staring into the fiery fragments of charcoal.

'Be careful about what you say,' Bray hissed. 'I am sure these walls have ears as well as eyes.'

'Yes, you are right, my friend. We found what we thought we would.' That was our mistake, Urswicke mused. Undoubtedly the Garduna had taken over The Chasuble some time ago. God knows what happened to its former tenants – probably floating deep down in one of the marshes which surrounded this tavern. The Garduna had set up a vigil. They would soon establish a pattern by which travelling tinkers, journeymen, peddlers, moon people and pilgrims travelled through their territory. Bray and he had seriously miscalculated. But what now? Urswicke closed his eyes and once again reflected on what he'd learned the previous evening. He had already established a hypothesis and worked that to a logical conclusion. He also recognised yet again how deeply involved was his devious father. At the thought of Sir Thomas, Urswicke leapt to his feet.

'Christopher?'

'In God's name, Reginald. I now recognise that red-haired archer. He's in my father's retinue. I am certain of it.'

Bray swung himself off the bed.

'Yes, yes, you are right,' he replied. 'And I've just heard more horsemen arrive. Christopher, how strangely fate turns.'

Urswicke thought the same when, a short while later, his father, accompanied by two archers, sauntered like the Great Cham of Tartary into the fetid bedchamber. He bowed mockingly at his son, totally ignoring Bray as he always did. Urswicke senior, the great Lord Recorder of London, drew off his gauntlets, snapping his fingers at one of the archers to move the room's one and only chair before the brazier so he could sit opposite his son. He unclasped his cloak, letting it fall to the floor. The Recorder then dismissed his escort; stretching out his hands to be warmed, he beamed across at his son.

'So, Christopher, this little venture comes to an end. And what have you discovered, eh?' He undid the top lacing on his expensive Lincoln-green hunting jerkin.

'Strange,' Urswicke senior went on in a murmur, 'that our paths should cross at such a time in such a place.'

'A coincidence or fate, father? Mere chance, eh? Though I suspect you come here often, don't you? You and your escort and, if not you, then Mauclerc, Clarence's creature.'

'I would say that's true. You're just fortunate that I arrived this morning, otherwise you would have been kept until I did. Anyway, as I asked: What have you discovered, Christopher? What have you found? What conclusions have you drawn?'

'Well, for a start what you call this venture, esteemed father, was all your own creation, wasn't it? You must take ownership of it. You can't wriggle out of what you've done.'

Christopher watched the shift in Sir Thomas's eyes. He recalled playing chess against his father years ago. He would glance up and catch those beautiful eyes staring benevolently at him. Urswicke senior had enjoyed such trysts until he began to lose. This was no different. Christopher folded his arms and stared down at the floor. He could deny, obfuscate or even refuse to talk, but where would that lead? No, he decided he'd play the game, keeping his figures hidden deep in the shadow of his hand.

'Well, beloved son?'

'Very well, esteemed father.'

Bray coughed noisily, tapping his booted feet against the floor.

'Those archers, beloved son.' Urswicke senior stared across at Christopher. 'They are armed and very dangerous, so no more interruptions.'

Christopher gestured at Bray, who just grinned mischievously back.

'I could arrange,' Urswicke senior rasped, 'that we talk alone.'

'In which case, esteemed father, you would be talking to yourself and never discover how this game played out. Well, you would but, by then, it would be too late for you.' Christopher watched the smile fade from his father's face.

'First, esteemed father, why are you here on this day and at this hour? I strongly suspect you have come to pay the Garduna, yes?' The Recorder just grinned and gently shrugged. 'But there's more to your arrival, isn't there?'

'Of course, beloved son. I understand that the countess has moved to her manor but then journeyed on to Chertsey. You are correct. We do keep this tavern, the countess's manor and Chertsey Abbey under close scrutiny. It's logical and necessary. Anyway, I intend to visit the abbey – to view the damage done to that tomb, and of course present our compliments to the countess, as well as to ensure that all else is well.'

Urswicke kept his face schooled to hide the surge of fear. He dared not look at Bray, yet he knew his comrade would recognise the real danger of Sir Thomas visiting Chertsey Abbey, poking and probing about. Would Katarina, Jasper and Henry remain safe?

'Esteemed father, why don't we begin there? Our beloved countess. You may well present your compliments, not to mention those of the King, his brothers, the royal court, but in a word that's all mendacious. You truly hate her. You despise everything she stands for. You'd like nothing better than to despatch her into the dark.'

'I don't agree.'

'Don't lie, father. If you're going to lie, you might as well leave.'

'I don't hate Margaret Beaufort,' his father snapped back. 'But she is a dusty relic of a House now destroyed. A cause truly shattered. She boasts a name now cursed. The Beauforts were my implacable enemies and those of my royal masters. The Beauforts were annihilated at Tewkesbury and afterwards. Their purpose is done. Their time has passed. They are for the dark, for the midden heap of history.'

'Esteemed father, thank you for your honesty. However, Margaret Beaufort still remains, a reminder of things past and perhaps of things yet to come.'

'Never!'

'Whatever,' Christopher retorted, 'Margaret Beaufort is of royal blood. A noble woman much loved and revered by the great and the good both within and without this kingdom. The Brothers York cannot afford anything to happen to her during this turbulent period. If it did, it would provoke the anger of Holy Mother Church, not to mention the great princes of Europe. Moreover, residing here as she does, Margaret Beaufort must gnaw at York's peace of mind, for she is a living reminder of the House of Lancaster, whilst her son is a direct threat. Yes, father?'

'Do continue, beloved son.'

'Margaret is powerful in her own unique way, but she's also very vulnerable. True, she resides in a splendid townhouse in the city and a spacious fortified manor here in the shires.'

'So she's not as vulnerable as you describe.'

'Oh for goodness' sake, esteemed father, think. She is a widow, and you know that Stafford her husband has only recently died. Buckingham and his coterie may be well disposed to her, but that's more out of courtesy than a matter of blood. Oh believe me, Margaret – the last of the Beauforts – has become very vulnerable, though as I have said you cannot exploit that here in England. Any unseen accident or mishap and you,' Urswicke pointed dramatically at his father, 'you and your Yorkist masters would be held to strict account. You know that and you act accordingly. You do not use any riffler band in the city, that would be too dangerous. No, you turn to the Garduna. Oh yes, I know all about them, father. You really do sup with demons. You should also remember one of your own pithy comments.'

'Which is? There are so many.'

'If you lie down with wolves, when you wake – if you wake – you do so howling.' Christopher paused. 'You brought the

Garduna into this kingdom to frighten Countess Margaret. They attacked her manor of Woking as well as her house in London. Bray and I were also swept up in the violence they unleashed. Very clever. Little real damage is done to the countess. Bray and I were left exposed and, of course, there were the proclamations posted in Cheapside and at St Paul's denigrating our mistress. However, let me leave that for the moment. Father, did you worry about me?'

'My orders were very precise,' the Recorder retorted. 'One of you was declared safe.' Urswicke's father glanced swiftly at Bray, smirked then looked away.

'In the end,' Christopher continued, 'you created an aura of threat, of fear, of menace. Yes, esteemed father?'

'I don't want to answer that, except to say that I have always believed, and I still do, that Countess Margaret should adjourn across the seas. We still hope she will.'

'You worked hard, esteemed father, to achieve that; the arrow storms and so on and so forth, and of course the emergence of Eglantine and Clairvaux. Rest assured, father, we do know the truth behind all that nonsense. Those two mummers from the masque, *The Scholars' Song*? You hired them, you trained them, you bribed them into posing as clerks of the Secret Chancery, then you despatched them to the countess's household so that they could mysteriously disappear. The only real evidence that something hideous had occurred were those two severed fingers, each adorned with a chancery ring. All your work. The fingers were hacked from some poor corpse. One of the many wretches you hang. Those two mummers served their purpose. You could proclaim that you had even sacrificed two of your precious clerks in an attempt to safeguard the countess and it was all brought to nothing. More pressure on my mistress to leave this kingdom and seek refuge elsewhere. Of course we now know the truth, both about them and about you.'

'Oh, don't worry,' the Recorder declared. 'I shall deal with those two villains on my return to London.'

'I doubt it, both are dead. We captured them. Bray and I. We kept them close in a cellar beneath the countess's house. Somehow, and only the good Lord knows the who, the why and the how, they were murdered. Crossbow bolts shattered their skulls.'

Christopher watched as his father's self-satisfied smirk faded and was replaced with that wary look that appeared when Urswicke senior was no longer convinced of certainties; when life took a sudden, unexpected twist, which it certainly had. Christopher again recalled those games of chess, so long ago, of playing his moves on one side of the board whilst planning a threat his father had not even glimpsed on the other side. So it was now. *Alea iacta est* – the die had been cast. Christopher was prepared to gamble all. The game had now changed.

The Recorder turned slightly in his chair, trying to curb his agitation.

'Haven't you realised, father? Do you think we are the only players here? Don't you realise others deep in the darkness are readying their strategy as well? The murder of the Frenchman Bernard, the killing of Hardyng, the countess's steward. Were you solely responsible for that?'

The Recorder just blinked, licking his dry lips.

'And of course you must know the Luciferi are in London.'

'They always are.'

'They too are involved in this secret, deadly game.'

'Well, that's what they're good at. Meddling in business that does not concern them.'

'Oh believe me, father, they are meddling in a game which could well cost you your head.' The Recorder made to protest, but the expression on his son's face made him sigh and almost crumple. 'Listen father, you hired the Garduna. How did you arrange that? Through the Count of Burgundy? You are dealing with a veritable hive of poison, murder, blackmail, and all kinds of sorcery and sacrilege. You brought that nest of vipers into England. In your eyes they had one task and one only: to make a lonely and vulnerable countess more so – and they did. They set up camp in this lonely, sombre tavern and despatched their mischief-makers through the forest and into the city. We now know the damage they wreaked. They would have been under strict orders not to harm the countess. The attacks on Bray and myself were part of the ploy. You probably dismissed the deaths of that visiting Frenchman and, more recently, that of Hardyng as not part of your scheme, though you would have welcomed them. They increased the air of danger and threat around the countess.'

'You said I could lose my head,' the Recorder demanded abruptly. 'Christopher, define the threat.'

'Of course, esteemed father. Listen intently. Last May, only last May, the House of Lancaster was truly shattered at the Battle of Tewkesbury. Henry the King was murdered. Yes, murdered, you know he was, as was his son within hours of the battle. The Lancastrian Queen, Margaret of Anjou, was captured. She is now a hapless prisoner, broken in body and spirit. All of Lancaster's henchmen went into eternal night.'

'Except for Henry Tudor, hiding like a rabbit in the wet forest of Brittany.'

'Oh, more than that, esteemed father. Tewkesbury is recent. Its devastating effects are still to be felt. One of these was that the House of Lancaster's claimants had been ruthlessly swept aside, leaving only—'

'The upstart Henry Tudor.'

'And, dear father, no less a person than Charles, Duke of Burgundy. Haven't you realised that?' In any other circumstances, Christopher would have laughed out loud at the abrupt change in his father's face. He glanced quickly at Bray who, equally astonished by his comrade's assertion, rose and walked to the window, muttering to himself.

'Charles, Duke of Burgundy,' the Recorder stuttered. 'Impossible.'

'Scrutinise the genealogy, look at them with fresh eyes. See how most of the Lancastrians were annihilated during the great bloodletting last summer, leaving Henry Tudor and one other, Charles Duke of Burgundy. He is a direct descendant, a great-grandson of John of Gaunt and Blanche of Lancaster. A legitimate claimant to the English Crown. Indeed, Duke Charles has as much English royal blood in him, perhaps more so, than Henry Tudor or Edward of York.'

The Recorder sat as if poleaxed, eyes blinking, mouth gaping.

'Proof!' he muttered.

'Proof,' Christopher snarled. 'We don't need proof, it's a fact. Now to develop my argument, let me educate you, father. Burgundy was prepared to shelter the countess, her household and eventually her son. Indeed, I think Duke Charles would have been delighted. Once there, however, I do not think that stem of Lancaster would have lasted too long.' Christopher waved a hand. 'Some accident, some unfortunate incident, and young Henry would be gone, leaving Burgundy as the leading, if not only, Lancastrian claimant.' Urswicke hid his growing glow of holy glee at his father's constant change of expression. 'You ask for proof, esteemed father. So tell me, what on earth were the Garduna doing here at Chertsey, digging up a royal grave and removing the corpse?' Christopher gestured at his father. 'Come sir, tell me.' Christopher paused for effect. 'I'll answer for you. The Garduna didn't dig up that coffin at your behest but that of Duke Charles. They did not have your support for such an enterprise, which is why you and Mauclerc came hurrying here to demand an explanation. They would simply reply that they were doing it at Burgundy's behest to demonstrate, perhaps, the duke's support of Countess Margaret. York, of course, would simply accept this – be pleased to see the coffin plucked from Chertsey. Indeed, you'd find it rather amusing because the casket does not contain a royal corpse, but the tangled remains of a traitor mixed with animal offal. Duke Charles, like the Garduna, might well be surprised but he would still use it. Yes?'

'To establish a shrine,' the Recorder blurted. 'The Garduna would take the casket to Burgundy. The duke would create a memorial to the last Lancastrian King of England and so enhance his own claim. A shrine to a family saint, a beacon light to all those Lancastrians seeking a banner to rally around.'

'Very clever, father. Yes, I suspect that was, and is, Burgundy's plan. Somewhere in this benighted place lies Henry's supposed coffin, waiting to be transported across the Narrow Seas to one of Duke Charles's churches in Arras. Burgundy, as I said, might well be surprised but continues the pretence over Henry's tomb. And what can the English Crown do but acknowledge this? After all, the truth does Edward and his minions great harm. A sham tomb containing tangled animal and human remains, buried in a holy place to replace Henry's sacred corpse. How could York explain that? Whilst no one, apart from me, knows the true whereabouts of those royal remains. Oh yes, father, the game becomes even more complicated.'

Bray came back to sit on the edge of the bed, scratching his head as he stared in disbelief at Christopher. Bray always maintained that when it came to digging up the truth and drawing up an indictment, nobody was more skilled than the innocent-looking

Christopher Urswicke. Bray tried to hide his surprise. He now realised Fleetfoot's message must have precipitated this revelation. It also explained Urswicke's brooding silence ever since they had left Chertsey.

'Now, father,' Christopher pressed his case. 'You can see why the Garduna pillaged the royal grave. More importantly, it explains the involvement of the Luciferi and the Cabinet Noir at the Louvre. Father, you are skilled and experienced. You know full well how the French would view this. They confront two great enemies, Burgundy and England. It's only a lifetime away when both these kingdoms, united under John, Duke of Bedford, almost annihilated the Crown of France. The situation became so dire for the royal line of Valois that God had to raise a saint, Joan of Arc, to deliver France from its enemies. Can you imagine what was supposed to happen? Margaret, Countess of Richmond and her son go into perpetual night. Bray and I might well follow. The deck is cleared, leaving no Lancastrian claimant to the English throne except for Charles, Duke of Burgundy. He is of the direct line and a legitimate heir of John of Gaunt. Duke Charles unfurls his banner and all the Lancastrian exiles, as well as those disaffected by York, flock to join. An invasion is mounted. Father, how many invasions have there been in the last ten years? At least three, ending with Edward of York's successful venture last summer. Indeed, reflect on that invasion. Edward of York was financed and supported by Charles of Burgundy. The great Burgundian cog, *The Saint Anthony*, was placed at York's disposal and carried a greater part of York's invasion force. What can happen once, can happen again. Of course, the French view all this with horror. This is a true nightmare for them. The past is summoned up and once again the Valois are fighting for their lives. Can you imagine Charles, Duke of Burgundy crowned King of England?' Christopher paused. He had two last powerful moves to make. His father was now openly agitated, scratching at a bead of sweat running down the side of his face. 'Father, you never saw this? You never perceived the possibility?'

'It's a fiction. It's a . . .' The Recorder fell silent, eyes blinking, lips silently moving.

'Is it, esteemed father? Let me develop my argument further. Charles Duke of Burgundy is married to Margaret, Edward of

York's sister; their offspring would unite the families of Lancaster and York. Can you imagine how this would be proclaimed through Europe? The Holy Father would see it as a path to eternal peace. Charles would inherit the mantle of empire and, once he was consolidated here, he would use the military might of England and Burgundy to bring the House of Valois crashing to the ground.' Christopher glanced at Bray and winked. 'Moreover,' he continued, 'there is more. Charles's mother is Isabella of Portugal, also a Lancastrian descendant of John of Gaunt's daughter, Philippa. Now heed this, father. On the third of November last, in his ducal chamber at Arras, Charles formally transferred the rights of Isabella to himself. The duke then registered his legitimate claim to the English throne in the presence of notaries and lawyers. This news was garnered by a Benedictine monk, who has no reason to lie and who has proved to be most trustworthy.' Christopher rose and walked over to the window. He pulled back the shutters and peered through the dirt-smeared, oiled sheet which covered the gap.

'I do admire your scheme,' Christopher declared over his shoulder. 'The removal of Countess Margaret both for now and in the future. However, unbeknown to you, your stratagem concealed another one, most dangerous to the Crown of England. Tell me, father, what would happen if the full truth emerged? If this hideous plot reached full fruition. The Brothers York would not be pleased. They would go searching for the origin of all this – namely you, my beloved father.' Christopher turned and walked back to sit down. He had one final move to make. 'The countess,' Christopher declared, holding his father's gaze, 'will not be leaving England.'

'Of course not.' The Recorder forced a smile. 'It would be against her interests. Moreover, after what you have informed me, her departure would not be in the best interests of the Crown. Yes, yes.' The Recorder's voice grew stronger. 'All such licences and permissions granted to her are now revoked. I shall order that immediately.'

'There is no need, father. Countess Margaret wants to stay, especially now. She is in deep negotiation with Lord Thomas Stanley who, as you may know, is one of this kingdom's most powerful barons. He has asked my mistress for her hand in marriage. The countess has responded most favourably. Lord

Thomas has given her the most solemn of assurances of his protection and support. Indeed, on your return to London you will discover this to be a matter of court gossip. More importantly, you will also find that mailed squires and clerks, boasting the Stanley blue and gold, have taken lodgings close to my mistress's house.'

Urswicke senior just sighed deeply, looking at a point behind Christopher's head.

'Father, if I had not shared my thoughts with you, what would have happened to Bray and myself once you had left?'

The Recorder pulled a face. 'I would have issued an order that you be released.' The Recorder gestured languidly around the chamber. 'From these comfortable quarters, once your mistress had left England.'

'And now?'

Again the Recorder sighed and glanced swiftly at the door.

'Christopher, what you have told me means that I must ride with all haste to Westminster. I must put certain matters in place. Seek out my own spies. Discover what is happening in the Burgundian court. You may well leave here but be warned. The Garduna see you and others with you as mortal enemies. They lost members of their company in London and they hold you responsible for their comrades' deaths.'

'They are dead,' Bray exclaimed, 'because they are murderous bastards who tried to kill us. Indeed, both your son and myself were only saved by the intervention of the Luciferi.'

'Be warned,' the Recorder, ignoring Bray's outburst, gazed sorrowfully at Christopher.

'I am warned, esteemed father, and if it hadn't been for your meddling, we would not be so exposed to our enemies.'

Urswicke's father just shrugged, picked up his cloak and got to his feet. He fastened the clasp and adjusted his warbelt.

'I must be gone, Christopher,' the Recorder said softly. 'I will wait for you below.'

The Recorder left. Urswicke, holding a finger to his lip for silence, urged Bray to prepare. A short while later they went down the stairs and across the taproom. Christopher could sense the animosity of those sitting around the dimly lit room with its fluttering light and juddering shadows. The same was true of the courtyard beyond. The ostlers and guards begrudgingly gave way, jostling both Bray and Urswicke until they were out onto the trackway. Here, the Recorder and his escort milled about in a clatter and jingle of harness. The air was ripe with the smell of leather, sweat and horseflesh. The Recorder was having quiet words with the dark-faced leader of the Garduna. He simply looked over his shoulder at Christopher and Bray then spat into the dust. Christopher's father urged his mount forward towards his son. He leaned down, stroking his horse's neck, as he spoke swiftly in Norman French.

'Christopher, I need to be in Westminster.'

'Will you visit the countess at Chertsey?'

'No, that will have to wait.' The Recorder smiled wryly. 'Please present my compliments and my apologies to your mistress.'

Christopher nodded, hiding his deep sense of relief as he stared up at his father.

'Christopher, I cannot spare any mounts. These gentlemen will allow you safe passage from here but they will not provide any assistance. You killed their comrades and they have invoked the blood feud. So take care.'

The Recorder turned his horse, raised his hand, and led his cavalcade off in a clutter of hooves and harness, thundering into the mist which swirled along the trackway.

Urswicke adjusted the pack on his wooden frame. Bray did likewise and both men walked forward. Once again the Garduna grudgingly gave way. Urswicke tried to maintain a brave face despite the scowls and stream of hissed abuse, but at last they were free. Once they had rounded the bend they stopped and undid their packs, drawing out the small arbalests which they primed. They took whatever else was of value and threw the packs into the undergrowth.

'Do you think they'll pursue us?'

'Christopher, they will already be deep in the forest either side. They will outflank us and choose the best place to strike.'

Urswicke glanced up at the blue sky, strengthening under the light of a weak sun. The forest mist had now dissipated. The air was clear. Nothing but the trackway unfolding before them. The only noise being the constant rustle from the thick undergrowth which stretched between the path and the dense cluster of ancient trees.

'The perfect day,' Bray murmured. 'For a perfect ambuscade. Your father could have . . .' He broke off.

The trackway was now narrowing, no broader than a coffin path. Black shapes abruptly appeared from the thick bushes either side. Sinister figures, hooded and masked. Two carried crossbows, the rest held sword and dagger.

'My friends,' Bray called out, 'stand aside, let us pass.'

'You killed our brothers and sisters in some stinking London alleyway.'

'Ah, so you are villains from The Chasuble. Didn't your leader promise my father, Sir Thomas, that we would have safe passage?'

'From the tavern yes, and you had that. This place is different. We are the Garduna and we answer to no one.'

One of the Garduna raised his arbalest, then lurched back as a long arrow shaft thudded into his chest. He tried to turn back but another arrow zipped into his exposed throat. The rest, confused and agitated, turned and twisted to face the unseen enemy. Bray held Urswicke by the shoulder, warning him to keep rock-still. The air seemed to sing as a rain of long shafts, loosed from powerful war bows, hissed through the air to find their targets. The Garduna spun around, searching for their foe, as even more shafts whistled into them. The last Garduna collapsed, gargling, the arrow shaft through his throat. Urswicke and Bray remained stock still, not daring to move, as they watched the Garduna shudder and moan in their death throes. At last all sound and movement died, replaced by a brooding stillness unbroken by any birdsong or movement in the undergrowth.

'Greetings, my friends.' Figures emerged from the green darkness. Four archers, master bowmen, arrows still notched, bows at the ready. They moved amongst the fallen Garduna, searching for any signs of life as well as anything of value.

'They're dead,' Urswicke called. 'All dead now.'

'True true.' One of the bowmen undid the visor across his face and pulled back his hood. Urswicke immediately recognised the captain of archers he had glimpsed in the taproom. The man lifted his hand in the sign of peace before joining his companions in plundering the dead. Once finished, the captain of archers pushed his way through the gorse to clasp hands with both Bray and Urswicke.

'Your father realised that the Garduna did not wish you well and that they would choose their time and place.' The captain unstrung his shiny new bow. 'And they chose this, not a good place, but they weren't forest people. Not like us, raised in the darkness of Sherwood. We tracked them like lurchers. Anyway,' he turned and shouted at his companions, 'are you done, my friends?' They shouted back that they were, their hands full of warbelts, boots, purses, and anything else of worth. 'Come, you can mount up behind two of my men. We will take you to Chertsey but no further. Sir Thomas told us to leave you there. He also wished to inform you that the Garduna no longer enjoy his protection.' The captain gave a gap-toothed grin. 'Your father, our noble Recorder,' Urswicke caught the tinge of sarcasm in the captain's voice, 'Sir Thomas said the Garduna were now wolfsheads, beyond the law, to be destroyed on sight . . .'

'And so they should be.' Countess Margaret heard Urswicke's account then made her own pronouncement.

'The Garduna,' she affirmed, 'must be destroyed root and branch. They cannot be allowed to act with such impunity. Sir Thomas is a demon incarnate.' She stared bleakly at Christopher then stretched out to grasp his wrist. '*Pax et bonum*, my good friend, yet what Sir Thomas devised against us was truly dire.'

'No need, my Lady. No need to apologise and defend my beloved father. He has sown his poisonous seed but it is up to us to reap the harvest and make him account.'

The countess nodded, letting go of Christopher's wrist and settling back in her chair. She and her two loyal henchmen had gathered in her chamber shortly after the archers had left them outside the main gate of the abbey. Katarina, Jasper and Henry were busy about their duties, maintaining the pretence they had so carefully constructed. Urswicke had reported to his mistress all that had happened at The Chasuble. He deflected the congratulations of both the countess and Bray, pointing out that Fleetfoot's messages had proved to be the catalyst in reaching a solution to all these mysteries.

'Your father, Christopher, was truly cunning and deeply devious,' Lady Margaret declared. 'Hiring a gang of rifflers from the city or elsewhere was too dangerous. Treachery and greed are rife and can be so easily exploited. Desperate wolfsheads can turn King's evidence. Outlaws can dream of receiving pardons and rewards. Above all, such people have a deep sense of self-preservation and change sides on a breath. No, your father chose well. The Garduna are not of this kingdom and they field a war band with no allegiance accept to themselves and the indenture they have sealed. I suspect your father contacted them through the good offices of Charles, Duke of Burgundy. Now,' she continued brusquely, 'forgive me, as it might appear in this matter I simply sat and watched. This is not true. You know full well that I have spies in both the English Court and abroad. Men and women who pass on to me the chatter they have heard or the information they have collected. It is no different here. I had to keep certain issues well hidden. My projected alliance with Stanley is one of them. The Stanleys have great ambitions. They see themselves as filling the gap left by the destruction of other great lords during the recent wars. Stanley and I will make a perfect match. They are a power both north and south of the Trent. They can field troops and whistle up their retainers like a huntsman can his dogs. Now you can see why I was so perturbed about those filthy reports posted about me at St Paul's and in Cheapside.'

'The Stanleys must have been concerned?'

'No, Reginald, in fact they were not. Such attacks are so blatantly false that they can in fact enhance your status rather than denigrate it. Lord Thomas, or so he said in his letters, wonders why individuals should go to such lengths to try and bring me into disrepute. Oh no, Stanley is keen for the marriage, so I dropped all intention of journeying to Burgundy or anywhere else. No, I have unfurled my standard here at the very heart of this kingdom, so here will I stay. As for Burgundy himself, the arrogant Duke Charles? Oh yes, I acknowledge his claims, but what can I really do except let Burgundy dash himself against the power of York?' The countess sipped from her goblet then carefully placed it down. 'My son was a different matter. I wanted to see him.' The countess blinked away her tears. 'Because I needed to see him. Just as importantly, I wanted to establish from him, Lady Katarina and Lord Jasper whether Charles of Burgundy, or indeed any other prince, had approached them offering refuge or sanctuary. That is why they came here, so we could discuss the future.'

'And have they been approached by Burgundy?'

'Oh ever so cleverly, ever so discreetly. A conversation here, a conversation there. Never mind,' she snapped, 'neither myself, my son or anyone of my household will seek the protection of Duke Charles. However, these matters are still not finished, are they Christopher?'

'No, they are certainly not. For a start we must deal with the Garduna at The Chasuble.'

'You've despatched Malachi, the courier? You know he is François' son?'

'I have noticed the family likeness, my Lady. Anyway, Malachi is now riding as swift as an arrow to alert his father in London. I have urged François to come here and bring all his power with him as swiftly as possible.'

'And when the Garduna are dealt with, we shall move to resolve other problems.'

'Oh yes, Reginald.' Christopher smiled at his comrade. 'We certainly shall.'

PART SIX

*'The Garduna sell their services of murder, kidnapping,
robbery and so forth to anyone who could afford them.'*

Three days later Urswicke and Bray were summoned down
to the main gate of the abbey. A biting-cold afternoon, with
the first hint of a mist-hung dusk closing in. François, one
hand resting on Malachi's shoulder, was waiting for him, flanked
on each side by a line of torch-bearers. Urswicke and Bray clasped
hands and exchanged the kiss of peace with the new arrivals.
Urswicke then invited François back into the abbey, ushering him
into the porter's lodge. Once settled, with Bray looking on,
Christopher informed the Frenchman of all he had discovered
about the memorandum that Duke Charles had drawn up in his
ducal palace in Arras.

'We thought as much.' The Luciferi Captain fought to curb his
agitation. 'We knew something was truly amiss. We also heard of
the work being carried out at Saint Vedaste, but at the time we
thought it a matter of little consequence. Duke Charles is very
cunning. We have all tended to think that the only opposition to
York was Countess Margaret and her young son. We were wrong.
We should have reflected more carefully, more deeply. I tell you
this. What you describe, Christopher, is the Cabinet Noir's
perpetual nightmare, even worse! A military alliance between
England and Burgundy, only this time the threat to France runs
much deeper. A total fusion of the military power of both England
and Burgundy. Such a move evokes the deepest fears of my royal
master. France would be plunged back into the horrid, heinous
wars of some fifty years ago. Last time God sent a Maid to deliver
us. God knows what would happen this time.'

The Frenchman paced up and down. 'Of course this could still
all happen. Burgundy could invade England and seize the Crown
as the Conqueror did some four hundred years ago.'

'Or as King Edward did only a few months ago,' Bray declared.

'France would have no other choice but to choose a side, seek an alliance, but it really would be sharing your meat with wolves. You see, Christopher,' the Frenchman stopped his pacing, 'your young prince must survive. As long as he does, he is the true beacon light for all who oppose Edward of York. Henry is of royal blood; the perfect champion in this kingdom of the rights of Lancaster.'

'But in the meantime, my friend,' Urswicke walked to the door, staring out at the gathering dark, 'we must deal with those who work for Burgundy. What power have you brought?'

'You best see for yourselves.' François led them out of the porter's lodge, through the main gate and into the line of trees. At first Urswicke thought he was having a vision, for a veritable army seemed to have risen from the earth. Well over a hundred men, armoured and harnessed for war; hobelars, men-at-arms, archers and even a cohort of slingers. All were dressed for battle, and behind these a line of war carts carrying trebuchets, catapults as well as a small but powerful battering ram.

'You are surprised, Master Christopher?'

'I am truly astonished. Where did these come from?'

François, holding up a blazing torch, stepped closer. 'We have our war cogs at Queenhithe and elsewhere. Ostensibly they are merchantmen, but in truth they are floating castles. This was easy to arrange. We came upriver on specially hired barges and so we are ready.'

'Will the authorities interfere?' Bray demanded. 'Those in London or here in the shire?'

'I don't think so,' Christopher replied. 'Remember what my esteemed father said. The Garduna are now forsaken. The Lord Recorder will only be too pleased by the total annihilation of these wolfsheads. So,' Urswicke patted François on the shoulder, 'tell your men to camp in the courtyard, orchards and abbey gardens.'

'Do you think the Garduna will know about your arrival?' Bray demanded, preoccupied with his own anxieties. 'They must keep the abbey under close scrutiny.'

'True, they do,' François laughed. 'Or rather they did. My cohort includes professional assassins, more skilled than any Garduna. I sent them ahead of us. Six Garduna kept the abbey gates and posterns under sharp watch. They are now dead, throats cut, corpses slung into the nearest marsh.'

The young courier Malachi pushed his way through the throng to stand beside his father who warmly embraced him.

'Your son, Monsieur?'

'My only son, Master Christopher.' François pulled Malachi a little closer. 'A warrior and the swiftest of messengers. Now,' François drew a deep breath, 'we must not linger long. I regret the slight delay in our arrival here, but this took some time to organise.'

The Luciferi paused at the eerie hooting of an owl deep in the trees behind him. 'A French owl,' François joked. 'One of my scouts telling me all is well. But not for long.' The Frenchman glanced up at the sky. 'Ideally we should attack now but it is growing late. At first light, Master Christopher, we will launch our assault. Until then, let me present my compliments to the countess and the lord abbot, then I will rejoin my men.' François extended a hand for Christopher to clasp. The Frenchman held him fast. 'Remember monsieur,' François hissed, 'what we have agreed. No quarter given. No prisoners taken. No pardon offered. No mercy shown, and everything the Garduna own is ours.'

'I remember.'

'Good, then let us proceed . . .'

Christopher Urswicke, Bray crouching beside him, watched the tendrils of forest mist dance like so many wraiths across the open ground, stretching up to the locked gates of The Chasuble. It was still dark; the undergrowth they had surged through felt icy to the touch. Darkness all around, covering them like a shroud. A silent mass of armed men bent on the total annihilation of their foe. François's assassins, skilful and sly as any hunting pack, had slipped through the darkness to silence forever the few scouts the Garduna had sent out in search of their comrades. The Luciferi had prepared well, now they were ready. The war carts, their axles soaked in grease, their wheels coated in thick, muddy straw had been noiselessly pushed forward. Each of these carried a small catapult, throwing arms pulled back and primed, the cups ready to receive tar-smeared bundles. Between the carts, lines of archers, bows at the ready. François came hurrying up to crouch beside them.

'Ready?' he whispered.

'As we shall ever be,' Urswicke retorted.

François got to his feet. 'Display the Oriflamme.'

Malachi, who had followed his father, now climbed on to one of the war carts holding aloft the sacred blue and gold colours of the French Crown. This was immediately greeted with shouts and cries of 'Saint Denis, Saint Denis'! Horns brayed. The archers swung their bows back, loosing a hail of shafts against the lightening sky. The war carts were pushed forward out of the line of trees. A pot of fire was swiftly started. The oil- and tar-drenched bundles burst into flames. Fiery missiles scored the darkness, falling like the devil's own brimstone on to the buildings behind the tavern walls. Tongues of roaring fire pierced the murk. The noise and clamour deepened. Men and women screaming; horses, driven mad by the flames, kicked their way out of the stables. The firestorm intensified, the flaming arrows dropping like hail beyond the walls. Bray quietly murmured his appreciation of François's tactics. The Luciferi captain was determined not to lose men in a futile storming of the tavern, but instead to drive the enemy out, and eventually his patience was rewarded.

The great gates of the tavern were flung open. The defendants were no longer able to bear the blazing inferno now ravaging the buildings. Nor did they have a place to hide from the constant rain of arrow shafts and fiery missiles. Urswicke, clutching his kite shield, joined Bray in the deadly dance of battle. Shapes and shadows broke from the dark, bearded faces, eyes glaring, mouths spluttering curses. A Garduna lunged at Christopher with a spear. Urswicke, trained in the tilt yards of the Tower, sidestepped, slashing the man across the chest. A woman, face all bloodied, tousled hair swirling in the strong breeze, came screeching at him only to collapse as an archer behind Christopher loosed one shaft after another. The noise was deafening. The Chasuble became a furnace of leaping flame, timber and stone cracking and collapsing in the heat. The roar of the conflagration almost drowned the screams, yells and curses of the bitter struggle being waged only a few yards away.

The Luciferi had unfurled their sacred banner, the Oriflamme, a sign that they would offer no quarter in what would be a battle – 'à l'outrance – usque ad mortem'; a fight to the death' with no

mercy given, no pardon shown. Urswicke realised the battle was
theirs yet the Garduna seemed totally devoted to what was really
a suicide conflict. Three of their company even retreated back into
the fire to be consumed by the greedy flames.

The hand-to-hand fighting continued but the struggle was really
over. François' archers, now fully protected, were able to move
freely, choosing their targets. At last the clamour and clash of
combat began to fade into a deepening silence, broken only by
the clatter of the burning tavern and the pitying pleas of the
wounded. Urswicke and Bray withdrew, sheltering behind
the high-sided war carts. François, his face all black and bloodied,
joined them.

'It's finished,' he gasped, wiping the filth from his face. 'I've
asked my men to draw water from the well, to drink and wash
away some of the dirt.'

'No prisoners?' Bray queried.

'Come and see. Very few and all injured.' François led them
across to another cart. The wounded Garduna, only eight in number,
had been made to squat with their backs to the wheels. All displayed
bloody wounds. Three of them had lost consciousness. François
knelt down beside one prisoner whose wounds were not so
grievous. The Luciferi questioned the man using the lingua franca
– the patois of the Middle Seas – but the prisoner just shook his
head, forced a laugh, then spat in François' direction. The Luciferi
captain got to his feet, brushing his mail jerkin.

'Garduna,' he declared, 'will not confess. They'll concede
nothing. I will give their throats the mercy cut and that will be it.'
François glanced up at the freshening sky. 'Daylight soon,' he
murmured. 'The forest people must now know what's happening.
I do not want the sheriff's men, or your father, Master Christopher,
interfering in our work.'

'I doubt if that will happen,' Urswicke retorted. 'Believe me,
my friend, my father will be quietly relieved at what you have
done. But, I agree, you should withdraw your men as swiftly as
possible.' Urswicke stepped closer. 'I have kept my word, François.
Now we need to ask something of you before you go. We will
leave all this to you but could you then come to the abbey? We
need to discuss certain matters. Shall we say after the Angelus
bell tolls at midday?'

Urswicke and Bray returned to Chertsey. They washed and changed and became involved in a spirited discussion with Katarina and Jasper. They informed both of these, as well as the countess, about the total destruction of the Garduna battle group. How its members had been annihilated and all its possessions and papers destroyed in that furious conflagration.

'And now what?' Katarina demanded. 'The Garduna may be annihilated but those who hired them remain deep in the darkness. Are we safe here, Master Christopher?'

'At this moment in time I believe Chertsey Abbey provides the best sanctuary for us all. Whoever enters this holy place is subject to the law of the Church rather than the demands of the Crown. Nevertheless, I admit I am becoming nervous. Woking Manor, The Chasuble and Chertsey are places of great commotion and tumult. The sheriff and the Lords of the Soil must be growing increasingly apprehensive about what is happening. So yes, you are safe here at Chertsey, but for how long I truly don't know.' Urswicke fell silent at a rap on the door. Katarina answered it and ushered in Abbot John and a hooded figure. The black robe the stranger wore was fresh and clean though the leggings beneath were caked in mud. Abbot John ushered his companion to a stool and told him to pull back his cowl, which he did.

'Alcuin!' Katarina clapped her hands. 'My Lady, Master Urswicke, Master Bray, this is Alcuin, who played the hero in safeguarding us here. Without his protection, Brother Sylvester would have betrayed us and Mauclerc would have had his day.'

Urswicke nodded understandingly. Shortly after their arrival here, Katarina had informed the countess and her henchmen about the danger Cornelius and Sylvester had posed and how these two treacherous informants had been dealt with. Katarina was now being tactful, not wishing to repeat the sordid treatment inflicted upon this young man. Urswicke and the others clasped Alcuin's hands. The young man then sat staring at the floor as the abbot described how Alcuin had presented himself at the postern gate, formally requesting sanctuary in the abbey.

'I have granted him that, he is safe here. But he has more to tell.'

'Alcuin.' Katarina, now sitting next to the young man, stroked his hair. 'You came back here for many reasons, didn't you? You missed the abbey?' Alcuin, eyes all tearful, nodded. 'But you also have information, haven't you? A great tumult has swept the forest. The Chasuble has been burned to the ground after the most ferocious, bloody struggle. God knows the strange sounds and sights you and others may have seen. So . . .?'

Alcuin nodded, struggling to control his sobbing breath.

'Tell them,' Abbot John urged. 'As you did me.'

'I left the abbey,' Alcuin blurted out. 'At first I was glad to be free. But that soon died. I travelled the forest, begging from woodsmen and others. I became lost, not just losing my way but I believed I had made a mistake. I didn't want to go forward. I realised I didn't want to leave Chertsey, so I remained in the forest and found myself at The Chasuble.' Alcuin grinned in a display of sore gums. 'I now know what happened. Gossip and chatter are rife amongst the forest folk. I admit it came as a surprise. I thought the tavern people were strange but not dangerous. They were kind enough to me.'

'In what way?'

'You are Master Urswicke?'

'That's how I introduced myself. Alcuin,' Urswicke reassured, 'we are all friends here. What you have learned out in the forest will, I suspect, be of great use to us.'

'Very well. The tavern people questioned me closely. I was blunt and honest. I explained how I had been a lay brother at Chertsey but then decided to flee.'

'And they asked why?'

'Of course, Master Urswicke. I told them that I was tired of living in an abbey. They laughed. They let me sit before the fire and served me food and wine. I assured them that I was a good worker and could I join their company? They replied they would see. Their leader was a tall, swarthy man with long black hair, moustache and beard. He called himself the Master; his word was law. Do you know, Lady Katarina, I'm sure he was the one who came to Chertsey, walking like a prince up and down the refectory. However, I wasn't certain, and I thought it best to keep my mouth shut and ask no questions. I felt comfortable but still wary. Once I had finished my meal, the Master and his henchman Alphonso took me to an outhouse where they questioned me more closely.'

'About what?'

'My origins. I was truthful. I told them all about being an orphan from Essex. That I had been placed, or really been taken in,' he added hastily, glancing at the abbot, 'yes, that I had been taken in to Chertsey Abbey. How I had worked in the refectory. I told them everything except about Brother Sylvester.'

'And they accepted you?'

'Yes. When they were finished, the Master clapped me on the shoulder. He called me his little goat, sturdy and strong. He added that if all went well I could join their company, but I must prove myself first.' Alcuin pulled a face. 'Naturally I accepted.'

'That's logical.' Urswicke turned to the countess. 'From what I have learned, the Garduna recruit young people like Alcuin. They train them and watch. If they are acceptable they are initiated.'

'What? Who are the Garduna?' Alcuin asked. 'Is that their real name?'

'Yes, it is my friend and, believe me, the Garduna are the devil's own minions. You are fortunate, my boy, but I think your appearance, your speech and your honesty protected you. Anyway, what happened then? Why are you here, Alcuin? What do you want to say?'

Alcuin swallowed nervously as he stared at the abbot and Katarina. 'I-I-I . . .' he stammered, 'I heard you in the cellar when . . .'

'When we dealt with Brother Sylvester,' Katarina added softly.

'Yes, you mentioned a man Mauclerc, York's henchmen, and a countess.'

'Yes, yes I did,' Katarina retorted. 'Why?'

'Well, I was immediately put to work in the kitchen. My main task was to collect kindling and dry logs for the great fire in the taproom. Early one morning, in fact I think it was the day after I arrived – sorry, but I do become confused . . .'

'You're safe here,' Katarina soothed. 'You were saying, early one morning?'

'Ah yes. A stranger, booted and spurred, swaggered like God Almighty into the tavern. He wore the Yorkist colours, definitely a man of war, close-shaven both head and face. Slit eyes like those of a dog, high cheekbones, his skin all pitted.'

'Mauclerc!' Urswicke interjected.

'Yes, that was his name. He was in a furious temper. He took off his warbelt and slouched in a chair before the fire. He didn't even give me a second glance. I didn't like the look of him and I was wary of his boot. The Master and Alphonso joined him before the fire. They spoke in the common tongue, I know that.' Alcuin grinned sheepishly. 'In the abbey, we servant boys chatter away in the common tongue so the novice master cannot understand.'

'Oh yes he does,' Abbot John interjected. 'Which is why we so often catch any mischief-makers.'

'Be that as it may,' Urswicke snapped, 'so they talked in the lingua franca? Of course, they would think you did not understand. So what did you learn?'

'Mauclerc was as angry as a muzzled mastiff. He cursed Chertsey, its abbot and all who dwelt here. On his return to London, he threatened to get royal warrants to raid God's Acre, digging up every grave.'

'Why should he want to do that?' the countess asked, turning to her companions. 'Mauclerc knew the Garduna had already pillaged the tomb.'

'He also knew,' Urswicke retorted, 'that the so-called remains dug up in the lady chapel were a macabre mockery, the tangled rotten limbs of an executed rebel. Mauclerc was logical. He would realise that the true corpse of our martyred King must be buried somewhere close to the abbey. God's Acre would be a natural choice.'

'And would he find the true coffin?' Katarina asked.

'Undoubtedly in time, yes,' Urswicke replied. 'Mauclerc is not a man to make idle threats. I appreciate that matters have moved on since he visited The Chasuble, which is now no more. Nonetheless, despite the destruction, Mauclerc will return here with a vengeance. So the genuine coffin casket containing the martyred King has to be moved.'

'Where?' Bray demanded.

'I know,' the abbot retorted. 'We will arrange a simple ceremony, exhume the coffin, Master Urswicke knows where it is buried. We will move it back to lie beneath the flagstones in the lady chapel. No no,' Abbot John stilled any protests, 'it's the safest, wisest and most prudent thing to do. The burial chamber in our abbey church is both honourable and holy. A suitable resting place for any corpse. More importantly, Mauclerc, for all his mockery and threats, is not of the Garduna. He may well trample through God's Acre, waving warrants from the King—'

'But the sanctuary of a Benedictine abbey', the countess exclaimed, 'is sacred and consecrated. What does the inscription read above the main door? "This is the House of God and the Gate of Heaven". Any violence shown to the shrine, to the tomb, or to Henry's remains, would incur the full fury of Holy Mother Church. So yes, the coffin should be exhumed and moved and it would be best if it was done quickly.'

'And so it shall be.' The abbot breathed. 'Oh yes today, before nightfall. It should be easy enough. Master Christopher knows where it lies buried and the resting place is already prepared.'

'I agree,' Urswicke declared. 'It's for the best. Anyway, what else did Mauclerc say?' Urswicke queried.

'He was ranting like a dog barking at the night. As I said, he cursed Chertsey. He believed some treacherous subterfuge was being plotted. He vowed to have the abbey ringed and to set close guard on what passed along the river. Careful inspection would also be made of all foreign merchant cogs along the London quaysides.'

Urswicke glanced sharply at his mistress and repressed a shiver.

'And Minehost and all his company at The Chasuble?' Bray asked. 'The ones we call the Garduna? What did they say?'

'Oh, the Master seemed satisfied enough. I got the impression that a great deal of money had changed hands. The Master and his henchmen seemed pleased. Remember I was only there for a very short while, but I picked up whispers that they were leaving and everything was being prepared.'

'So the attack on The Chasuble was clearly unexpected?' Bray asked.

'Yes, it certainly was. There was some debate about scouts who had not returned. I believe this was going on when the attack began. I only escaped unscathed because I lodged in one of the outhouses built alongside the curtain wall. When the attack began and the first hail of fire arrows fell like lightning, I grabbed my bundle, climbed the wall and fled.' Alcuin gulped from the goblet Katarina thrust into his hands. 'The forest folk are greatly afeared. They say all the demons from The Chasuble have not been killed but lurk like night wraiths desperate to break free.'

'So the Garduna were not all killed, some escaped?'

'I never saw any, Master Urswicke, that's just the chatter amongst the forest folk. I couldn't really care. I was determined to save myself. I fled towards the abbey. And Father Abbot,' Alcuin joined his hands beseechingly, 'this is where I want to stay. I am at home here. I love the church, the brethren, the sounds and the sights of this House of God. True, I wanted to break free, but now Sylvester has gone, I have nothing to fear. I want to remain.'

'And so you shall.'

'Anything else?' Urswicke demanded brusquely.

'My friend,' Katarina rose from her chair and crouched beside Alcuin sitting on his stool next to the abbot, 'you said when you were in that cellar that you heard me mention the countess?' Alcuin nodded. 'Did Mauclerc make any reference to her?'

'Oh yes, he cursed her too. He called her "the Beaufort bitch".' Alcuin's fingers flew to his lips as he stared at the countess. 'My lady, I am sorry.'

'Don't be, boy. I have been called worse. Just tell us what Mauclerc said.'

'He cursed you and said England would be well rid of you. That you would soon be bound for foreign parts, though he doubted very much whether you would ever reach there.'

Alcuin's reply created a deep stillness. Urswicke asked the young man to repeat what he said and Alcuin did so word for word.

'So,' Urswicke declared, 'now we know the real truth. Mauclerc, like all of us, has been overtaken by events. The Garduna have been annihilated, though a few may have survived. The Chasuble is destroyed. My father greatly frustrated, yet the danger remains. We confront an enemy who wanted you, my Lady, to leave this kingdom, not to shelter in some foreign court but to sustain some murderous mishap on the seas. God forgive me, I never thought of that. Yet how many cogs disappear? How many ships never reach port? How many passengers are washed overboard? We are confronting such hellish malice, but that will have to wait for a while. First, we shall restore the late King's casket to its rightful place. Yes, my Lady, Father Abbot?' Both murmured their agreement. 'Secondly,' Urswicke continued, 'there is a real danger of this abbey being cut off and controlled by Yorkist troops. Thirdly, the destruction of the Garduna, and perhaps the flight of some of them, might lead to a closer scrutiny of all foreign cogs along the London quaysides.' Urswicke drew a deep breath and gestured at Katarina. 'You, my lady and your companions must leave as swiftly as possible but in a manner that no one dare accost you either by land or sea. I have an idea which can be seen through before sunset. So Lady Katarina, Lord Jasper, and you my young prince,' Urswicke bowed towards Henry, 'swiftly gather your possessions, keep hidden, whilst you prepare to leave.'

'How?' Jasper demanded.

'With the help of my good friends, the Luciferi.'

'And me?' Alcuin demanded. 'What will happen to me?'

'As I said, you will stay here.'

'To do what, Father Abbot?'

'I have an idea.' Lady Katarina spoke up. 'Listen, Abbot John. Alcuin loves Chertsey, yes? The coffin of King Henry will be moved back to its usual sacred place. Now we have an empty anchorite cell with no anchorite. Why can't Alcuin become Custos – keeper of the tomb? Your recommendation would be hard to refuse. You could present Alcuin in the best of lights and emphasise the need for someone to tend the tomb, organise the offerings and make sure that all pilgrims acted in a devout fashion.' Katarina's smile widened as the others laughingly confirmed their agreement to such a proposal. The council meeting then ended, Urswicke and Bray leaving to prepare for the arrival of their visitors.

François and his henchman Armand, together with three others of their company, arrived at the abbey in the early afternoon. François immediately closeted with the countess, Urswicke and Bray. The Frenchman, as he sipped at his wine and helped himself to herb-encrusted morsels, explained how The Chasuble was now nothing more than a stretch of scorched earth, whilst the Garduna battle group had simply ceased to exist. He added that he was grateful to Abbot John for the burial of two of his comrades who had been seized and executed, their grisly remains brought into the abbey by the Garduna. Katarina had informed him about this and so had Abbot John. François promised that sometime in the very near future the Luciferi would return to collect their dead.

'And so you'll leave now?' Christopher asked.

'Most of my men are now aboard a war cog which will sail on the next tide. Others will remain, for we are not finished yet, are we, Master Christopher?'

'We are certainly not.'

'We also have a request to make.' The countess measured her words carefully. 'We have people, precious to us, hiding here at Chertsey.' She drew a deep breath. 'I would like them to be on board that French war cog, when it leaves London. Monsieur, can you accommodate that?'

'My Lady, I suspect who these precious people truly are. I have met one of them already. If my suspicions are correct, they should be gone sooner rather than later.' François paused, hand going to a crucifix on a chain around his neck. 'My Lady,' he continued, 'you and your henchmen have been most helpful. The Cabinet Noir will be delighted. An entire Garduna war band has been totally annihilated, and the most devious plot against us brought to nothing. What Burgundy wanted would have been most injurious to my royal master. We recognise the truth of the situation. Edward of York is truly powerful. In two battles last summer he virtually destroyed all opposition in this kingdom. There is no one to check his growing power, except you.' The Frenchman gestured towards the countess. 'Believe me, we have more than a vested interest in supporting you, my Lady. The presence of a Tudor, the true Lancastrian claimant to the English Throne, is the most serious threat to Edward of York and his coven. We want you to remain that hidden yet deadly threat. So yes, we will do all we can to accommodate you, to provide any assistance you need. But we must move swiftly. Your guests must leave with us.'

'Remember they are precious,' Urswicke declared.

'Master Christopher, we will provide them with swift, sure and safe passage to La Rochelle. Moreover, as a guarantee for their safety, I will leave my own beloved son Malachi with you.' He stretched out a hand and the countess clasped it.

'In return,' she declared, 'I solemnly promise that – as the future Queen Mother of the King, my own precious son – England will never, under his rule, go to war with France. You have my solemn oath on that.'

'And that,' François retorted, 'will be the foundation stone to build a secret yet strong alliance between the Houses of Valois and Tudor.' François rose to his feet.

'Armand waits. My Lady, if your party is ready to leave then we should depart as soon as possible.' He turned to clasp Urswicke, then Bray by the hand. 'I will be gone but I shall return to meet you in the city, yes? To plan the next moves on the chessboard. My Lady, you will keep my son safe?'

'As if he was my very own.'

François made to leave then abruptly turned, smacking the heel of his hand against his forehead. He stood, hands clasped, eyes closed, muttering quietly beneath his breath.

'François, what is it?'

'Christopher, I was so immersed in what was going to happen, I forgot one thing. Come, let me show you.'

They left the guesthouse and François, seeking the help of a lay brother, led them across to the mortuary close to the abbey church. He paused on the steps leading up to the sombre doorway.

'On my arrival here, I asked Father Abbot if the abbey could accept what had been stolen from it. Let me show you. He led them into the mortuary which reeked of pinewood juice and the tang of other herbs. The chamber was empty except for a battered wooden coffin on trestles in the centre of the chamber. François walked across and patted the lid.

'We found this at The Chasuble, the coffin which the Garduna stole from the abbey church. They kept it in a small outhouse in a far corner of the tavern gardens.' François' face creased into a smile as he moved the torch he carried and gestured towards the coffin. 'Perhaps that's the first miracle. The casket and whatever is in it survived. What do you want to do with it?'

The countess walked to the coffin, her cane tapping the mildewed paving stones. For a while she just stared at the tawdry remains, then glanced back over her shoulder.

'Christopher,' she declared, 'you will swear these are not the mortal remains of King Henry?'

'No more than I am.'

'Good. Then I will first seek the approval of Father Abbot on what I want. The coffin is to be emptied, its pathetic remains put in a new casket and buried somewhere out in God's Acre. However, and Monsieur will help us,' Countess Margaret tapped the top of the battered lid, 'this must be emptied and scrubbed clean. I then want a dagger fastened inside. The casket is to be sealed and despatched to Duke Charles of Burgundy in his ducal city of Arras. I need to give him a warning; that's all he will get if he pushes his claim to what is not his. He will understand my message: a dagger and a mouldy coffin are sombre reminders of the outcome of war.'

Urswicke nodded in agreement.

'My Lady, it will be done in a matter of days. I think it appropriate.'

'I agree,' François declared, his voice now taking on a lilting tone. 'We are also going to send Duke Charles a present. Not a dagger or a coffin, but the pickled, mummified head of the Garduna leader at The Chasuble tavern. If Duke Charles wants to, he can have it buried along with the coffin you will send. An appropriate end to his dreams of glory. However, for the moment, we are finished. Master Christopher, we shall meet in London.'

Three days later, the countess arranged a sumptuous feast in the small banqueting chamber of her house in London. The room had been lavishly decorated, its oaken woodwork polished, the walls bedecked with vividly coloured tapestries boasting the arm, colours and achievements of the Beaufort family. Urswicke and Bray had personally supervised the preparations. They gave the cooks detailed instructions on the delicious feast to be prepared: spiced minced chicken, fried loach with roses and almonds, marrow and fruit, tarte gelantine, beef pie, as well as rare dishes such as fried Valencia orange. The room was filled with winter flowers, whilst a host of beeswax candles provided light and fragrance to mingle with that from the roaring fire. The dancing hearth flames split the herb-drenched logs and sent puffs of perfumed smoke to mix with the other fragrances from the kitchen and spicery. The guests of honour, and the reason for the celebration, was the imminent departure of Sir John Stafford, Guido the physician and Squire Lambert. They were to leave on the morning tide aboard the Burgundy cog *The Pegasus*, moored at Queenhithe. All three guests had travelled with great haste from Woking Abbey. Nevertheless, when they arrived in the countess's house, they seemed subdued, impatient to leave so, as they loudly proclaimed, they could be back in the Burgundian court before Christmas. Of course, they were full of questions about what happened at The Chasuble. They had, like so many others, seen the columns of smoke rising above the trees whilst rumour ran rife amongst the forest folk about the fierce battle fought in and around the now destroyed tavern. When questioned by Urswicke, Guido the physician, who looked pale and drawn, admitted they had visited the blackened ruins.

'All gone,' he murmured as if to himself. 'No corpses, no possessions, nothing at all.'

Urswicke simply heard him out before diverting the conversation to Sir John's imminent departure. He also apologised to all three guests that he had been unable to obtain *The Book of Lancaster*. Sir John simply shrugged, as if he was no longer interested in the subject. During the conversation, Urswicke became acutely aware of the hateful glances from Squire Lambert who sat, all sullen and silent. Urswicke, however, had prepared well. On their return to London, he and Bray, together with François, had closeted in secret council, where Urswicke delivered his indictment. At first his two companions did not accept it. Christopher, however, skilfully argued about what he believed and the judgement he had prepared. This banquet was the lure. The countess's three guests were arrogant. They would expect such festivities, but it would also be where and when the trap was sprung. Urswicke was certain of his case; he just hoped and prayed that Sir John in particular would not suspect that an ambuscade was planned.

As it turned out, the festivities remained subdued, the guests of honour almost playing with their food, Sir John only becoming engaged when he announced that all their baggage was ready and they were impatient to leave. Urswicke nodded understandingly. Once the servants had poured the sweet wine, Bray took up guard at the door. Urswicke rose and, lifting his chair, placed it before the samite-draped table behind which the three guests now sat.

'Master Christopher, what is this? My Lady?' Stafford gestured across the dais, to where the countess sat. She just stared bleakly at him. Sir John turned back to Urswicke.

'You sit before us like a plaintiff in Westminster Hall.'

'Or a judge,' Urswicke countered.

'A judge? In God's name what is to be judged?'

'Your treachery, your violation of everything I hold sacred. Your litany of crimes is long and serious. You,' he pointed at Sir John, 'along with your accomplices, were hand in glove with the Garduna. You know who they are and what they do. Indeed,' Urswicke now jabbed a finger at Guido, 'I believe your origins are Spanish. More relevantly, I maintain you are a leader, if not *the* leader, of the Garduna. What's your title, El Hermano Majo?'

'Garduna,' Guido snarled. 'What nonsense is this?' He made to rise but sat down when Bray lifted the powerful arbalest, its cord already winched back.

'Good sister,' Sir John pleaded, 'what is this nonsense?'

'Good brother, let us be honest. You never had much time for me. I know from my late husband that you were bitterly opposed to our marriage, maintaining the Beauforts were upstarts with no rights or claims.'

'I—'

'No brother, don't lie. Isn't that one of the reasons, if not *the* reason, for your quarrel with Sir Henry and why you left England to lodge in Burgundy?'

'You meant my mistress ill,' Urswicke accused. 'You came like Judas crying all hail when you meant all harm.'

'Preposterous!'

'No no,' Urswicke declared. 'I believe my mistress. As I also believe you are part of the present conspiracy against her.'

'Again, nonsense.'

'You lodged in Burgundy. The impact of the great battle at Tewkesbury made itself felt. The board had been cleared. Beaufort and all their allies cut down like flowers in the field. York was intent on destroying Lancaster root and branch. He almost did, except for two powerful claimants: Henry Tudor and Duke Charles of Burgundy, who has a strong and – we concede this – legitimate claim to the English Throne. In the aftermath of Tewkesbury, with the death of King Henry, the flight of Tudor and the destruction of all things Lancaster, a most deadly and subtle conspiracy was formed. As I said, Lancaster was uprooted. Edward of England wanted this complete. To be rid of the countess but a lasting solution, one which could not be placed at his door. He, you and Burgundy plotted a way forward, Edward of York's participation being firmly in the hands of my beloved father. To be blunt, Margaret and her household were to be harassed beyond belief until we had no choice but to flee England for Burgundy. Once at sea, and I would take an oath on the truth of this, some unfortunate accident would be arranged; a heart-chilling calamity, but that would be it.' Urswicke sat rubbing his hands as he stared at these three most devious opponents.

'The harassment of my mistress, however, had to be carefully managed. In such a way that no allegation could be levelled against you or York. Nonetheless, you had to be careful. It was far too dangerous a task to entrust to rifflers in London or some coven of outlaws from the shires. Tongues clack. Souls can be bribed. Loyalties suborned. Fealty bought. No no, you needed experts, skilled in the business of murder, and the Garduna were a most logical choice. As I said, Physician Guido, you know full well what I am talking about. I do wonder what you really are? A senior commander? Even the Grand Master, yes?'

'Even if I am what you say,' the physician blustered, 'what real proof do you have? What evidence that I have broken any law? Even if you are correct, I could plead that I had the support of the English Crown in driving from its territories a woman well known for her opposition to King Edward and all his company.'

'Ah, but just wait for a while,' Urswicke replied. 'I haven't finished my indictment. You see, the first conspiracy was only a catspaw, a shield, a cover, to hide an even more sinister plot. Both of you . . .' Urswicke gestured at Sir John and the physician, studiously ignoring Lambert, who sat all solemn. Urswicke wondered if he could drive a wedge between this sinister young man and his two patrons or, even better, provoke him into some outburst. The squire refused to meet his gaze, however, and sat staring down at the table top.

'Go on,' Sir John taunted. 'Urswicke, what were you going to say next?'

'Ah yes, both of you came to England to attend the funeral obsequies of the countess's late lamented husband, but that was only a device to get close to her. You also came to make careful study of the Stafford family history. A laudable enterprise, but in truth you journeyed to the chancery at Westminster to collect as much information as possible on one Lancastrian lineage, that of Charles, Duke of Burgundy. You know, as I do, that he can claim clear descent from John of Gaunt, the founder of the Lancastrian dynasty. You searched for every scrap of information on this issue. No no, don't deny it. My friends in the chancery will confirm what I have said. This also explains your need, Sir John, to consult *The Book of Lancaster*, held in Chertsey Abbey.' Urswicke paused, allowing the silence to deepen. He noticed how all three of his opponents had kept the sharp table knives close to hand. 'Master Bray,' Urswicke turned, 'you have more than one arbalest?'

'I do and they are all fully primed.'

'Good.' Urswicke smiled dazzlingly at his opponents. 'And so we come to the real plot. Margaret, Countess of Richmond, her son and probably myself and Master Bray would travel to Burgundy and, at an appropriate time and in a mysterious way, we would be despatched to judgement. Of course,' Urswicke shrugged, 'if we ever survived and reached land, either on your cog or anyone else's, fresh mishaps would occur. Oh, Edward of York would mourn, he would dab his eyes and wipe the tears from his cheek whilst he attended our requiem Mass. Secretly, of course, he would be delighted. A woman he hated and feared, silenced for good with no blame laid at his door. I suspect only then would Charles of Burgundy publicly proclaim his right to the English throne. A true nightmare for Edward, and indeed for France. This was no spurious claimant but one of the most powerful rulers in Europe. The danger would be very real. Charles has the wealth and the military might to pursue such a claim. We have proof of that.'

'What do you mean?'

'Earlier this year, the Brothers York invaded England, but the means of supply was Burgundy. This could well happen again.'

'Politics.' Sir John shrugged. 'This is all politics. We all meddle in politics.'

'True, sir, but you also meddle in treachery and murder. Both of you should be shamed. You are responsible for those poisonous proclamations about the countess. You wrote such filth when you visited the chancery offices at Westminster. You were closeted together. No one could really see you and no one would even suspect what you were involved in.'

'Proof,' Sir John shouted. 'What proof do you offer?'

'Oh, very simple. The parchment and ink used in the chancery offices are most distinctive. I compared them to those filthy broadsheets. They matched. If you wish I could also seek confirmation

of that from my good friend, the former Head of Chancery.'
Urswicke sat back in his chair, staring at these three reprobates
who had dared to malign his beloved mistress. 'You sustained that
nonsense, as you did those attacks on Woking Manor as well as
this house. You portrayed yourselves as victims when in fact
you were the perpetrators, hand in glove with the Garduna, your
companions in crime.'

'They are not—'

'They certainly are. They, you and my father were the prime
movers behind the campaign against the countess and those vicious
attacks on myself and Bray. And before you ask for evidence –
you are my evidence. You had the means and the motive. You are
steeped in sin and it's time you confessed it. We now turn to
murder. Your first victim was our French visitor, Monsieur Bernard.
Yes?'

'We had nothing to—'

'You had everything to do with it, physician. You knew, you
must have known, that if the Garduna were hunting us, then the
Luciferi, despatched by the Cabinet Noir in Paris, were hunting
the Garduna. The Luciferi were convinced that the Garduna were
bent on mayhem most injurious to the French Crown. What they
didn't realise until much later was that you and my father were
close allies of the Garduna. A most unholy trinity, bent on Lady
Margaret's total ruin. Think of a rope being fastened around my
mistress's neck, one noose made up of three strands! I cannot
say where, when or how all three of you met to conspire this or
that. However, the noose, or should I say the garrotte, you
fashioned, was real enough.'

'Listen.' Squire Lambert pulled himself up in his quilted chair.
'Listen,' he repeated in his heavily accented voice, 'you talk of
us as being hand in glove with the Garduna, but we were here,
we never received visitors.'

'You think we are as stupid as you are. I have just answered
that,' Urswicke riposted. 'You, my treacherous guest, could slip,
like the snake you truly are, out of this mansion on some pretended
errand. Moreover, your two companions often journeyed across
the city. It would be easy for one of you or all three of you to slip
into a tavern or alehouse where the Garduna envoy would be
waiting.'

'Easier still out at Woking,' the countess intervened. 'A lonely manor, deep in the countryside, surrounded by thick forest. It would not be difficult to arrange some midnight meeting.'

'Oh yes,' Urswicke leaned forward, 'you'd encounter no difficulty in meeting your fellow demons. Anyway, to return to the Luciferi. They brought this house under close watch, even though they were not sure whom they could trust. The only person beyond any suspicion was the countess, and so they decided to communicate with her, probably on the principle that any enemy of the Garduna must be their friend. They sent in Bernard, a seemingly honest ordinary visitor. You, of course, suspected who he really was. A Frenchman asking to see the countess, it must be urgent, it must be important. As I said earlier, the Garduna kept a close eye on us but they would be constantly looking over their shoulder for the Luciferi. Now, on that fateful day, Hardyng lodged our visitor in the waiting chamber which can be locked from within and without. Our steward was a good and honest man and, before leaving the visitor, he served him a goblet of wine.'

'If I remember correctly,' Sir John almost yelled, 'Hardyng left that chamber locked both within and without.'

'Of course he did, but listen. You, Guido, acting all innocent, perhaps accompanied by Sir John and Lambert, decided to intervene. Lambert would be your guard, your spy, vigilant against anyone seeing you knock on the door of that waiting chamber. In brief, you wheedled yourself in, acting the friend when in fact you intended murder. You chatted with Bernard.'

'Proof, evidence?'

'Oh, don't worry, I will come to that by and by. Anyway, you put Bernard at his ease. I suspect you were carrying a wineskin. Whatever. You talked to him and that's where you discovered his first name, Andre. You later mentioned that in passing, but no one else knew that name. I asked Hardyng shortly before you murdered him. The Frenchman never gave his first name; he was simply Bernard.'

'You cannot—'

'Hush now, our late lamented steward maintained that the only name the visitor gave was Bernard, nothing more, nothing less, nothing else. So when did you learn it?'

Guido just gazed sullenly back.

'The wine was not poisoned,' Lambert protested.

'Oh yes it was. Whilst Guido was busy with Bernard, he distracted the Frenchman and slipped a deadly potion into the man's goblet.'

'But the wine wasn't poisoned,' Sir John blustered, standing by the table. 'It was fed to rats and they remained unscathed.'

'Oh yes, the rats,' Urswicke mocked. 'I certainly remember Guido seizing the goblet and sniffing at it. He then said he'd take it to the cellars. Another lie! The wine left in the cellar was probably from the wineskin Guido kept hidden in his cloak, not the poisoned wine in the goblet.' Urswicke paused to collect his thoughts, marshalling his argument against this unholy alliance. The only matter he was uncertain of was whether or not his opponents were allies of the Garduna or leading members of that sinister coven. He strongly suspected the latter.

'So you are claiming,' Sir John demanded, 'that I got rid of the poisoned wine and substituted it with the good? Where's your evidence for that?'

'Hardyng the steward. Didn't he talk, drunk though he was, of seeing dead rats where he least expected them? Dead rats in a sewer near the scullery? But that's where you poured the tainted wine, wasn't it? Down some jakes hole. Oh yes, Hardyng wasn't as stupid as he appeared. Like me he began to sense the real danger, the deep threat to the countess, was not from outside but from within. I suspect he saw other things as well, but of course he was only a servant. He had to be very careful about commenting on certain matters. Nevertheless, Hardyng suspected things. Reason enough to kill that poor man and silence his clacking tongue.' Urswicke studied the manuscript before him. He glanced up and smiled thinly. 'One reason for murder, although there are undoubtedly others, but I will come to that in a while. In the meantime, back to Andre. You had silenced him and sent a warning to the Luciferi, who could only speculate on the identity of a traitor lodged deep in the countess's household. For a while they had to be most cautious regarding anyone they approached.'

'Master Urswicke,' Guido pointed towards the hour candle. 'Hurry now, we wish to be gone. This is a farrago of lies. We are envoys of Burgundy. We are not subject . . .'

'Subject or not,' Urswicke retorted, 'you will sit and listen to this indictment. Until then,' Urswicke shrugged and waved a hand, 'if you try to leave before I am finished, Master Bray will kill you.' Urswicke's voice and the naked threat rang like a tocsin through the chamber. Guido and Sir John looked at each other while Squire Lambert's hand crept towards a sharp, pointed carving knife. He hastily withdrew when Bray coughed threateningly. 'Two more murders,' Urswicke continued. 'Or should I say three. You kept this household under close watch. Despite our best efforts, you discovered we had captured and imprisoned those mummers Eglantine and Clairvaux. Two fools who pretended to be clerks of the Secret Chancery. A subtle ruse planned by my illustrious father. Of course he informed you about what he had done. I would add that he also provided a cover, a pretence, for the mysterious disappearance of both those clerks from this house. Again, we see the chains of this conspiracy link up. It was probably nurtured and planned in Arras, where you would meet the Garduna and my father's emissary somewhere in Duke Charles's palace. Once you were agreed, the Garduna went their way, you would go yours, and of course my Father would wait here, smirking like a cat waiting to pounce. As I said earlier, it would be so easy for you to meet, be it with the Garduna or one of my father's spies from the Guildhall. You were all intent on harassing the countess. Those two mummers were part of this persecution. They played their roles well. Eventually they had to leave whilst the rest of the household were distracted by the mummers' troupe performing their masque. Again I wonder about Hardyng. Did he see, hear or feel something untoward? Did he wonder why those two clerks disappeared at the very time entertainment was being provided so close to the countess's mansion?'

Urswicke paused as Sir John leaned across and whispered in Guido's ear. Guido nodded in agreement to whatever was said. He then turned to murmur to Squire Lambert, who just pointed to Guido's chancery satchel which he had now placed on the table before him.

'As I said,' Urswicke declared, 'you discovered what we had done capturing those two mummers. You certainly couldn't allow them to interfere with the web being spun. God knows what they would have said.' Urswicke shook his head. 'All three of you are killers; you take to murder as a bird to flying. You plotted the assassination of Eglantine and Clairvaux as you did poor Hardyng. He had to die, so you could seize his keys, get into that cellar and murder the two mummers. Hardyng, of course, was an easy victim. Totally overcome by what was happening in the countess's household, he became sottish with drink, a toper from dawn to dusk, constantly mawmsy, deep in his cups. He wandered this mansion, muttering to himself. He'd have seen this, glimpsed that. He certainly discovered, when he least expected it, the corpses of those rats apparently poisoned. He would reflect on that. He would remember that the wine taken to the cellar was supposed to be poisoned but, surprisingly, later found to be free of any noxious substance. And yet, on the other hand, there was poison lying about. Hence the dead rats, but where had this come from? And why? Who was responsible?' Urswicke fell silent, letting his words hang like a noose in the air. 'Hardyng would chatter,' Urswicke continued. 'He had to be silenced, his mouth closed forever and his murder used to perpetrate two more killings. We held one key to the cellar where we had lodged the mummers. Of course there were two keys, the other being held by Hardyng the steward. To cut to the quick, you followed our poor steward into that copse of trees in the countess's garden.'

'Oh for heaven's sake,' Guido shouted.

'Oh for heaven's sake, yes. Hardyng was your prey. The poor man was constantly inebriated. Perhaps you slipped a potion into his wine to render him even more incapable. Hardyng often went into that copse for his secret drink. You,' Urswicke pointed at all three, 'you forced him onto that stool then kicked it from beneath him holding his arms and legs to hasten death. However, you made two serious mistakes. First, Hardyng was a short man. Even standing on the stool, he couldn't possibly have reached the branch to fasten that rope. And had he been able to, I suspect he was so drunk, he'd have fallen off. Any court would accept that a man in Hardyng's condition, given the height of the stool and his own size, could never have stretched up to tie a perfect knot before fashioning the noose around his own neck. Hardyng was so inebriated, his bladder so full, it emptied in his death throes.'

'And the second mistake?' Lambert slurred.

Urswicke glanced at him swiftly. He could not prove it, but he was certain the squire had played a principal part in Hardyng's hanging. Lambert would like that, watching a man choke to death. A sinister soul who perpetrated dark deeds.

'Your second mistake,' Urswicke retorted. 'Hardyng was left-handed, very much so, as I have recently learned. Now he would have tightened the noose here,' Urswicke tapped the right side of his own neck, 'but the noose which strangled him was positioned on his left.'

'All of this is pure speculation,' Sir John scoffed.

'With no real evidence,' Squire Lambert echoed.

'Hardyng was murdered,' Urswicke continued remorselessly. 'You took his keys and, with Lambert standing on guard, you went down to that cellar. Both of you were armed with a crossbow which, I am sure, I could find amongst your possessions.'

'Our possessions are under the Seal of Burgundy,' Guido snapped. 'They are precious. We are envoys.'

'You entered that chamber.' Urswicke ignored the interruption. 'Your quarry were easy victims, being chained and manacled. Both men were killed with a bolt to the head. You then locked that door and returned the key to the now dead Hardyng, hanging like a piece of rag from that branch, his face cruelly mutilated by the crows. Once more you created murderous mystery and mayhem. In the end you strove to create a world of deep chaos so as to compel the countess to flee this kingdom.' Urswicke rose to his feet. 'But you failed. The Garduna failed. My father failed. Despite your best efforts, you arrogant peacocks, you made errors from the start!'

'What do you mean?'

'Oh, let me see.' Urswicke stared at the ceiling, tapping his chin. 'For example, you never really, in fact not at all, answered the countess's question about the ambuscades perpetrated outside Woking Manor. How did those mysterious assailants know when you were leaving? Where you were going? What path you would take? Of course your allies the Garduna were very close. They had set up camp, created their lair in that lonely forest tavern, The Chasuble. Using Squire Lambert as your courier, you would inform them of what you were doing, where you were going and how it was to be arranged.' Urswicke snapped his fingers as if he'd suddenly recalled something. 'Oh, by the way, Sir John, what is your true relationship with the squire?'

'None of your business.'

'Oh it certainly is, because it's all very strange. He must trust you and Guido implicitly.'

'What do you mean?'

'Well, Squire Lambert was allegedly poisoned: a box of tainted sweetmeats delivered to the mansion. I never saw that box, we never really examined it. In fact our devious young squire was not poisoned. You, Guido, gave him some harmless potion to disturb the humours: a situation which could be easily rectified. Nevertheless, the good squire must trust you to take any strange potion, harmless though it might be.'

'And why should we do that?'

'Oh, Physician Guido, to depict yourselves as being victims, being mysteriously attacked because of your relationship with the countess. You were trying your very best to sustain the appearance of being the loving, supportive guests, astonished, angry and concerned at what was happening. And of course it was more trouble for the countess, not even members of her household were safe. You deepened the fear and intensified the nervousness of all her servants.' Urswicke waved a hand. 'All hypocrisy, a sham, a mask, to conceal the dreadful truth about your malicious treachery towards our mistress.' Urswicke stared at each of the accused. He was certain of their guilt and determined on their punishment.

As if he could almost read Urswicke's thoughts, Physician Guido sprang to his feet, patting his quilted jerkin.

'I have in my pockets and in my chancery satchel,' he declared, 'sworn letters, signed and sealed by His Excellency the Duke of Burgundy, proclaiming my two comrades and I are sacred envoys, honoured members of his household: the same has been confirmed by the King of England.'

'And so!' Bray yelled.

'You uncouth bastard,' Sir John retorted, pushing away the chair and getting to his feet. 'This nonsense is at an end. We shall adjourn to our chamber, collect our baggage, then we shall leave. You cannot stop us.'

Urswicke glanced at the countess who merely shrugged. Urswicke could sense that his mistress did not wish to be drawn by these traitors. She would follow the Latin motto 'to watch and stay silent'. She would be determined not to give these three reprobates the satisfaction of knowing how wounding and grievous their conduct had proved.

'We will not stop you.' Urswicke turned back to the accused. 'So you will leave for the city?'

'Oh no,' Guido smirked maliciously. 'I do not trust you, Urswicke. The streets of London are dark and lonely. We will hire a barge from here to take us along the riverbank to our ship *The Pegasus*. However, to avoid any mischief, I have asked for your father, Sir Thomas, Recorder of this City, to come here to ensure our safe departure as accredited envoys who must be treated according to all the protocols.'

'I assure you,' Urswicke snapped, 'it will be in accordance with all the protocols.' He shrugged. 'More proof of your guilt.'

'What do you mean?'

'You're not proper envoys, you are Garduna. You were aware of their depredations including the secret instructions to seize and remove the remains of King Henry. The Garduna have been truly annihilated. You must have deduced that the finger of accusation would eventually be directed against you. You failed. The countess and ourselves survived your onslaught. You probably sensed the change of mood in her and certainly my father. It's time for you to go and, like the cowards you are, you plead for protection. Oh well, in God's name go!'

The three guests left, kicking aside furniture, slamming the door behind them. Bray, who watched them go, quietly cursed as he placed the crossbow on the table.

'Very clever,' he breathed. 'They want to leave here. What a pity! I could have met them in the streets below and meted out justice.' Bray then turned. 'Christopher, I suspect you knew they were going to leave from here, didn't you? You made no objection.'

'Of course I did.' Urswicke smiled back. 'And no, I don't have the gift of prophecy or of seeing the future. My good father, who now knows better, informed me precisely of their plans. We agreed to that. Believe me, Reginald, my esteemed father, the Recorder will be only too delighted to see the back of these malignants.'

Two hours later, a cohort of Tower archers arrived. Countess Margaret welcomed them, saying the Recorder's escort could gather in the buttery while she and Sir Thomas would officially take their leave of Sir John and his companions. Urswicke and Bray remained deep in the shadows, carefully watching proceedings. The countess's guests remained in their chambers until Lambert, armed with a lantern, summoned in a war barge to the jetty beyond the water-gate. The guests mustered and left. Urswicke followed them out. He watched the countess, who stood still as a statue. She made no attempt to communicate with her three dishonoured guests, whilst they responded in kind. They clambered aboard and took their seats in the canopied stern. Ropes were cast off and the war barge, its lanternhorns flaring on the stern and prow, edged away, the echoing splash of oars receding as the barge entered a bank of rolling river mist. Once it had disappeared, they all returned to the solar. The countess claimed she was tired and, after taking a frosty farewell of Sir Thomas, retired to her chamber. Once she'd gone, Sir Thomas sat down on a cushioned chair, sighed noisily and put his face in his hands. He sat like that for a while before taking his hand away and staring tearfully at his son.

'We were deceived,' he rasped. 'I admit, I confess that we, my royal masters and myself, would dearly love to see the back of the Lady Margaret. Once she'd gone, perhaps her cause would fade and crumble away. Burgundy, however, wanted to remove her and seize her claim.'

'I agree, esteemed father, and Duke Charles would prove to be a most dangerous opponent with all his wealth and power . . .'

'The King must never find out what has happened, beloved son.'

'Of course, esteemed father.'

'God knows what those three will report when they reach Arras.'

'I don't know,' Christopher retorted, 'and before God I don't care.' He walked over to a mullioned window and stared through the thick concave glass. He really wanted to go out onto the jetty, but what was the use? The mist had blanketed everything. Urswicke narrowed his eyes and smiled to himself. He and François had cleverly plotted their enemy's departure. Urswicke reckoned that Sir John would want to reach *The Pegasus* as swiftly and as safely as possible and a river journey was the surest way. This had been confirmed by his own father, who'd also revealed that Sir John had demanded his presence at the countess's mansion and, because they were envoys, he had no choice but to agree. Urswicke and François had been truly delighted. It would be so easy for the

Luciferi to have their war barge close by, lurking in the dark, waiting for the invitation to approach the jetty. A second barge would patrol nearby to warn off other craft. The Luciferi would be cloaked and hooded. Sir John and Guido would never dream that they were walking into such a deadly trap.

Urswicke leaned his hot brow against the cold glass. He closed his eyes. Everything so far had gone to plan. He imagined what would unfold during that river journey. Sir John, Guido and Squire Lambert would think they were safe. They would be smug, congratulating each other on what they had achieved. How they had perpetrated hideous mischief against the countess and then walked away scot free. They would suddenly become aware of the trap closing in on them. The barge would move away from the riverbank to the splash of oars, the rowers pulling vigorously as they leaned over. Then the captain, François, would shout an order. The Luciferi, who acted as oarsmen, would soon deal with their enemies. Death would be sudden and abrupt. Crossbow quarrels loosed into each of them. Once completed, the corpses would be stripped and searched and, with the weights brought specially, tossed into the Thames. If the cadavers were ever discovered, a rare enough event, they would be regarded as more victims of some river pirate. And who could protest? Duke Charles could make enquiries, even send envoys to Westminster. The English Crown, or rather his father, would simply lift his hands, commiserate, and declare that all three had been sent off, hale and hearty, by no less a person than himself, not to mention Sir John's revered good sister Countess Margaret. Of course, the Secret Chanceries of both Burgundy and London would wonder exactly what did happen, but there was really nothing anyone could do.

'One more thing.' The Recorder coughed and cleared his throat. Christopher turned and went back to his seat. 'I received a present,' Sir Thomas declared, 'if you could call it that. Two severed heads in a basket. I do believe,' the Recorder added wryly, 'they both belonged to the Garduna. Now I have no doubt they were despatched by the Luciferi as a mocking farewell.' There was a tag fixed to the basket with a message scrawled on it: 'Hermano Majo and friend.' The Recorder blew his cheeks out. 'I don't think so.'

'What is this, father?' Urswicke repressed a shiver.

'The Luciferi believe they have severed and despatched the head of the Garduna leader and his henchman Alphonso. They are wrong. Before I had the gruesome tokens tossed into the Thames, I carefully examined them. The Garduna leader had an old but deep scar here.' The Recorder tapped just behind his right ear. 'Neither head bore that mark. They sent the wrong one. This means that the Garduna Master, or whatever status he might claim, may have survived that bloody battle at The Chasuble. Oh yes,' the Recorder whispered, 'I now know all about that. At first, like you and your friends the Luciferi, I thought the Garduna had been totally annihilated, wiped out, every last one of them. It's to be expected: the Luciferi never take prisoners. However, if the Garduna leader escaped, he will be intent on returning and striking back.'

'Against me?'

'Against you,' Sir Thomas agreed.

'No father.' Urswicke tried to control his temper. 'You hired the Garduna. You signed an indenture with them, or perhaps you did not, just a pact confirmed by oath and a handshake.'

The Recorder stared wearily back.

'The Garduna will certainly invoke the blood feud,' Urswicke declared, 'against you and I concede against me, but,' Christopher gestured at his father, 'you above all.'

'Why?'

'You allowed the Luciferi to attack The Chasuble. You sent no help, no warning. Esteemed father, if I were you, I would be most prudent.'

'And of course, there's danger from our three departed guests.'

'Esteemed father, don't worry about them! There's many a slip between cup and lip: their departure may well be one of those occasions.'

'What do you mean?'

'Wait and see.' Urswicke grinned. 'By the way, father, who was the supreme leader of the Garduna – the villain at The Chasuble? Sir John? Physician Guido? I have never really decided.'

'And neither have I!'

'But they've all gone!' Christopher whispered.

'In which case,' the Recorder got to his feet, 'beloved son, think kind thoughts of me.'

Urswicke simply stared back. Sir Thomas made his farewells

and promptly left. For a while, Bray and Urswicke just sat in silence, listening to the different sounds of the house. Bray rose and put two more logs on the fire. He then went to join Urswicke sitting at the chancery desk. The clerk was studying a memorandum describing the genealogy of Charles Duke of Burgundy.

'Is he still a danger, a threat?'

'No.' Urswicke shook his head. 'I've talked about our noble duke with our even more noble countess. Burgundy is no threat. Duke Charles is what he is, Reginald, a foreign prince. He would receive little support in any claim for the English Throne as long as Henry Tudor lives. Now, God forbid, if Henry Tudor died, then Duke Charles could emerge as a powerful claimant to the English Throne.' Urswicke pushed the manuscript away. 'But that won't happen, will it? This can be consigned to history.' Urswicke laughed softly to himself.

'Christopher?'

'The Garduna have a long-standing blood feud with the House of Lancaster dating back to its founder, John of Gaunt. These recent revelations now depict Duke Charles as a leading Lancastrian claimant. The Garduna may well invoke the blood-feud, especially after they lost an entire battle group on his behalf. Oh yes, my friend, Burgundy has released a monster which could well turn on him. Moreover . . .' Urswicke paused at a knock at the door. He and Bray rose as it opened and the countess slipped into the solar. She performed a mock curtsey then moved to embrace each of her henchmen before sitting down at the top of the council table, with Bray and Urswicke either side.

'Well done,' she whispered. 'Well done indeed. You sent our noble Recorder packing. I glimpsed him leave like the beaten dog he is.'

'He will return,' Bray countered. 'He will go back to his chambers at the Guildhall. He'll hide away, rest, lick his wounds then rise for fresh mischief.' Bray spread his hands. 'Christopher, my apologies, Sir Thomas is your father.'

'He is also my enemy and, as we've just demonstrated, a deadly one.'

'Deadly indeed,' Bray agreed. 'Though now that he has incurred the full wrath of the Garduna, they may well go hunting him.'

'Rest assured, Reginald, my father is Recorder of London. He controls most of its underworld as a huntsman does his lurchers. He will let these loose against any quarry. They'll cast about and track down any Garduna who escaped. I am sure,' Christopher added wryly, 'that the forests around Chertsey and Woking are being thoroughly searched. Oh, don't worry about Sir Thomas. I assure you he has a sense of self-preservation which is a wonder to behold.'

'Nevertheless, he has failed the Brothers York,' the countess murmured. 'I, you, we are still here, hale and hearty.' She smiled. 'To quote scripture, "we flourish like the cedars of Lebanon".' She played with a quill pen on the table before her. 'Yet I agree, Sir Thomas Urswicke is a mortal danger to us and our cause.'

'And always will be.' Bray leaned over the table, using his hands to emphasise his argument. 'Christopher, I appreciate I speak about your father but the countess is correct. Sir Thomas is a deadly threat to all three of us, not to mention Prince Henry, Lady Katarina and Lord Jasper, now safely on board that French war cog.' Bray sipped from the goblet he'd filled earlier. 'Our Recorder is truly dangerous and murderous. We thought we were being driven into exile, in fact we were literally being driven into the sea. We were to be drowned. We would never have reached Burgundy or anywhere else. Whatever ship we, or the countess boarded, would have been attacked. I am sure the Garduna have war craft and would only be too willing to finish the task assigned to them. If we had boarded *The Pegasus*, some unfortunate accident would have occurred, such incidents are common enough. Oh yes, we would have perished at sea. And how long would Prince Henry have survived that?' Bray held up his hand in a sign of peace as the countess quietly moaned to herself. 'Now we are all safe,' he comforted. 'Prince Henry is in good hands and Stanley's men will soon arrive in London. Even the servants are returning.' Bray took a deep breath. 'All good, except we know that Sir Thomas persecutes us. Time and again we have to fend off his attacks but then he returns.'

'What do you suggest?'

'Christopher, we should take the war into the enemy's camp; in fact I have already begun to do so.'

'Reginald?'

'Christopher, my Lady.' Bray rose and walked over to his

chancery satchel. He brought it across to the table, opened it, then took out a scroll of parchment. He unrolled this, placing small chancery weights on each corner. Urswicke rose to stand over the rich yellow manuscript, the pen strokes so clear, the deep black ink catching the eye. 'Read it,' Bray urged. 'Read it, Christopher, for our mistress.'

'Listen, you citizens of London,' Urswicke began. 'And remember this warning when judgement falls on that most unjust judge, Sir Thomas Urswicke, Recorder of London. He will not change his ways. He will not reform himself. He is guilty of disobedience to us. He will return like a dog to its vomit. He sees and sees again but does not perceive the real evil he has committed against us. He hears and hears again but does not understand his perfidious conduct. He has betrayed the Garduna. He has tricked, deceived and deserted our comrades. He stands accused of rank treachery. Very well then, he and his creature Mauclerc have sown the tempest, so now they must surely reap the whirlwind. We have marked them both down for vengeance and our vengeance will snap close like a trap. Given under our hand in this City and set to be proclaimed to whom it matters because we are the Garduna and we answer to no one.' Urswicke glanced up. 'My Lady?' She just made a face, shook her head and glanced at Bray. 'Reginald?' Urswicke demanded. 'What is this farrago of nonsense? Who wrote it?'

'I did, and what is more, last night I stole into St Paul's and posted it up on the Cross. I did the same at the Standard in Cheapside.'

'In God's name why?'

'So your father, Christopher, is served back in the same coin he dealt out. I heard what Alcuin said when he returned to the abbey. How some of the Garduna may have survived. If that's true and their leader has, they will invoke the blood feud.'

'This will vex my father?'

'No Christopher, it will also frighten him. He is not used to being threatened in his own city. Secondly, it might well distract him from us. Thirdly, those who read it will be most curious about what prompted such a broadsheet. They will ask who are the Garduna? They will wonder what Sir Thomas has done to provoke them.'

'Do you think my father is in any real danger from the Garduna?'

'No, no I don't.'

'Are you sure?' the countess asked, openly fascinated by this sudden turn of events.

'The Garduna are few and gravely weakened,' Bray replied. 'Any survivors of that violent clash at The Chasuble will be wary and watchful. They are greatly depleted in resources, strangers in a foreign land, without a lair to hide them or a lord to protect them.'

Urswicke sat down, tapping the broadsheet.

'You have posted this already?'

'Well yes, or something akin to it. The broadsheet you have just read will be proclaimed in the same places over the next few days.'

'Reginald, was it wise to include Mauclerc? Was it necessary? The Brothers York may well wonder if we have a hand in this.'

'I doubt it, Christopher. Both these limbs of Satan, the Recorder and Mauclerc, nourished the Garduna. They were their allies, and that is well known to those who should know such things. Oh, I appreciate our hatred of Mauclerc is also well known, but the fact is that he dealt with the Garduna and they with him. Your noble father withdrew all support and protection. Mauclerc was his messenger boy. More importantly, it affords me deep satisfaction that both Sir Thomas and Mauclerc will feel more than a tremor of fear.'

'It will certainly cause trouble.' The countess laughed drily. 'Between Sir Thomas and Mauclerc, their murderous venture failed. And, as you know, passing the blame is as old as Adam and Eve. Christopher, are you really worried that the Brothers York will see through Bray's plot and blame us?'

'I don't think they will move to that conclusion immediately. But, what happens if the Garduna have all been killed? My father would certainly reflect on the true source of these broadsheets. What if,' Urswicke pressed on, 'the Garduna themselves made it very clear that they have invoked the blood feud but these proclamations are not their work?'

'Highly unlikely.'

'Thirdly,' Urswicke continued, 'Reginald, if you are caught . . . and heaven knows my father spins a truly tangled web. He has a net which covers a legion of informants, Judas men, bounty hunters and all that tribe. Even if you post such proclamations after the chimes of midnight, there will be watchers in the dark. I repeat, if you are caught, God help you and God help us, especially my Lady. You know the finger of accusation will be pointed at her, she will be dragged off to the Tower for questioning.' Urswicke narrowed his eyes as he gazed at Bray, a true comrade, more dear to him than any brother. Bray could not hold Christopher's gaze but glanced away and Urswicke felt a prick of clammy fear. 'Reginald,' he leaned across the table, 'Reginald, look at me.' His companion did so. 'Reginald, where is this path really leading? True, we can cause great irritation and vexation to the Yorkist Lords and my father in particular but, if matters turned awry, what you plan could do great harm to the countess. So Reginald, where is this truly leading?'

'The death of both your father and Mauclerc.'

'By whom?'

'By us, Christopher, or rather by me. Sir Thomas dies and Mauclerc too. However, I will arrange it so their deaths, their sudden slayings, will be laid at the door of the Garduna.'

'And how will this be done?'

'That's my secret, Christopher.' Bray now asserted himself. 'Sir Thomas and Mauclerc loose one assault after another against our dear mistress and against us. Do you fully understand what they were planning in this enterprise, for her? For us? Brutal death, swallowed up by the sea and forgotten in its depths. How long will this go on? We must end it. But,' Bray breathed out noisily, 'only if you agree. I swear to that.'

Urswicke glanced at the countess who gazed bleakly back. Urswicke rose and walked to the window, staring through the heavy glass. He recalled his father, years earlier, teaching him chess or how to draw a bow. He blinked back the tears, quelling his anger at what their relationship was rather than what it should be. As a boy Christopher had adored his father, regarding him as strong, vibrant and full of courage, quick of wit and sharp of mind. Then the dream had died when his mother grew sad and withdrawn, always tearful, never to be comforted.

'My friend,' the countess called out, 'what Reginald says is the truth. Sir Thomas and Mauclerc deserve death, but that is down to you.'

'He is my father and yet . . .'

'And yet what?'

'He killed my beloved mother. He didn't give a whit for the pain she felt or the sorrow it caused her.' Urswicke turned and retook his seat. 'Oh yes,' he whispered, rubbing his hands together, 'Thomas Urswicke and his string of doxies, like a whore master with his chorus of strumpets. So yes, in my eyes he deserves death for that alone.'

'And yet?' the countess demanded. 'Tell me, Christopher, what do you think your mother would say?'

Christopher closed his eyes and bit his lip to control a sob which seemed to course through every fibre of his being. He recalled his mother sitting on her favourite garden chair, calling all excited that Sir Thomas would be coming home soon. Urswicke opened his eyes. 'Leave my father to his sins,' he declared. 'If we meet in combat, hand to hand, sword to sword, that is different. But to kill him, to cast him down by stealth, to become assassins . . .' Urswicke shook his head. 'I beg, I ask you not to follow that path.'

The countess proffered her hand, which Christopher kissed. He then turned to clasp Bray's.

'You have my solemn oath, Christopher, I will not make any further move in this matter.'

'I agree,' the countess interjected.

'So.' Christopher drew himself up. 'Leave the Garduna to their devices and my father to his. At least for the moment. But rest assured, my friends: Sir Thomas Urswicke, Recorder of London, is never far from my thoughts.'

AUTHOR'S NOTE

D ark Queen Watching is of course a work of fiction, though strands of history are woven deeply into the narrative.

1471 was a glorious year for the House of York. Edward and his brothers were now unchecked, free of any real threat, be it from within or without. Edward, encouraged by his wife Elizabeth Woodville, worked hard to emphasise and enhance his own status as a victorious general and divinely appointed king. The Sun of York blazed strongly, only one shadow persisted: Margaret Beaufort, the Countess of Richmond, never gave up her plan to bring about the fall of the House of York and the ascendancy of her own son Henry Tudor. In my belief, Margaret was a truly brilliant, charismatic and determined woman. Twelve years later, the harvest she had sown was brought to full ripeness. In the end she proved to be the dark nemesis of the House of York.

The role of France in these opening years of Edward's reign is as I have described in the novel. Louis XI was perpetually fearful of an English invasion, which would bring back the bad old days and the misery France had suffered until the emergence of Joan of Arc. In the end, it wasn't Brittany or Burgundy which played a key role in Henry Tudor's successful invasion of England in 1485. French mercenaries and French gold helped Henry Tudor to make his successful landfall at Milford Haven. The Tudor never forgot. Despite some sabre-rattling, England did not go to war with France during Henry VII's twenty-four-year reign.

The two mummers mentioned in the novel are not to be dismissed as nigh impossible. Indeed, the last decades of the fifteenth century saw the emergence of pretenders who made outrageous claims and acted the part to suit them. Imposters such as Lambert Simnel and Perkin Warbeck were real people who claimed to be royal princes; such claims were supported by many who should have known better.

The posting of broadsheets in St Paul's and Cheapside was also a growing feature of the age. During the reign of Richard III

(1483–1485), such proclamations became commonplace, probably inspired by Richard's inveterate opponents, Margaret Beaufort and Christopher Urswicke. On 18 July 1484 'Seditious Rhymes' appeared on the doors of St Paul's. One of them ran as follows: 'The Rat, the Cat and Lovel the Dog rule all England under the Hogge.' A scathing reference to King Richard (his insignia was a white boar) and his three henchmen, Ratcliffe, Catesby and Viscount Lovell. On the eve of the Battle of Bosworth, Howard of Norfolk, Richard's principal commander, found the following note pinned to his pavilion. 'Jockey of Norfolk ride not so bold, for Dickon [Richard III] your master has been both bought and sold.' Psychological warfare in the hands of people like Christopher Urswicke was certainly alive and flourishing in the fifteenth century!

Margaret did marry Lord Stanley and the marriage proved to be a great success. At the Battle of Bosworth, Richard III and his commanders foolishly expected Stanley to support them. Richard paid the price of such stupidity when Stanley, at a vital part of the battle, promptly changed sides.

Duke Charles of Burgundy's claim to the English throne was as it is described in the novel. Duke Charles did formally file his claim in November 1471. In the end it came to nothing. Charles was drawn into different conflicts in Northern Europe and was killed at the Battle of Nancy in January 1476.

The corpse of King Henry VI eventually rested in peace. In fact, in August 1484 Richard III ordered it to be moved from Chertsey to Windsor. At the same time relics of the dead King began to proliferate: these included the dead King's coat, not to mention the 'holy dagger' which killed him, along with the late King's spurs, a chip from his bedstead and the dead King's red velvet hat.

Finally, the Garduna did exist and, for centuries, flourished most vigorously in Spain until November 1822, when its Grand Master, along with sixteen of his henchmen, were hanged in the great marketplace of Seville. Some people claim the Garduna in fact survived this and that they still exist to intervene and cause mischief wherever and whenever they wish.